DO NOT REMOVE
CARDS FROM POCKET

A Bridge to Hope

The Stafford Chronicles, Book 1

Patricia Harrison Easton

Servant Publications
Ann Arbor, Michigan

Vine Books is an imprint of Servant Publications especially designed to serve evangelical Christians.

This is a work of fiction. Apart from obvious references to places and historical events, all characters and incidents in this novel are the product of the author's imagination. Any similarities to people living or dead are purely coincidental.

Published by Servant Publications
P.O. Box 8617
Ann Arbor, Michigan 48107

Cover design: Diane Bareis
Cover photos: Wildflowers by Malcolm Lockwood and covered bridge, used by permission, Stock Imagery.

96 97 98 99 00 10 9 8 7 6 5 4 3 2

Printed in the United States of America
ISBN 0-89283-950-3

LIBRARY OF CONGRESS CATALOGING-IN-PUBLICATION DATA

Easton, Patricia Harrison.
A bridge to hope / Patricia Harrison Easton.
    p. cm.   — (The Stafford Chronicles : bk. 1)
ISBN 0-89283-950-3
I. Title. II. Series.
PS3555.A7335B75   1996
813'.54—dc20   96-16519
                                                                    CIP

Dedication

As always for my husband Richard,
because he is so much a part of all I do.

Also for Bert Ghezzi and Kendra Marcus.
Thanks for believing in me. I love you both.

O N E

Marty Harris took her eyes off the Interstate to sneak a look at her sleeping children. Fifteen-year-old Jeff sprawled across the seat next to her, his face for the first time in weeks giving the illusion of peace. Annie snuggled into her pillow with a half-dozen stuffed animals around her as she dozed on the backseat. Good. Marty needed to deal with her own emotions now, not theirs. In the eight months since Dan's death, all she'd thought about was the children, helping them to cope with the loss of their father and planning for their future on her limited resources. For months before that, all any of them could think of was Dan, as he became more and more weakened, slowly erased by leukemia.

Now back among the familiar hills and valleys of her childhood, all kinds of odd feelings churned in her. She ran a hand through her short curls, not the long auburn waves Dan loved. Her first independent act had been the hair cut. Now she regretted it. She took a deep breath and refused to give in to another rising wave of sadness.

"Are we almost there, Mom?" Annie's small round face appeared beside Marty's shoulder.

Marty reached back to rub her eight-year-old daughter's cheek. "We're coming up to our exit," she said, glad to have the company to distract her. She had never been much good at dealing with her own feelings. "Are you all right, sweetie?"

"Sure," Annie said. "Do you think Grandpap and Uncle Kyle will let me ride today?"

"What's the hurry?" Jeff growled. "There'll be nothing for any of us to do all summer but ride horses, shovel manure, and watch the corn grow."

Marty turned the Volvo off the Interstate and onto old Route 23. "Please, Jeff, try to be pleasant. We all know that Washington County, Pennsylvania will never be Washington, D.C., but we simply don't have enough money to continue to live in D.C.

It was very nice of Grandpap and Uncle Kyle to ask us to spend the summer here. I need the time to plan for our future."

Marty braked as the car in front of her turned into the truck stop. The old building had a clean coat of yellow paint, green trim and a new name—Patsy Malone's Family Restaurant. She'd gone to school with Patsy Malone. Patsy had wanted to be a nurse. But then Marty knew about life's left turns.

"I think the summer will be fun," Annie said.

"That's the spirit, Annie," Marty said.

"Yeah, right," Jeff muttered. He turned on the radio and the unmistakable fiddle riff of a country tune filled the car. "Oh, man," Jeff said, reaching to find another station. When the next three offered the same, Jeff slammed the radio off. "Hicksville!"

Marty tried to swallow her anger. Sometimes Jeff was so much like his father, quick to judge anything that didn't meet his standards. Marty turned the radio back on to 89.3, a PBS station. The soft moan of a blues sax floated into the car. "There! You know, we're not that far from Pittsburgh and it *is* a modern city."

"It's not D.C.," Jeff said.

"No, and some things about it are a lot nicer—like the cost of living and the crime rate," Marty snapped. "And it has a world-renowned symphony and excellent ballet, opera, and theater, all of which are affordable. Unlike D.C., here we can occasionally afford to attend one of those events." Annie shifted back onto her seat and Jeff turned from Marty to stare out the window. "I'm sorry, Jeff, but this isn't easy for me either."

After an uncomfortable silence, Jeff whispered, "Sorry, Mom." Marty reached across the seat and Jeff took her hand, giving it a squeeze.

"I love you, kid," Marty said. She smiled. Like his father, Jeff was also caring, quick to apologize, and honest enough to admit his own mistakes.

Marty turned off the air conditioning and pressed the buttons to roll down the windows. "What we need is a little fresh air."

Annie stuck her head over the front seat and sniffed loudly. "It smells green, Mom."

"It sure does," Marty replied. "Like growing things."

Jeff grabbed his throat, pretending to choke. "I guess I'll get used to it."

Annie's infectious giggles made Marty laugh. When she looked over at Jeff, he grinned, too. Jeff also had Dan's sense of humor. The hole Dan's death had left in her heart asserted its presence.

The Volvo rolled down the hill and onto Clayton, one long street of shops and turreted Victorian houses with a few red-brick Federal period survivors. Many of the shops were hung with familiar names—Patterson's Hardware, McCary's Pharmacy, Raynak's Service Station. People strolled the hilly sidewalks that ran the length of Main Street. The bright June afternoon was invitingly warm, the kind that lured everyone into town to see what was happening.

"Look, Mom," Annie said, pointing over Marty's shoulder, "Grand Opening—Ceci's Ice Cream Parlor." The old Simmons house had been painted an earthy beige with the elaborate Victorian trim and shutters colored green and blue and red. It looked like a gingerbread house. "Can we stop for ice cream?"

"We'd better go home first. Grandpap's waiting." Marty wasn't ready to deal with old friends and she was certain to see some if they stopped. Most of her friends had never left the county. Next to the ice cream parlor, a shiny red truck bore the sign—Derry Brady, Blacksmith. Marty's stomach fluttered. She sure wasn't ready to run into him. She'd spent most of her adolescence either running after or away from Derry Brady. Marty pressed on the gas pedal, anxious to get out of town.

Feeling ridiculous, she set her jaw and tried to focus on the road ahead. She was a thirty-eight-year-old widow with two children—much too old to still get a rush from that irresponsible, womanizing jerk. By the time she turned the car off the main road, she was feeling like herself again. She drove across a covered bridge and wound along the county roads that led to the farm.

"Come on, Annie, a quick game of Cemetery," Jeff said. Without waiting for her answer, he began to count the Black Angus steers that dotted the field on his side of the car. "Fifteen, sixteen, seventeen…"

"Not fair," Annie wailed. "I didn't even say I'd play."

"Look, Annie," Marty said, pointing to the sheep on their side of the Volvo.

Marty slowed the car and Annie began to count.

"Twelve," Annie said. "I have twelve."

"I'm still winning, Peewee," Jeff teased.

"Look up ahead, Annie," Marty said. Ahead, on the right side of the car, was Trinity Methodist Church, the tiny country church Marty had attended throughout her youth. Behind the church the burial ground held graves from the early 1800s.

"Cemetery! Cemetery!" Annie yelled. "Jeff loses all his points."

Jeff and Marty laughed until they saw an old woman kneeling by a grave planting flowers. A quiet that was more than silence crept into the car.

Annie was the first to speak. "I miss Daddy," she said.

"I know, honey. Me, too," Marty said.

Jeff slumped in his seat and turned to look out the window.

"Dear Lord, please help us," Marty prayed silently. After years of not practicing her faith, that was the only prayer that came to her, that and the Lord's Prayer repeated like a mantra on sleepless nights when loneliness and fear threatened to crush her. She'd traveled far from her beginnings in that little church where God had been real to her.

Morgan Road curved to the right, cutting through the farm where generations of Morgans had been raised since the late 1700s. Marty had been the maid of honor when her best friend, Gayle, had married MacKenzie Morgan one year after graduation. The black-and-white Holsteins of Mac's dairy herd grazed the hillside. Gayle had written regularly, no matter how infrequently Marty answered. From her letters Marty knew that Gayle and Mac and their son and daughter had been happy here. Maybe Marty and her family could be, too.

Marty fought the impulse to pull onto Morgan Road. A visit with Gayle and Mac would fortify her, help her to make the last mile to her family's farm. She hadn't been back since Mama died six years before. She simply hadn't been able to face Duke's sadness and Kyle's chaos and what she knew would be the general deterioration of the place. For all the big holidays she had insisted that her father and brother come to her and Dan, where they would be sure to be on their best behavior. So what made her think she could cope with it all now? Yet now, she had no choice; she had to deal with it. No, there was more to it than that—now, she needed family and home and old friends in a way she never had before.

Morgan land lay on her right as she crossed the old iron bridge over Five Mile Creek and pulled onto the unpaved farm lane beside a dented mailbox with "Stafford" hand painted in uneven red letters on the side. Here the creek turned, dividing the Morgan property from theirs. The creek, twelve feet across and three feet deep, tumbled over rocks as it rolled past the farm. The house was not yet in sight when Marty stopped the car.

"Are we there?" Annie asked.

"Yes, we are," Marty answered. "The house is just around that bend ahead." On a hillside above the creek, Marty looked for the ledge that had been her special childhood place, where she had sat and read for hours, dreaming about escaping from the farm and living an exciting life in a distant city. Well, she had, and it had been a good life, though not as exciting as she'd imagined. But she had never really been able to escape the farm—she carried it with her. Marty didn't mention the rock ledge to the children. The steep path looked more dangerous than she remembered.

She took her foot off the brake, put the car into drive, and started toward the farmhouse. To her left, a sagging barbed-wire fence enclosed a pasture that rose gently away from the lane. What kind of shape was the rest of the place in? Duke had admitted that he was having trouble keeping up with all the work. Although no one had said so, Marty was sure Kyle didn't help much. He never had. Mama had been the one who held everything together, making sure the work got done even if she had to do most of it herself. The doctor had said an aneurism in her aorta had killed her, but Marty believed that she had just finally worn herself out.

"Look, Mom," Annie said, pointing to a big white-faced sorrel horse, his head hanging over the fence.

"That must be Uncle Kyle's gelding. He's supposed to be really nice." Marty rolled closer to the house and stopped the car. "Go ahead to pet him if you want."

Annie leaped out of the car, running toward the horse.

As she got out of the car, Marty looked around. Nothing seemed that different. The old clapboard farmhouse sat in a kind of bowl above the creek, the land rising gradually behind and to the left. The barn nestled on a ridge halfway up the hill.

As she started toward the house, she smiled. Someone had started painting the porch. The first step and part of the floor were a deep forest green. Then she saw the layer of dust covering the new paint—another half-done job. She looked back at her children, Annie gingerly stroking the face of the big sorrel and Jeff leaning against the car. Marty took a deep breath and climbed the steps.

The front door flew open and there stood Duke, trying to tuck his stained T-shirt over his belly and into his baggy jeans. His fringe of gray hair was wispy and uncombed. Two dogs charged after him. Jake, Duke's huge old Australian shepherd, began to lick Marty's knee. The other, a gangly speckled puppy, jumped and nearly knocked her off the porch. A third dog growled and dug at a door somewhere behind Duke.

"That other one is Kyle's blue heeler. She can get nasty," Duke explained, pushing his dogs aside. "Cody—this crazy pup—is all that's left of her and Jake's last litter."

Marty threw her arms around her father, blinking back tears. "Hi, Daddy," she said.

Duke held her tight, squeezing so hard Marty couldn't even find the breath to protest. Through the open door she could smell an unmistakable dog odor. The pup slipped back into the house behind Duke and lifted his leg.

Marty couldn't help herself; she started to laugh. No doubt about it—she was home.

T W O

Marty sank down on the bed and looked around the bedroom. Nothing had been changed in the twenty years she'd been gone. The quilted pink bedspreads on the twin beds had faded, as had the matching rosebuds on the wallpaper. The same ruffled curtains now hung limply at the big square windows. Someone, probably Duke, had run a dust cloth around the room, missing a few places on the white dresser. Dan had called the decor "cutesy Pennsylvania farmhouse." Marty didn't care. When she was ten years old, she and Mama had decorated this room together, picking out the bedspread and curtains from the J.C. Penney catalog and the wallpaper from the hardware store. Mama had convinced Duke to pay Marty twenty cents for every stall she cleaned and Mama had taken on extra lessons to help pay for it all.

Annie struggled into the room with her biggest suitcase, dropping it by the door. "I like this room," she said. She ran over to one of the windows. "I can see the creek and the woods."

Marty smiled. "I know. That's what I always loved about my room."

"But now it's *our* room, right?"

"That's right," Marty answered. "Yours and mine." Surprisingly, the idea of sharing the room was comforting. The awful late-night silence had haunted her since Dan's death. Now, even if dreams startled her awake, she wouldn't be alone.

Duke came to the door, a lopsided grin on his face. "I have a little surprise up at the barn. Let's go."

Wary, Marty peered at her father. His surprises were never practical and usually ended in disaster. "We should unload the car."

"Oh come on, Marty," Duke urged. "The luggage can wait."

Annie hurried to the door and took the hand Duke extended to her. Her eyes were shining. "Please, Mom," she said.

"Oh... I guess so," Marty said. She followed Duke and Annie down the stairs and out of the house. Jeff shuffled toward them, a small African drum under one arm, a string of South American seedpod clappers around his neck, and a suitcase in his other hand. "We're going up to the barn, Jeff," Marty said. "Want to come along?"

"No thanks. I'll have more fun unloading the car."

Marty forced a smile, trying to encourage him. She knew she'd have to take special care to meet his needs while they were here. It had been so hard for him to leave most of his instruments in storage with the furniture. With Duke and Annie, Marty climbed toward the barn. When they got close Annie skipped ahead into the barn, but Marty stayed behind with Duke who had stopped to catch his breath.

"Are you all right, Dad?" Marty asked.

"Sure. This old hill seems to get a little steeper every year."

When they reached the barn door, Annie ran out and threw her arms around her grandfather. "Is it for me?" she squealed.

"Sure is," Duke said, "But I expect your mom's going to get as big a kick out of this as you are." Duke walked over to a stall and slid the door open. Inside, a swaybacked, sunken-eyed pony stood looking at them through half-closed eyelids.

"Dad! It couldn't be!" Marty said, walking into the stall and stroking the pony's forehead. This muddy beige animal with the white mane and tail didn't look much like the chocolate brown dappled pony with the blond mane and tail that she remembered.

"Yes, indeed it is. Annie, this is Miss Cocoa, the pony your mom and Uncle Kyle learned to ride on."

"I got her when I was eight and she was three. Dad, that makes her thirty-three years old! How in the world did you find her?"

"I never lost track of her," Duke said. "After Gayle's kids outgrew her, she sort of passed from family to family. Old Man McCary had her last. His grandkids outgrew her years ago, but he never had the heart to get rid of her until he heard you were coming nome with your kids. I expect Jeff's a bit big for her, but you're just right, aren't you, Annie?" Duke scooped Annie up and set her on the pony's back. Cocoa's head sunk lower. She shifted her weight, cocking a back foot to rest on its toe. Marty thought she heard the pony groan.

"Hold on to her mane," Duke said, as he pulled on the halter. Finally, the pony stepped forward, limping badly on the back leg.

"Dad, she's lame," Marty said.

"Well, at thirty-three you didn't expect her to be in good shape, did you?" Duke said. "Actually, she's not in too bad a condition, considering. I think her chief problem in the back is a cracked hoof. I have Derry coming to trim her."

Marty felt her heart nearly bounce out of her chest. "When?" she asked, her voice cracking on her.

Duke chuckled. "Tomorrow or the next day. Whenever another call brings him out this way. What's with you? Did someone tell you that Derry's between wives?"

"Dad!" Marty could feel her cheeks getting hot. Actually Gayle had written that Derry and his second wife were having problems, but she didn't know that the marriage had ended. Still, she wasn't surprised. Derry Brady had a habit of hitting on every girl in the county over twenty—not a good way to keep a marriage intact.

"Just remember, girl," said Duke, "he hasn't changed much."

"I didn't imagine he had," Marty said, concentrating again on the pony. Poor Cocoa. There seemed a lot more wrong with her than a cracked hoof. Marty guessed that she hadn't been wormed in quite a while, and she didn't look like any oats had been her way either. Well, she'd drive over to the feed mill in the morning and buy some vitamins and wormer paste, and see if there was special feed for old horses.

The old pony still stood with her head down, breathing hard after carrying Annie only a few steps. "Come on, Annie," Marty said. "Let me help you off her. I don't think she's up to being ridden yet. It's going to take time to get her back in shape."

Marty almost laughed hearing herself. Cocoa could never be brought back to any kind of robust health. They'd probably have to fight just to keep her alive, yet Duke was grinning as if he'd pulled off the horse deal of the century. Marty had a feeling it was going to cost her a bundle in feed and vet bills.

"I better get to my unpacking," she said, turning to leave the barn before she became any more irritated with her father. He wouldn't understand that although she needed to come home, she didn't want to feel trapped here.

"Is it okay if I stay with Cocoa for a while?" asked Annie.

"Sure," Duke answered. "We'll give the old girl a good brushing."

Duke had already headed for the tack room to fetch the brushes and Annie had a look of such delight on her face that Marty only said, "All right, honey. Just be careful she doesn't step on your foot." Duke came back grinning widely and carrying two worn brushes. Marty wanted to say, "Don't brush too hard or the old girl will fall over." Instead, she headed toward the car.

A truck parked next to the house hurried Marty's step. It had to be Kyle's.

"Mom!" Jeff called, fear in his cry.

Marty turned toward the voice to see Jeff standing on the roof of the Volvo. On the ground crouched a stocky, dark-colored dog, probably Kyle's Australian blue heeler. "I'm coming," Marty said, moving quickly toward the house to find her brother. The dog spun toward Marty, growling. She froze and tried to stay calm. There was no surer way to get bitten than to run from a bad dog. Now barking deep in its throat, the dog began to run toward her.

"Down, Bella!" The dog dropped to its stomach as Kyle stepped off the porch. "Come," he said, and the dog, tail wagging, ran to him. "Sorry, Sis, she's real territorial."

Marty cautiously moved toward her brother. "Will she eat me if I give you a hug?"

Kyle laughed. "Probably. Let me lock her up." He snapped his fingers and the dog followed him into the house.

"Are you all right, Jeff?" Marty asked.

Jeff climbed down from the car roof. "That dog would have torn me apart. I had nowhere else to go but on top of the car."

"That's all right, as long as you're okay. She didn't bite you?"

"If you hadn't taken off running, she would have just circled, holding you in place until I got there," Kyle said, banging the screen door behind him.

"You saw what happened and didn't call her off?" Jeff snapped.

Kyle grinned, a boyish lopsided grin a lot like Duke's. "You did look pretty funny dancing around on top of that fancy car." He leaned against a porch post, folding his arms across his broad chest and crossing one blue-jeaned leg in front of the other. With his brown hair looped over his forehead and curling longer behind his ears, he looked more like a kid in his early twenties than a man of thirty-two.

Jeff stomped by his mother and Kyle into the house.

"Guess he didn't think it was too funny," Kyle said. He wrapped his arms around his sister. "Don't worry, Sis, we'll toughen him up."

Marty pulled back. "Kyle, life is toughening him up. He's lost his father. Remember?"

Kyle bent to kiss Marty's cheek. "Give us time. Jeff and I will get along just great."

Marty hugged her brother hard. "I sure hope so. What about that beast of yours?"

"Bella? She'll get used to you."

"But Kyle, what about Annie? She's little. Bella could swallow her in one bite."

"Bella loves kids. She's great with anyone under five feet tall." With his arm around her shoulder, he turned Marty toward the house. "Help me with dinner. I picked up some steaks."

Marty threw her arm around his waist to walk into the house with him. She did love him, this Peter Pan brother of hers. She always had. She swallowed the lump forming in her throat. "Steaks, huh," she teased.

"Sure thing. To celebrate your homecoming." He jumped up the porch steps ahead of her and gallantly swung the door open. "After you, my lady," he said with a bow.

Marty led the way into the house and to the kitchen. Four

brown bags filled the counter by the refrigerator. Marty smiled at the five huge T-bones she pulled from the first one. She and Annie could never eat a whole steak each. Kyle began to pull lettuce, tomatoes, cucumbers, potatoes, and salad dressing from another bag. The remaining bags held two three-liter bottles of pop and a quart of milk.

"I figured Annie still drank milk, but Jeff would rather have pop," Kyle said.

"Everything looks wonderful," Marty said. Jeff usually went through two or three quarts of milk a day. She'd tell him to go easy tonight. She'd go to the store tomorrow.

"How about I grill the steaks? You fix the salad and nuke the potatoes," Kyle said.

As Kyle, his arms loaded with steaks and cooking utensils, pushed his way out of the door, Marty went to work scrubbing the counters. No food was going to be prepared in this kitchen until it was cleaned. It really wasn't too awful, but a lot dirtier than Marty found acceptable. Occasionally, she glanced through the window to check on Kyle's progress. When she saw him placing the steaks on the grill, she put the potatoes in the microwave.

Annie and Duke came laughing through the front door just as Marty was finishing the salad. "Get your hands washed, Annie," she said. "Then come and help set the table." She heard Annie and Duke talking as they crowded into the powder room under the stairs to clean up. Marty walked down the hall to the foot of the stairs. "Jeff," she called, "dinner's ready."

He didn't answer but she heard his feet hit the floor above her. Annie and Duke were setting the table when she walked back into the kitchen. Through the window she saw Kyle making his way across the lawn with a tray full of steaks. Marty hurried to open the door for him.

Soon they were all seated around the big round kitchen table ready to eat. Kyle picked up his fork and knife. "All right," he said, "dig in."

"Just a minute, now," Duke said. "I'd like to say a blessing."

"You old hypocrite. You haven't been to church in ages," Kyle said.

"No matter. I'm feeling a need to talk to the Lord and I'm sure he understands, even if you don't." Duke reached out and took Marty's and Annie's hands. They all linked hands to finish the circle. "Dear Lord Jesus," Duke began, "two of us are missing today—my Betty and Marty's Dan. I know you're taking good care of them and I believe they're smiling down on us, because we're all together again, like a family should be. I thank you for that. We thank you, too, for this bountiful meal brought home by my son and cooked by him and my daughter. It is a great blessing for me to have my children and grandchildren seated together around my table. Help us to love and care for each other. Amen."

"Amen," Marty echoed, squeezing her father's hand. Everyone began to eat, Kyle teasing and Annie and Duke chattering between mouthfuls. Jeff ate silently. Marty knew it wasn't going to be easy for this group of very different personalities to get along, no matter how much they loved one another. And Marty did love them all. She said her own silent prayer asking the Lord to give them patience with one another.

T H R E E

Marty woke early the next morning and felt rested for the first time in months. She looked over at Annie, her brown wavy hair fanned across the pillow, a slight smile on her lips as she breathed the small even sighs of sound sleep. She was a beautiful child, a gift of joy and light.

Marty reached for her watch—seven o'clock. Early for D.C., but late for farm time. She slipped out of bed and dressed quietly before tiptoeing downstairs. She could smell coffee and headed for the kitchen. Kyle was hunched over his coffee cup reading the paper.

"Good morning," Marty said.

"Umm," Kyle mumbled.

Marty glanced over his shoulder to see what he was reading. "That's yesterday's paper," she said.

"Yeah, well, I'd rather read yesterday's news than walk all the way down the lane this early to get today's."

Marty chuckled and patted her brother on the back. "Never change, do you?"

"I suspect I change some, but not so it's noticeable. My fans would be too disappointed."

Marty went to the cupboard and finally finding an uncracked mug, poured herself a cup of coffee. "Are you referring to female fans?"

"Of course," Kyle said, grinning.

"Anyone special?"

"Naw. The young ones are too silly and once they're over twenty-five they're too smart to fall for my lines. I guess I'm destined to be a bachelor."

Marty heard a sound at the door. "What's that?"

"The dogs. I let them out when I got up and they're ready to come back in."

"Lock up that dog of yours."

"Just sit down and let her check you out. She'll be fine," Kyle said, walking to the door. He threw the door open and all three dogs squeezed through at once. The pup gamboled up to Marty; lifting his front legs into her lap, he licked her cheek.

Laughing, she pushed him down. "Sit," she ordered. To her surprise, he obeyed. He cocked his head, wrinkled his forehead and gazed at her out of white-rimmed eyes. Marty gave his head a pat. "Good boy, Cody," she said.

"Like I told you before, he likes you," Kyle said.

Bella, approaching from the opposite side, sniffed Marty's leg suspiciously and then trotted off to sink onto the floor next to Kyle, her head on his boot. Jake plodded by them to the water bowl.

Kyle finished his coffee. "I better get to work."

"Where are you working?"

"I'm putting on a deck for Doc Harbison. Pete Thomas is helping me. We'll be done by the end of the week and that will give us enough money to hit the roping circuit for a few weeks." Kyle stood and stretched. Bella jumped to her feet beside him, waiting for his next move. "Old Pete is a much better header than he is a carpenter. Lately, we've been making more money team-roping than we have at carpentry." Kyle snapped his fingers and Bella followed him to the cellar door. "I'll lock her up, so she doesn't scare the kids when they come down. Let her out later. Okay?"

Marty picked up her coffee mug and followed Kyle to the door. She watched him cross the lawn and hop into his truck cab. After all these years, he still played cowboy, using the rest of his life to support his play, yet never getting quite good enough to make it big time. He hadn't really committed himself to either carpentry or roping. But wasn't she a fine one to be critical of him, she thought. After eighteen years of living in the shadow of her professor husband, who was she? What did she want? There had to be something out there for her, a job she'd be excited about. And if she found it, could she balance the demands of work with duty to her children? On one of his last lucid days Dan had said, "You and the children will be fine. Just love each other and remember how much I love all of you. You're stronger than you think you are, Marty." Had he been right? Was she strong enough to raise the children by herself? Hard questions, but they were the ones she'd come home to answer.

Kyle pulled up beside the porch and called, "I already fed the horse and pony. I do early duty and Duke does the evening feeding. If you want to ride Red, go ahead. Your old saddle is still up in the barn." He smiled broadly, waiting for her reaction.

"Thanks. I just might do that," Marty said.

"I'm really glad to have you home, Sis."

"I've missed you, little brother," Marty said, realizing how much she meant it and how deep inside there gnawed a longing for all the years they'd lost. He was twelve when she went off to college, hating the smallness of rural life and coming home as little as possible. She hadn't realized that she was giving up as much as she was gaining. She waved after Kyle as he drove down the farm lane to the road.

Marty sat down on the porch, leaning against a post and dangling her legs over the edge as she sipped her coffee. Behind her the pup whined and pawed at the screen door until he pushed it open. He wiggled up beside her and flopped down, rolling belly up, his long legs waving in the air. Marty scratched his stomach. Dan and she had been talking about buying a puppy just before he got sick. His idea of a dog was "the bigger, the better." He'd have liked this pup.

Feeling twinges of self-pity stirring, Marty jumped to her feet. "Come on, Cody," she said, "let's take a walk." With the puppy right on her heels, she went back into the kitchen where she left a note for the kids—"Gone for a walk. Be back soon. Love you, Mom."

The warmth of the morning sun in a cloudless sky promised a beautiful day. Marty took deep breaths as she strode toward the creek with Cody trotting beside her. She never had much patience with whiny, dissatisfied people and she wasn't going to allow herself to become one. She and Dan had led a good life. She was only twenty when they married and he a twenty-four-year-old graduate student. By the time she graduated, he had received his Ph.D. His dissertation, judged brilliant in his field of political theory, brought job offers from all over. They chose the most prestigious and moved to Washington, D.C.

Dan never quite got used to the reality that *prestigious* didn't mean *lucrative*. Nor had he understood why a shortage of money didn't bother Marty. She had never told him how poor parts of her childhood had been. When Duke was a mechanic for the Clayton Coal Company, and the miners went on strike, the mechanics went out with them. Periodic strikes ate up any money they managed to save and then put them deep enough in debt that it took them until the next strike to dig their way out. She remembered winters when all they ate was venison or rabbit Duke shot and vegetables Mama canned from her garden. Christmas presents were homemade—puzzles and toys crafted by Duke and candy, cookies, mittens, and sweaters made by Mama. Yet, the Stafford kids always had everything they needed, and the childhood Marty had dreamed of escaping was now a mostly happy memory. Love had come in abundance even when worldly goods were in short supply.

She turned to walk along the creek toward the road. She'd get Duke's paper for him. Cody ran ahead and took a big slurping drink from the creek. A pair of mallards coasted on the surface of a deep pool in the creek's center. Cody spotted them and with a yelp leaped into the water. The mallards lifted off, squawking, and flew upstream, just skimming the surface of the creek. Cody splashed after them until they rounded the bend behind the house and disappeared from sight.

"Cody, come!" Marty called and the puppy ran back through the creek. He jumped onto the bank right in front of her and vigorously shook himself. Marty stepped away from him only to have him follow her. Laughing, she pushed him away. Cody acted like that was the signal to play. He bounced at Marty, catching her behind the knees and toppling her to ground. Then he wiggled and shook and threw himself all over her, licking her face. The harder Marty laughed, the more excited he became and the faster he licked. When she rolled onto her stomach and hid her face, he nibbled her hair. "Cody, sit," she yelled. Amazingly, he did.

Marty sat up and the puppy offered her his paw. "Truce," she said, shaking it. Her peach-colored T-shirt and pale blue jeans were covered with mud and grass stains. Her hair was sticky with dog spit and her face felt slimy. She grabbed the puppy and pulled him onto her lap, squeezing him and kissing the white triangle on top of his gray head.

The sound of a truck turning onto the lane startled her. She was still on the ground when she recognized Derry Brady's red truck slamming to a stop next to her. She was standing by the time he leaped from the truck and ran toward her. Before she could stop him, he scooped her into his arms and twirled her around. "It's about time you came home!" he said. He held her at arm's length, amusement evident on his handsome face. "Good grief, what happened to you?"

Marty ran a hand through her rumpled hair and tried to brush away some of the filth on the front of her T-shirt. "I was playing with the puppy," she muttered. She managed a feeble grin. Cody trotted over to sniff Derry's leg.

He bent and scratched the puppy behind one of his floppy ears. "Looks like he drug you through the creek for a mile or two," he said, smiling so that tiny wrinkles formed around his violet eyes. Those wrinkles and just a touch of gray glimmering along the temples in his black hair were the only changes she noted in him. If anything, they made him less perfect and so more attractive. "Oh, Marty," he continued, shaking his head, "I'm sure glad the rumors aren't true."

"What rumors?"

"Everybody was saying that after all those years in D.C., there wasn't much 'country' left in you."

"What are you doing here so early?" she asked, not willing to fall so easily into his teasing banter. As she remembered only too well, Derry Brady could charm the spots off a leopard.

"I'm always on my first call by eight and since I saw you speeding through town yesterday, I decided to make you my first call."

"Good. That pony's feet are in bad shape."

"Well, hop in the truck and let's get to it then," he said. He opened the passenger door and Marty climbed into the cab. The puppy jumped in after her and sat on the floor at her feet.

"Stop at the house. You can have a cup of coffee while I change," she said.

"Maybe the rumors are true. You don't have to change to go to the barn, you know."

"At least, let me wash my face and change my T-shirt. I promise to leave on the dirty jeans so you don't think less of me." She was doing it—firing back at him. That's how he used to lure her in. He'd start flirting and then she'd flirt back, and pretty soon she'd start believing he meant the sweet things he said. Well, she was older and wiser now.

He pulled up close to the porch. They stepped from the truck and he followed her into the kitchen. Duke stood at the stove in faded green boxer shorts and a raggedy T-shirt frying eggs. "Hey, Derry, want some eggs?"

"Naw, just a cup of coffee. The princess here needs to change her clothes." Derry helped himself to a mug.

"I'll be right back," Marty said.

Upstairs, Annie was just waking. "Morning, Mom," she said. Loud laughter drifted up from the kitchen, first Duke's and then Derry's. "Who's downstairs?" Annie asked.

"The blacksmith, sweetie. Better get dressed in a hurry if you want to watch him trim Cocoa's feet," Marty said, hoping that Annie would jump out of bed and come to the barn with her and Derry.

Annie was dressed in pink shorts and a flowered top before Marty decided what shirt to change into. She grabbed a cotton Aztec print and threw it on. "Annie, please wash your face and brush your teeth before you come downstairs," she said. Then Marty hurried into Duke's room and ruffled through his closet until she found an old brown robe for her father. Some culture shock would be inevitable for her children here, but she knew Annie wasn't ready for the sight of Duke in his skivvies.

In the kitchen Duke and Derry were still laughing, no doubt amusing each other with off-color jokes that were sure to embarrass her. They used to delight in seeing her cheeks redden. Marty handed her father his tattered terry-cloth robe. "Annie's on her way down," she said.

Duke quickly slipped into the robe. "Sorry," he said. "I guess your brother and I have been baching it out here too long."

"Don't worry, Duke. Now that Marty's back, she'll remind you about your manners," Derry said.

"I never succeeded with any of you. You're barely civilized," Marty said, pouring herself another cup of coffee.

"This is just like old times, with you two sitting around this kitchen snapping at each other," Duke said.

Annie walked into the room before Marty could manage a comeback.

Derry leaned back in his chair. "I don't believe it, Marty. She looks just like you when you were a kid. Except she doesn't have your red hair."

"Her father was dark," Marty said.

"You knew my mom when she was as little as me?" Annie asked, her eyes round with surprise.

"I sure did," Derry answered. "I went all the way through school with her from kindergarten through twelfth grade. What grade will you be in next year?"

"Third," Annie said.

"Well, your mom was the prettiest girl in third grade, like you will be," Derry said. "But, you know what, she just got prettier every year. I'll bet you will, too."

Yeah, thought Marty, *but that didn't stop you from cheating on me with every girl in the county.* Derry looked up at her with that smile that always melted her and made her give him one more chance. She frowned. "Let's get that pony done. I'm sure you've got a full day ahead of you."

Derry Brady was as good looking and smooth as ever, and loneliness made her vulnerable. But she was on her guard and, with the good Lord's help, she'd keep him at a safe distance.

FOUR

Annie marched down the barn aisle with the ancient pony hobbling behind her on a lead rope. Annie looked as proud as if she were leading a Kentucky Derby winner. In spite of Marty's growing discomfort with Derry's familiar banter, she smiled.

"Yes, ma'am," Derry said, "you've got a reason to be proud with a pony like this."

Marty glared at him. Surely he wouldn't mock a little kid. Derry looped an arm around the pony's neck and scratched under her bushy mane. "She's always liked a good scratch, haven't you, Cocoa girl," he said, his voice as soft and gentle as the look on his face. He laughed as the pony leaned into his hand, nodding her head as if to encourage him. "Miss Cocoa and I are old friends, Annie. I was real pleased when I heard she'd come back here."

"Don't tell me you remember this pony?" Marty said.

"She was still around, Marty, when you and I..." he looked at Annie and winked, "were seeing each other. But I shod her for Morgans and most of the other families who had her." He looked at her hooves which were so long they curled on the ends. "As you can see, no one has trimmed her in a while." He bent and examined her feet.

"Grandpap says she just needs a good trimming and she'll be fine," Annie said.

"Annie, I..." Marty began.

"Annie, good trimmings are the only kind I give, so let's see what we can do for the old girl." He bent to work. Marty could see the pony shift her weight and lean into him every time he picked up a foot, but Derry didn't once push her off and make her balance herself, like blacksmiths usually did with the animals they shod. His shoulder and back muscles bulged under his red T-shirt as he supported the pony while nipping and filing her feet.

Marty looked away, not liking the effect those muscles we.e having on her. She walked to the end of the aisle, checking the condition of the place. From the amount of manure-caked straw in each stall, Kyle had apparently just rotated Red all winter. When one stall got too filthy to deal with, he moved the horse to the next one. When this had been ripe, the smell had to be nauseating. She felt her anger rising. How could Kyle and Duke have stood it? Now that Red stayed out in the field all the time, the manure had dried and just added to the dry, musky smell of the barn.

She was embarrassed to have Derry see the place like this. She glanced toward him as he worked on the pony's feet. Annie sat on a tack box and held the lead rope, laughing and talking with him. Obviously, his charm worked even on eight-year-olds.

Marty fetched the wheelbarrow and a pitchfork from the supply room and went to work on one of the stalls. This barn had been a showplace once, with its oiled oak doors and freshly painted trim. Mama used to laugh that Duke kept the barn in better repair than the house. But Mama had been the driving force behind it all. Now cobwebs draped in ghostly swags from the rafters. The broken asphalt in the aisle made walking treacherous. The stall fronts and doors which she and Kyle had been made to oil every six weeks were caked with grime. She had been too tired last night to notice the horrible details.

She hauled five wheelbarrows of filth from the first stall to the manure pile behind the barn. She nearly cried as she opened the next door. The manure was so deep she had to step up into the stall. There was no way she could do all twenty stalls by herself. This Augean stable needed Hercules.

"Mom," Annie called, "come see Cocoa's feet."

Marty forced a smile and walked toward her daughter who now hugged the pony around the neck. Derry leaned against the wall, watching her in a way no one had in years. "Your pony looks wonderful, Annie," she said, her voice sounding phoney even to her own ears. She felt the heat rise in her cheeks. She had almost reached them when she stepped on a piece of broken asphalt and lurched forward—right into Derry's arms.

"A lot of women have fallen for me over the years, but your mom always did it most dramatically," Derry said.

Marty straightened herself, readjusting her shirt that had bunched up above her waist.

"Hey, Marty. You're blushing."

Annie giggled. "You are, Mom. Your face is all red."

"Derry, cut it out! Annie, don't listen to him."

"I like him, Mom. And he asked me out for ice cream tonight."

Marty stared at Derry, who grinned back at her. "She said she wasn't allowed to date yet, but she could go if her mom went along."

"Can we go, Mom, please? He's going to take us to that place we saw in town, the one that looks like a gingerbread house."

He was as sneaky as ever. This time he'd wheedled Annie onto his side. Well, she wasn't that easy. "Not tonight, honey," Marty said, and looked away from Annie's disappointed face. "Why don't you brush your pony while I say goodbye to Mr. Brady?"

"Forget the Mr. Brady stuff, Annie. Everybody calls me Derry." He looked sharply at Marty and strode from the barn. She followed him down the hill at what seemed to her an appropriately casual distance.

"Derry, thank you so much for coming right away," she said. She straightened her shoulders. Keep to business. "Now what do we owe you?"

"Nothing, not for that pony."

"Derry, I insist."

"I'm not doing you a favor. It's that pony. I won't charge for her." He looked uncomfortable. "Do you have any idea how many kids around here had their first ride on her? Quite a few of them are horse people today because they loved riding on that pony. This is between Miss Cocoa and me. Old Man McCary never had her feet done. I used to sneak into his field in the morning on the way to my first job and trim her. Lately, I've been too busy."

Marty's smile became genuine. "Thanks," she said.

"I had to put some epoxy in that crack. I'll check it regularly.

If I were you, I'd give her a little bute in her feed—every other day should do it. She's got a lot of arthritis in those old legs of hers. She's not going to take any heavy riding, but I'm sure you know that."

"Yeah, I do. I think Annie's just as content to brush and play with her."

"She's a nice little girl, Marty. You're lucky."

"I know I am. Wait until you meet Jeff."

Derry stepped up into his truck before turning back to her. "I'm sorry about your husband."

"He was a good man. We were happy together," Marty said, she looked away from Derry toward the barn.

"You better get back to Annie. Listen…" he began, reaching through the open window and taking her chin to turn her face back to him. "I'm not playing with you. We're both too old for that. I really would like to take you and Annie—your son, too, if he wants—out for ice cream tonight. It will be fun. You can get into town and see some old friends."

"Not tonight," she said. A look of disappointment crossed his face. "How about tomorrow night?"

The broad smile that flashed across his chiseled lips and shone out of his violet eyes warmed her. He was above all else an old friend, and Derry as a friend was kind, generous, and dependable.

"Great! Pick you up at eight," he said, as he started the truck. He winked at her and was gone. She was glad she'd changed her mind. Derry was so much fun. She remembered how he used to make her laugh. She needed to laugh like that again. She'd wear her flowered sundress, the one for which she'd paid more than she should have at that little shop in Arlington.

She watched until his truck and even the dust trail was long out of sight. As she headed back to the barn, reason returned to her brain. He'd done it again… he'd reeled her in like a trout on the end of a fishing line. She supposed she'd have been disappointed if he hadn't at least tried to connect with her, even though it made her feel uncomfortable at the time. She focused on her memory of Dan, her honest, straightforward, dependable man. And Dan had been a lot taller than Derry and just as good looking, with his broad forehead, dark eyes and square chin.

Still, Derry had invited the kids, so it wasn't like a real date. She certainly wasn't ready for that. Besides, she'd managed to put him off a day, so he couldn't think he'd just bowled her over.

After praising Annie on her grooming of Cocoa, Marty picked up the pitchfork and went to work, hoping to numb the confusing emotions racing through her.

FIVE

Marty turned the shower on hotter than she normally would have on such a warm day. She picked up the soap and washcloth and scrubbed hard—especially on her arms and neck, which were particularly grimy. The musty dust still clung inside her nose, and all she could smell was dried manure. She let the water run over her head and down her face. She'd worked all morning, and had managed to get only five of the stalls cleaned.

She shouldn't have done it. The work was empty drudgery, and it wasn't her responsibility. But the pain in her back almost made her forget the weird flutter in her stomach caused by Derry Brady. She let the hot water hit her back between her shoulders. Her back muscles felt stretched and strained, but they were still strong, capable of hard work. For that she could be grateful.

Just as her muscles began to loosen, the stream from the shower cooled rapidly to a lukewarm spray and then an icy trickle. She'd forgotten about this side of country living. She rinsed quickly and jumped from the shower, slipping into her soft, terry robe. Then she stepped from the bathroom, ready to face her day. She had to get to the feed store. Not only did she need supplies for the pony, but she also needed lime, a lot of it, to disinfect those stalls.

Before she reached her room the phone rang. Duke and Annie had gone for a walk in the woods. Jeff was apparently still asleep, although it was after eleven. She ran for the phone in Duke's room. "Hello," she said, breathless.

"You rat! You've been here since yesterday and haven't called me. Meet me at the rock ledge."

"Gayle!" Marty said. But Gayle had hung up. Marty gave her hair a quick drying with the towel and then fluffed her short curls with her fingers. She dressed for the heat in a pair of cutoffs and a T-shirt and pulled on her sturdy hiking boots, hoping that she could still climb to the rock ledge.

Jeff opened the door to his room as she hurried by. Ignoring his sour look, Marty kissed his cheek. "Your sister is taking a walk with your grandfather. When she comes back, keep an eye on her. I won't be long."

"Where are you going?"

"To meet my oldest and dearest friend at the rock ledge," she said. She laughed at his puzzled expression. "I'll explain later." She charged down the steps and out the door, no longer feeling tired. A good talk with Gayle was just what she needed.

The puppy loped to meet her. "All right," she said, scratching him behind the ear. "You can come." He gamboled along beside her, occasionally leaving her side to splash through the creek. She squared her broad shoulders, lengthened her stride, and inhaled deeply. How she had missed that fertile earth smell of June in Washington County—a smell that combined all the odors of the creek, the grasses, the wildflowers, and trees mixed with the warm essence of animals. When she reached the section of the lane below the rock ledge, Marty peered up through the trees to see Gayle had beaten her there. "Hey, Friend!" Marty called.

"I'm still faster than you are," Gayle teased from the ledge.

Marty looked at the tree trunk bridge and hoisted herself onto it. "I'm hoping I can still do this." The pup jumped into the water and splashed across. Fortunately, the creek narrowed to about ten feet across and two or three feet deep at this point. By balancing carefully and quickly putting one foot ahead of the other, Marty joined the pup on the other side.

"So far so good," Gayle called. "Now for the tough part."

Marty started the climb. The old path was still evident, worn into the cliff face of rock and dirt. Her leg muscles seemed to retain a physical memory of the climb, pulling her steadily upward until the ledge jutted just a step above her. The puppy clambered past her, nearly knocking her down. When he landed on the rock, he almost bowled Gayle over.

Gayle laughed that deep warm laugh that Marty loved and believed could come only from an untroubled soul. Gayle extended her hand and Marty grasped it, leaping onto the ledge and throwing her arms around her friend.

"Boy, have I ever missed you!" Marty said. She clung to her friend as if she hadn't seen her in years, even though Gayle had driven Duke to D.C. when Dan had died. Gayle had been the one to keep the family running through seemingly endless days of visitations and the funeral.

"Well, now you're home," Gayle said, as if Marty were a traveler completing a journey.

"For the summer anyway."

"All right, so I'll take a summer." Gayle's smile spread across her face, a broad-featured, striking face that became beautiful when she smiled. She plopped cross-legged on the rock ledge, looking like a slightly older version of Marty's childhood friend, her figure still slim and girlish. She even wore her thick blond hair in the same kind of short ponytail, but smoothed straight back from her forehead without the square bangs she had as a kid.

Marty sat beside her and the puppy jumped into her lap and then into Gayle's.

"Cody, you are a hazard," Gayle said, pushing him back to Marty.

Marty made the pup sit between them. "How do you know Cody?"

"I think he eats every other meal at our house," Gayle answered. "And your brother talked Mac into taking one of his littermates." Gayle stroked the puppy's muzzle where the brown speckles turned black. "By the way," she said, mischief evident in her voice, "I hear Derry's been to see you already."

"For Pete's sake, who told you that? I saw him just this morning. I see gossip still travels with the speed of lightning around here."

"Relax. It's not general knowledge yet. Derry told us when he stopped to tack a shoe on one of our Belgian mares. Of course, after you show up in town with him tomorrow night, everyone will know."

Marty groaned. She drew her knees up and laid her forehead against them. "I'll try to behave properly so I don't give anyone, especially Derry, the wrong idea."

"I have great faith in your good sense. Besides, Mac gave Derry a talking-to. Told him that you are a grieving widow and he's not to try to tree you like a hound after a coon."

Marty smiled her appreciation. "Listen, I'm sorry I didn't call you yesterday. I was a bit overwhelmed."

"I told Duke to get a maid in, but he said he had the time to clean. I can just imagine."

"Oh, he did an okay job. I wasn't expecting House Beautiful, you know. The barn, however, was a bit of a shock."

"Knee-deep in horse poop?"

Marty nodded. "It's a miracle old Red's feet didn't rot off last winter. I got some of the stalls mucked out this morning."

Gayle leveled one of her "looks" at Marty. "Why?"

"I know, I know. I shouldn't have."

"You know Duke and Kyle. Filth and chaos don't bother them like they do most people. They won't even notice if you work yourself to death trying to fix the place up. Don't you let them dump on you. Your kids need you more than they do."

"You're right. I just can't stand the place a mess. I remember how nice Mama kept the house and garden and how much pride Duke used to have in the barn."

"You can't fix all those years of neglect in one summer, Marty."

"I know, but…"

"Is it just one summer?"

A sigh escaped from deep inside Marty and nearly brought a flood of tears. Marty bit her lip and willed the tears away. "I don't know. I can't afford to stay in D.C., but I don't know that I want to stay here either. Right now I think I'd like to teach, but maybe closer to Pittsburgh."

"Teaching jobs are pretty scarce in all of western Pennsylvania."

"That's what I've heard. I finished my student teaching after Jeff was born but never took a job, so that will make finding a position even tougher."

"Do you have some time to explore your options?" Gayle asked.

"I have enough money to get through the summer without touching my investments. If the house in D.C. sells, I'll have more time. The trouble is, I'm not sure I have any marketable skills. I've been a wife and mother for so long…" She hesitated and then, like a swollen stream breaching its banks, her words flooded the space that time had put between them.

She told Gayle her fears of not being able to care for the kids alone, either financially or emotionally; about not knowing who she was anymore now that she wasn't Dan's wife; about Jeff's unhappiness and Annie's uncertainty; and about the terror that sometimes shook her late at night. "I guess I don't even mind doing some work here, because I'm so glad to be someplace where I don't have to handle it all alone. But in moments of clarity, I know that Duke and Kyle can't take on my problems; they don't even deal with their own."

"Take it to the Lord, Marty. Pray on it and God will show you what to do. And he'll help you to do it."

Marty looked at Gayle in surprise. Gayle had always been the first to suggest sneaking out of Sunday school to go swimming in the creek or ice skating on the pond. She was ready to make a sarcastic remark, but Gayle's face seemed totally sincere. "Gayle, I'm not sure I know how to pray anymore."

"Just do it and you'll find it comes easier with practice. Why don't you start by coming to church with Mac and me on Sunday. Bring the kids and I'll gather some of our old friends for a picnic at our place afterwards."

"Do I have to go to church to come to dinner?" Marty asked.

"Of course not. Only if you want to. But, are you sure you don't?"

"I don't know where God and I stand right now. Dan, the great agnostic, made his peace with God before he died. He even asked for his mother's pastor to come and pray with him. Needless to say, my mother-in-law was thrilled."

She paused, jarred by her memories. "We all did a lot of praying those last months—for all the good it did. At first I felt guilty that maybe my faith hadn't been strong enough, that I hadn't prayed in the right way. Then I got mad at Dan for dying **and** furious with God for letting him die. I guess I have a lot of untangling to do on that subject."

Gayle reached for Marty's hand. She had always understood, except about how Marty had hated this place and her desperation to escape. But Marty hadn't been able to outrun all the bad feelings and she'd found that it wasn't this place she'd hated after all, only its limitations. For all her childish dreaming of a sophisticated world of art and culture, after she'd found that world, some nights she'd cried, missing the people and places of her home. Dan would try to tease her out of it, saying, "You can take the girl out of the country, but you can't take the country out of the girl." Then he'd kiss her and call her his "little hillbilly" and go back to sleep.

It had been the same about issues of faith, so she hadn't been able to tell him she had missed church, especially the old stone Methodist church on the hill at home. He'd laugh about Bible thumpers and cornfed preachers talking on cue with God. Finally, she'd just numbed herself to her longings. And now when she needed God, she was having trouble finding him. "Maybe I will come to church on Sunday," Marty said. "I don't know. If not..."

Gayle reached out and hugged her. "If you can't do church this week, then come for the picnic anyway. Okay?"

Marty blinked away the tears that stung the corners of her eyes and clung to Gayle. "I have missed you more than I ever let you know!"

By the time they parted the sun was way past the midpoint of the sky, and Marty and Gayle had caught up on all the news and renewed their friendship to its former closeness.

Cody scrambled down the hillside beside Marty, scattering pebbles into the creek below. She was glad for his company and touched by his simple affection. When they had made it across the creek, she reached down and scratched his head. She looked back to the far side of the creek where the occasional silver blue of a spruce or mossy green of native fir varied the brown and green of oak, maple, and locust trees. Several white-trunked sycamores grew beside the bank. It was in just such a sycamore, huge and hollowed, that her many times great-grandfather had survived his first winter on this land. With only the clothes on his back, his rifle, and what tools his knapsack could carry, he had walked into what was then called "The Big Shade" to stake out property for his family. It was down this lane that another grandfather had marched to help General Washington win the fight for independence. In those woods, that same grandfather and his sons and daughters had hidden their still during the Whiskey Rebellion, praying that they wouldn't have to fight again, this time against President Washington. During the Civil War, Staffords had left this farm to fight for the Union. Some of them had no doubt been as afraid and uncertain as she was now, but the Staffords were a tough lot. She broke into a jog, Cody loping beside her. Her strong legs pumped as she sped toward home. She had a feeling that whatever lay ahead, she, too, would need to be tough.

S I X

"Here he comes, Mom," Annie called from the front porch.

Marty glanced at her watch—8:10. Not bad for a guy who had once arrived three hours late to take her to a 4-H meeting that had already been over for an hour. "Annie, you run on down," Marty said. "I'm going to try one more time to get Jeff to come."

She could hear Jeff in his room beating on one of his many drums. It sounded like an African rhythm, but angry and insistent. She climbed the steps and knocked on his door loudly. The drumming stopped. "Jeff?" Marty said.

"Yeah," he answered from behind the closed door.

"May I come in?"

She heard the sound of feet hitting the floor and footsteps across the hardwood. Jeff opened the door and stared sullenly at her.

"Jeff, why don't you come with us? It will be fun."

"I'm not in a fun mood," he snarled, and returned to the bed where he flopped back against the headboard and again began to beat on the small carved drum from Zaire that Dan had given him.

Marty willed him to look at her, but he only stared down at his drum, his hands rhythmically beating it. "Hey," she said.

Jeff looked up, his hands still working on the drum head. "What's the deal, Mom? If you take the kids along on your date, is it going to make you feel better?"

"Jeff, I told you, this isn't a date."

"Yeah, right!" Jeff said, drumming hard and angry.

Marty sighed and shook her head. "Okay, Jeff, be as angry and miserable as you want, but I still love you."

Jeff's shoulders slumped. The drumming stopped. Marty waited. Finally, he said, "Yeah, me too, to you."

Marty crossed the distance between them and kissed his tousled hair. "We won't be late."

He nodded and went back to the rhythm which sounded slightly less angry. Marty stopped and looked once more at her reflection in the hall mirror. She fluffed her curls with her fingers. She'd have to do. She liked her green-and-navy checked blouse over her green tank top. With her denim skirt and good leather sandals, her outfit seemed appropriate, not as fancy as the sundress she'd thought about wearing, but dressier than jeans. Why was she fussing? Like she'd told Jeff, this was not a date, only going out for ice cream with an old friend.

Memories of her first date with Dan—a formal dance at his fraternity—flooded her mind. She darted into her bedroom and opened her jewelry box. She took out the antique locket Dan had given her on their tenth anniversary and fastened it around her neck as she hurried down the steps. She didn't open it to look at the two small photos, one of Dan and her when they were married, the other of the children when they were little. She just felt better with it around her neck.

Derry was waiting for her beside a shiny white sports car. Annie had already climbed into the backseat. Marty never could tell one car from the other, but she knew this was an expensive package. Duke had told her Derry had done very well for himself, working hard, making good investments and some profitable horse deals on the side. He slumped in studied ease against the side of his car, in tailored khakis and a purple knit polo shirt which did great things for his eyes. But he was trying too hard, which meant he was every bit as nervous as she was. Just the thought made Marty relax.

As she skipped down the steps, he gallantly swung open the passenger door. "I never mind waiting for a pretty lady."

Marty laughed. "After all the time I clocked waiting for you when we were teenagers, you better not mind."

When he circled the car and slid into the driver's seat, he whispered, "Don't forget—I've spent the last twenty years waiting for you to come home."

Marty's stomach flipped. This was not how she wanted the evening to go, particularly with Annie who was now giggling in the backseat. "Derry Brady, from what I've heard you've always had plenty of female company to keep you occupied."

Derry's laugh erupted from deep in his belly. "All right, so I wasn't totally lonely and pitiful, but I sure did miss you. No one has ever known how to keep me in my place like you do."

Marty looked at him sitting smart and sassy behind the wheel of this "look at me, baby" car, and for the first time since he'd rumbled back into her life, she felt safe. She knew she could keep him at a distance because she knew him so well. If she didn't, he'd use her up and quickly lose interest, like he did with all the women in his life. Marty didn't play those games. She playfully punched his shoulder. "And don't you forget it, Buddy."

"Good grief, Annie," Derry said rubbing his shoulder. "Is she this tough on you kids?"

Annie's face popped up between their seat backs. "Nope," she said. "She's the best mom in the world."

Marty kissed her daughter's cheek. "Only because I have the best kids in the world. Now you sit back and put on your seat belt."

She helped Annie adjust the belt and then fastened her own around her waist.

Derry smiled at her, a soft private smile. "I always knew you'd be a good mom."

"Thanks," she answered.

They had arrived at the end of the farm lane. Derry turned the car left and rattled across the old iron bridge and on toward town. "You know, I have a niece Annie's age," Derry said.

"That's right," Marty said. "Gayle wrote and told me Cam adopted a little girl from South America."

"From San Salvador. She was what they called a 'special needs' child. She was five and had some problems. He was down there on a wildlife rescue mission and stopped to see a friend who worked at the orphanage. Kika grabbed onto his leg and wouldn't let go. You know my brother—he couldn't just leave her there, so he set about to adopt her. I'm really proud of him. He's doing the single-father bit very well. I asked them to meet us tonight, but they have father-daughter Spanish lessons. He said to tell you he'd see you soon and..." Derry looked at her out of the corner of his eye and grinned sheepishly.

"Come on, what else did he say?"

"He told me to behave myself with you or I'd have my little brother to answer to."

"That's right. Cam always stuck up for me." While Derry had been the object of her rampant teenage desire, Cam had been her buddy, probably her best friend after Gayle.

"Kika will be going to school with you, Annie."

"If we stay here," Marty said.

Derry's head snapped around and gave her a quick hard look before turning back to the road ahead. "When Duke said you were moving home, I thought…"

"Grandpap told me that he was going to take care of us. That we were going to live here and go to school here and everything," Annie said, worry evident in her voice.

"Annie, I don't know yet where we're going to live. Grandpap knows that, and he shouldn't have told you we were staying."

Derry reached over and patted her arm. "You know Duke, Marty. He creates his own reality." Derry lowered his voice to a whisper. "The thought of Duke taking care of anyone is a little scary. Although, I must admit I like the idea of you staying here."

"Mom, if we go somewhere else, what will happen to my pony?" Annie asked, an edge of hysteria in her voice.

Marty wanted to scream. Duke had a way of scratching old wounds, which was precisely why she wasn't sure she could stay on the farm. He was so darn manipulative, bumbling along, making bad decisions and then getting Mama to clean up after him, make everything right again. Well she wasn't going to become Mama.

"Annie, that's not something you have to worry about now, all right? I'm sure Grandpap will keep the pony for you. After all, he's the one who got her." And Marty would use all her power to ensure that he did. Her little girl wasn't going to have any more losses. Not if she could help it.

Her words seemed to calm Annie, and while Marty sat and stewed, Derry talked to Annie about her pony, about ponies in general, about the small country school she'd attend, about all the fun things for a kid to do around the county. By the time they reached town, Marty determined to dispel her mounting agitation. It had been a long time since she'd had an evening out, and she was going to enjoy herself.

"Hey, look, Marty, Raynak's Service Station. Remember when we almost blew it up?"

"Derry! You are going to have my daughter thinking I was an arsonist or something."

"Fireworks, Annie," Derry said. "I had some fireworks my uncle had brought up from West Virginia and your mom and a whole group of us including Timmy Raynak set them off in that field across the street. A bottle rocket went a bit farther than we planned and landed in a garbage can by the station. Fortunately, Timmy's parents were right there to roll it away from the gasoline pumps."

"Or we might have blown up the whole town," Marty added. "And, in case you have any such ideas, Annie, I spent the next day, which was the Fourth of July, alone in my room. I missed the parade, the community picnic, the *real* fireworks, and everything."

"Well, you were lucky. I could barely walk when my old man got done with me," Derry said.

Marty noticed a tall fat man standing outside the hardware store, his T-shirt barely covering his belly. "It's Pudgy Patterson," she said.

Derry slowed the car and opened his window. "Hey Pudge," he yelled, "look who's home."

Marty laughed and waved as Pudgy grinned and peered into the car. "Hey, I heard you'd come back," he called.

"We're going up to Ceci's. Meet us there," Derry called.

"As soon as I close up the store, Derry," Pudgy called. As he waved after them, his limp T-shirt rose to expose most of his round stomach.

"There is the best-known bellybutton in the county," Marty said.

"Sure is," Derry said. "Pudgy played football with me, Annie.

The team's warmup exercise was getting him into his pants. They never seemed to stretch enough."

Marty's mood had lightened considerably and Annie's infectious giggle replaced any remaining shadows. They were all laughing as Derry pulled up in front of the gingerbread house.

Inside, the wall between the old parlor and dining room had been knocked out to make one large room, nearly half of the first floor of the big old house. The walls had been decorated in a paper of a Victorian design, pale blue and green stripes intertwined with flowers. Lacy curtains hung from brass rods over the floor-to-ceiling windows. Material matching the wallpaper covered the cushions on the banjo-backed wicker chairs.

Derry ushered them to the biggest table, right in the center of the room. Marty could feel her cheeks heating up. "Derry, the place is pretty crowded and there are only three of us. We better take that small table over by the window."

"Don't worry. When Pudge spreads the word that we're up here, we'll fill this table in no time," Derry answered.

A young girl squeezed by them with a tray laden with tall glasses filled with jewel-colored soda and scoops of ice cream and boat-shaped sundae bowls topped with mountains of whipped cream with a pirouette cookie stuck in like a flag.

Annie, her blue eyes big and round, patted Marty's arm. "Mom, can I have anything I want?"

"You bet you can," Derry said. "When you're out with me, young lady, nothing but the best."

Annie and Derry ordered first, each seeming to try to outdo the other with their impossible combinations of ice cream and sauces. When the waitress turned to her, Marty said, "A cappuccino and a single scoop of raspberry frozen yogurt."

"Booooo! Hissss!" Derry mocked.

Marty made a face at him. "It's what I want," she said. "I'm not a glutton, like some other people I know." But as the waitress went by with sundaes for another table, Marty's mouth watered. She hadn't ordered what she wanted, but what Dan, ever vigilant about fat content and cholesterol, would have chosen. And although she had never had any trouble with elevated cholesterol or weight gain, she had always tried to encourage him. She still had time to call the waitress back, but her mind went blank. She didn't have any idea what she really wanted.

SEVEN

"Derry, how good to see you!"

Marty looked up at a tall woman with sweeping blond waves, whose long elegant fingers were on Derry's shoulder. When he gave the woman a knowing, private kind of smile, Marty felt a green rage rising, and that surprised her. She didn't want that kind of a relationship with Derry or anyone. She wasn't ready for it.

Derry took the woman's hand and spun her onto a seat next to him. The woman's flowered sundress billowed around her and sent a whiff of pricey perfume toward Marty. She sported a tan that could only come from daily sessions at a tanning bed. Marty looked down at her own coarse denim skirt and the pale legs beneath it. She imagined how she looked compared to this woman—like Annie's pony next to a long-legged, shiny-coated thoroughbred.

"Marty and Annie," Derry said "this is Ceci Collins. She owns this place."

Marty pasted a smile on her face. So, Derry Brady was still up to his old games. He had always played all the girls against each other, loving to watch them throw jealous tantrums over him. Ceci began to prattle on to Derry about some horse of hers he'd recently shod. Apparently, she owned show horses, and was trying to impress everyone within earshot with how valuable this particular horse was. Marty scanned the room, hoping to find a familiar face to distract her.

Just then the front door flew open and slammed against the wall. Everyone turned to see Pudgy standing in the door, his arms spread wide, a huge grin on his face.

"Welcome home, Miss Marty!" he shouted. He ran across the room and threw his beefy arms around her. After squeezing her so hard she couldn't speak, he bounced her up and down a couple of times in the chair before planting a big wet kiss on her cheek. Marty knew her cheeks had to be scarlet. Out of the corner of her eye she saw Ceci cast a condescending look their way, but Derry, Annie, and Pudgy were laughing with such abandon that she couldn't help throwing her arms around Pudgy's shoulders to hug him back, her laughter joining theirs.

Pudgy threw himself into one of the small wicker chairs, nearly upsetting it. Ceci winced and excused herself to see some other customers. Pudgy turned his exuberance toward Annie. "I know you have to be Marty's girl 'cause you look just like she did when she was little." He held out his hand. Annie offered hers and he gently shook it. "I'm Pudgy Patterson."

"I'm Annie Harris. Did everyone around here know my mom when she was a kid?"

"Not everyone, Annie," Marty was glad Ceci hadn't been around then.

"I'm telling you, Marty, you'll be surprised how many of us are still around," Pudgy offered.

"Even some of the ones determined to leave town didn't get any farther away than Pittsburgh," Derry said. "Unlike someone else we know, most everybody shows up for our class reunions."

Before Marty could respond, the waitress arrived with their order. Glad for the reprieve, Marty watched as the waitress laid a colossal whipped and ice cream confection in front of Annie and then another in front of Derry. "Wowee," said Pudgy. "Will you look at those!"

As the waitress set Marty's frozen yogurt and cappuccino on the table, she asked, "What can I get for you, Mr. Patterson?"

"The flesh is weak, Melissa. As much as I'd like one of those," he said, pointing to Annie's sundae, "you'd better bring me one of those." He pointed to Marty's small scoop of raspberry yogurt. "As long as it's low fat, right?"

"Here, Pudge. Take this one." Marty said pushing it toward him. "And bring me one of the sundaes." She felt reckless and rebellious, like the kid she'd once been.

"You can afford it. You're almost as thin as you were in high school," Pudge said. "Me, I've got to watch my cholesterol and my blood pressure and…"

"And Darla must be joining us," Derry said, "or you'd be

47

snarfing down a sundae like the rest of us."

"You know me too well. She'll be here as soon as she gathers up the little ones. We've got four kids, Marty. Walter Jr. is thirteen. He's a good boy. I left him to close up the store. Then there's Kathy, Jennifer, and Mark who are ten, eight, and six." He dug in his pocket and pulled out a wallet, flipping it open to a photograph.

"Course, you know Darla," Pudgy said, pointing toward the woman in the photo. "Darla Green, a couple of years behind us. We married as soon as she finished high school and I've never had one moment's regret. I was working in the store with Daddy so I was able to put her through nurse's school. She's real smart and always dreamed about going on to school."

Marty looked closely at the pretty woman in the photo but didn't recognize the face. Yes, there had been a Darla Green—a scruffy, skinny little thing who had lived in a fallen-down shack outside of town with her drunken father and no mother that anyone could remember. Marty hadn't really known her, but she remembered the kids had called her Dirty Darla and stayed away from her. There were rumors, too—some of the guys claimed her nickname had nothing to do with her raggedy clothes or the fact that the shack had no running water. What Marty remembered most was the girl's sad, dark eyes and how she shrank into herself whenever anyone noticed her.

So Marty wasn't prepared for the pretty, round-faced woman who came into the ice cream parlor, the smile on her lips lighting up her whole face and shining out of her dark eyes. The two youngest children broke into a run when they saw Pudgy and threw themselves at him. He wrapped his arms around them and then stood to hug his wife and his older daughter. Both Pudgy and Darla beamed as the children were introduced. They all offered their hands for Marty to shake.

"Of course, Darla, you remember Marty," Pudgy said.

"Sure I do." She gave Marty a quick firm hug. "You might not remember me, though. We didn't know each other very well. You were always so popular," she said with a genuine smile. She sat next to her husband who scooped her hand into his.

Derry traded places with Annie so she could sit next to Jennifer and he next to Marty. He leaned forward and grinned at Darla. "You remember me, don't you?" he said, pretending neglect.

Darla laughed, a soft melodious sound. "Of course, Derry. You are unforgettable."

The waitress came back with Marty's sundae and took the Pattersons' orders. Marty looked over at Annie, deep in conversation with Jennifer. Marty joined in the easy banter with her old friends about what the ensuing years had held for all of them. They had been good years for Darla and Pudgy.

"Well, I might have known everyone in town would know you were back before we did," a nasal voice whined behind Marty.

"Renee!" Marty jumped from her chair to hug her cousin. Standing behind Renee, arms crossed under an ample bosom, loomed Marty's aunt. "Aunt Bertie!" A reluctant smile came to the old woman's face and she threw her arms open.

Marty moved into her arms and accepted her back-patting hug and kisses on both cheeks. When Aunt Bertie pulled back, she slipped a lace-edged handkerchief from under the belt of her green shirtwaist dress and dabbed at her eyes. "My only sister's daughter and I have to find out you're in town by overhearing conversation in the hardware store. Imagine my embarrassment."

"You could have told us you were moving home, Marty," Renee added, her habitual sour look on her face. "Somebody asked me about you last week, and I had to tell them I didn't know a thing, hadn't heard from you in ages." She narrowed her eyes and looked around Marty at Derry.

"I'm sorry. I've been here only a few days. I assumed Duke would tell everyone I was coming in for the summer."

Renee and her mother humphed simultaneously.

"Oh," Marty said, "you two still aren't talking to Duke?"

"Nor do we plan to any time soon," boomed Aunt Bertie to Renee's nodding agreement.

Marty saw Derry and Pudgy exchange amused looks. Darla

ushered the kids to a table for four right beside the big table to make room for Renee and Bertie who immediately lowered themselves into the empty seats. An awkward silence followed as the two settled in. Marty ran her fingers through her hair and considered only a moment before she said, "I was going to call you, Renee. I need to make an appointment to get my hair cut." Derry and Pudgy both nudged her feet with theirs. She could see them trying not to laugh. Apparently, Renee wasn't any better than she used to be at styling hair.

But Renee's sour look disappeared and she managed a proud half-smile. "Of course, Marty, but be sure to call. We style only by appointment these days. Wait until you see the shop. I redecorated, you know, and what with the new decor and the tanning bed, we are swamped." She fluffed her blue-black hair with her long nails. Her enameled bangle bracelets jangled.

"I was over at Donald's the other day and saw your new sign," Derry said. "Chez Renee in pink and purple with lots of silver glitter. Nobody coming down Main Street will miss you, that's for sure."

"Shut up, Derry" she snapped. "You wouldn't know class if it fell on you."

"I heard the shop's real pretty," Darla offered.

"Why thank you, Darla," Renee said crisply. "Feel free to stop by to see it. After all, we're practically neighbors."

"Everybody's talking about how nice it is," Aunt Bertie assured them.

The waitress came to deliver the Pattersons' ice cream and to take any new orders. "No, no," Aunt Bertie said. "We can't stay. I just stopped to see my niece." She drew herself to her full height and Renee, shorter and rounder, stood beside her.

"My goodness," Marty said, "you didn't see Annie. Annie, come here."

Annie bounced over from her table. "I really like Jennifer, Mom. When we're done eating our ice cream, can I walk down to her house? She wants to show me her kittens."

"Just a minute, Annie. I want you to meet your Aunt Bertie and Cousin Renee."

"Oh! Hi!" Annie said, looking surprised.

Aunt Bertie hugged Annie to her and again dabbed at her eyes when she withdrew. "You make this mother of yours bring you to visit, you hear? I promised your dear grandmother that I wouldn't lose touch with your mother and you children and now here you are, back home. We're still at the same address, Miss Marty."

Marty stood and hugged her aunt. "And do you still make the best peanut butter cookies in town?"

"Yes, indeed I do, and you might remind that brother of yours about how much he used to like my cookies. He seems to have forgotten where to find us," Aunt Bertie said, her face softer and more loving than when she came in.

Marty hugged Renee. "I'll call and come by soon. All right?"

The Pattersons echoed their goodbyes.

"Bye now, Renee. Bye, Mrs. Crawford," Derry said.

Again the two women humphed in unison. "Your mother would roll over in her grave, Missy," Aunt Bertie whispered. With Renee hurrying to catch up, she strode from the restaurant.

"Hey, Derry," Pudgy teased, "I don't think they like you."

Derry's violet eyes shone with mischief. "Aw, come on. You know they gotta love me—everybody does. They just don't approve of me."

"Relax, pal," Pudgy said. "There aren't many people around here that those two do approve of. Bertie has set herself up as the grand dowager of Main Street, the judge and jury of the whole town. Frankly, she finds most of us wanting."

"Walter!" Darla scolded. "Be nice. That's Marty's family you're talking about. Besides, Bertie is an angel at heart. No one in this town is on the scene faster than Bertie when someone needs a helping hand."

Annie and Jennifer rushed to their table. "Hey, Mama, Pop," Jennifer said. "I can't eat any more. Kathy said she'd finish my ice cream. Can Mark and me take Annie to see the kittens?"

"I still live in the big house behind the store, Marty. Walt Jr. should be there. They'll be fine. I mean... if it's okay with you."

"Sure. We'll walk down and get you when we're finished."

Annie grabbed Jennifer's hand and off they went. Marty smiled after them and scooped up the last gooey bite of her own sundae. She sighed in satisfaction. It had, indeed, been just what she wanted. Maybe figuring out what that was wouldn't be as hard as she'd imagined.

"This town hasn't changed much, Marty," Darla offered. "It's still safe; everybody watches out for everybody else's kids. It's a wonderful place to raise a family."

Marty nodded. That was what she was looking for—a safe and wonderful place to raise her family. Pudgy again gathered his wife's small hand into his own. They obviously loved each other deeply, so much so that Darla had been transformed from a gaunt, haunted creature to this lovely woman smiling into her husband's eyes. Marty fingered her locket. Dan had often looked at her that way. She wanted that back—not yet, but someday someone to look at her in total love and appreciation.

Derry went to pay their bill and she saw him huddled in the corner talking with Ceci Collins. Ceci laid her left hand against Derry's cheek for just a moment. As Marty watched, Derry turned from Ceci and, smiling broadly, came back to her. Satisfaction, like an electric current, ran from the small of her back to her shoulders, up her neck to her scalp making her light-headed. It occurred to her that it was possible to want something even though you knew it wouldn't be good for you.

E I G H T

Marty lay in bed and watched the light around the yellowed shades grow from gray-blue to golden. She looked at her clock—six o'clock. She swung her feet over the side of the bed. She'd been miserable and restless all night, possibly her stomach punishing her for her ice cream indulgence, but more likely the anxieties that had been raging through her for the last several days.

She listened for a moment, hearing only the gurgling of the creek and the early morning songs of birds through her open window. Annie stirred and turned in her bed. Marty slipped into clothes and tiptoed from the room so she wouldn't disturb her daughter.

The dogs were still quiet in the basement. The kitchen she'd left neat and clean the night before showed signs of late-night raids. In the sink, a thousand-legger crawled along the edge of a bowl glazed with the soupy remains of melted strawberry ice cream. An open bag of bread hung over the edge of the counter. A pile of scraps including the end of a tomato, a blob of mayonnaise and the lid to the mayonnaise jar, lay on the counter.

She sighed and replaced the lid on the mayonnaise jar, then opened the refrigerator, putting the jar inside and grabbing an apple from the fruit crisper. She ignored the rest of the mess. She hadn't risen this early to clean the kitchen.

What had she expected, after all? Duke and Kyle were slobs. They always had been. She hadn't come back only to live the life Mama had worked so hard to help her escape. But did she have any other choice? Her lip trembled and she bit it hard, willing anger to replace the fear. Anger, at least, was easier to deal with.

She gave the apple a quick rinse in the sink and bit into it as she stepped out onto the porch. Mushy. She should have expected as much from a summer apple.

Red nickered and trotted the fence line, his usually shiny coat matted with dried sweat. Marty walked over and fed him the rest of the apple, scratching his forehead where the white hair swirled. The poor horse had probably spent several sweltering hours on the trailer outside of some bar after the roping last night. Marty had heard Kyle stumble up the stairs a few hours ago and knew it was unlikely that he'd appear again before noon.

"You hungry, big guy?" she soothed. He tossed his head and pawed. "Well, if you and Cocoa are going to have breakfast, I guess I'd better get it for you." If last night was any indication of how Kyle usually spent Saturday nights, she imagined old Red had missed more than a few Sunday breakfasts.

In the barn, she filled the coffee can with sweetfeed and carried it to Red, now waiting beside his feed bucket. Back inside the barn, she fed the pony and stood a while, watching her eat. She smiled, remembering what this pony had meant to her at Annie's age. Cocoa had been her confidante and friend, sometimes the only one besides Mama she could count on in her crazy family. She remembered Cocoa pulling Gayle and her in the pony cart to their favorite picnic spot across the bridge and down the opposite lane near the creek. That spot hadn't been as pretty as some on the farm, but it made up for it by the adventure of stealing away, of leaving the property.

Marty opened the stall door and scratched Cocoa behind the ears. The pony raised her head and looked at Marty with remarkably clear eyes as if she, too, were remembering. Marty bent and kissed the pony's nose and then left her.

Outside the barn, Red had already gobbled his feed and was heading toward the shade of a large maple tree. Marty opened the gate and walked across the field to catch the big gelding. "Come on, Red. Let's clean you up," she said, as she took him by the halter and led him toward the barn.

After she fastened him in the crossties she went to work, currying and brushing his coat until its usual gloss returned. The warm, lively smell of horse filled her nostrils. She was doing Kyle's work again, but taking care of the horses had never felt like work to her.

She hadn't been on a horse in years. Duke had taught her how to stay on and, when she hadn't, to crawl right back up on the pony's back. But when she outgrew the pony, Mama had coached her for hours on Maisie, Mama's own mare, teaching her to run the barrels, the poles, and the keyhole race, showing her how to shave seconds off her time, to try always for first place. "My girl can ride with the wind," Mama used to say. "And she's tough to boot," Duke would add.

She rubbed the curry over Red's rump and the gelding stretched his nose forward, curled his lip, and nodded his head. "Feels good to get cleaned up, doesn't it?" Mama had always insisted, "Care first, ride later." But Kyle was more like Duke. All he ever wanted to do was ride, ride, ride.

She found a metal comb and pulled it through Red's mane and tail, gently untangling the coarse hair the way Mama had taught her. She lifted Red's feet and cleaned the caked manure and dirt from them with a hoof pick. The hoof seemed healthy, a miracle after the way he'd spent the winter. But even if thrush had started, keeping him outside would have helped. Or maybe he was just a tough old guy. He had to be, to survive Duke and Kyle.

Satisfied that Red was as clean as he could be without a bath, Marty dragged her old saddle from the tack room. Years of dust caked the old wood-treed Big Horn. She gave it a quick wipe, silently promising to do a proper saddle soaping soon. She found one of Kyle's saddle pads and threw it on Red's back before hefting the saddle up after it. In short order she had Red saddled and bridled.

"It's been a long time, Red," she sighed. "Go easy on me." She put her left foot into the stirrup and pushed off with her right. After a bit more struggle than she remembered, she landed in the saddle, her arms, hands, shoulders, back, legs, and feet falling into place as if she'd ridden yesterday. She hadn't forgotten. It occurred to her that Mama had made decent money running a boarding stable and giving lessons. Maybe that was an option she could consider, if she didn't get a teaching job.

She turned the gelding toward the upper pasture and found that even when he broke into an easy jog, she stayed right with him. By the time she'd reached the woods behind the house, her aching thigh muscles destroyed the illusion of time standing still. But if she was going to ride again, she'd have to push on through it. She nudged him into a lope at the top of the hill. He easily lifted into a smooth canter and the wind, warm but softened by the early morning air, brushed through her hair and across her face. She moved with Red—she hadn't lost the seat she'd been so proud of as a young rider.

As they came to the woods, she pulled him to a stop. The path through the woods was between two tall locust trees, but all the trees edging the pasture had grown tall since she'd last ridden here. Finally, she found the path. It was still passable, kept that way, no doubt, by deer. She and Red entered the world of shade and bird song that was "her" woods.

Red lowered his head and picked his way carefully along the trail. Marty guessed that Kyle had brought the horse this way before. In front of her a rabbit darted into the brush.

The path looped around the lower end of the ridge and then wound its way down the hill toward the house in the bowl-shaped valley below. Soon Red carried Marty into the pine clearing which, with its high arching branches, had always reminded her of a cathedral. One of the older pines had fallen across the path on the other side of the clearing, blocking the exit.

Marty pulled Red to a stop and looked around her. This, like the rock ledge, had been one of her favorite places. Right in front of her a shaft of sunlight suddenly cut between two trees and shot across the opening. Marty smiled and felt a song from years before start to form in her heart and throat. She hummed the tune without recognizing it until words came with the memory. "He walks with me and he talks with me," Marty sang softly, "and he tells me I am his own."

But then, the words were gone and only the tune remained and even that became strangled in the swell of loneliness Marty felt rising in her. Once she had had someone to walk and talk with and certainly she had been his own, forever she had hoped. She heard Dan's voice in memory calling, like he did most days when he came from classes, "I'm home. Where is my lovely wife?" She wasn't anybody's anymore. She remembered when

Dan had proposed. He had kissed her to seal their promise and then had wrapped her in his strong arms and held her close. She had loved him so, as well as everything he represented—education, stability, respectability. She had believed he would always be there to take care of her; as long as he held onto her, she would be safe, and he would make her dreams come true.

Red shook his head and pawed at the pine needles underfoot, obviously impatient to move on. Marty took a deep breath. Red and the strong scent of pine brought her back to reality. She would make herself crazy dwelling on losses. She had kids to raise, and she had to be strong.

Marty turned Red back the way they had come. Besides, Dan had made nearly all her dreams come true. They had enjoyed a good life together, a better life than Marty had ever imagined she'd live. And he had kept her and their children safe. He just hadn't been able to protect himself from the disease that took him from her, making her lonely again—lonely and afraid that there would never again be anyone to help her raise the kids or sort through life's problems.

She breathed deeply and the mingled smells of the woods and the farm reminded her that sometimes, even with Dan, she'd been lonely. As Red climbed the path toward the ridge, Marty realized that loneliness had always been with her. The only time she had eluded this feeling was when, as a very little girl, she had believed herself to be the center of her parents' world, a world that they had made safe for her.

Red broke into a trot as they neared the edge of the woods. Where the dark of the tree cover met the bright light of the sun-washed field, the big horse jumped forward as if leaping a barrier. Marty laughed and stayed right with him, pulling him back to an easy jog.

Like Red she had to jump out of the dark and head for the sunlight. She couldn't let fear and loneliness overwhelm her. She tried to remember the song she'd been singing, a song from her childhood. Again the tune came first and then, "… and he tells me I am his own." All the words came flooding back. It wasn't a love song. It was a hymn.

She had learned that hymn in the classroom in the basement of the church from Miss Pritchard, her Sunday school teacher. Miss Pritchard had also been the town librarian and Marty's special friend. The one-room library behind the fire hall had never been very busy, and often Marty was the only one there on a Saturday morning. Once she'd asked Miss Pritchard if she ever got lonely. "My no, dear," the old woman had answered. "Jesus is always with me, even in the dead of night when not another soul's around."

Although it sounded like one of those stock answers Sunday school teachers give to difficult questions, she still believed that Miss Pritchard had meant it. Maybe that was why she'd taught them the song, so they would know Jesus was with them. Marty had believed it then, because she wanted to believe everything Miss Pritchard told her. But, looking back, Marty couldn't remember ever really feeling the presence of God in her life. Not then, and not now.

She pulled Red to a walk and let him find his own footing as he stepped off the ridge and headed toward the barn. It couldn't be more than nine or nine-thirty. She had time to shower and still make the church service Gayle had invited her to. She pushed Red to walk faster. She had a need to sit in that old stone church and feel like the little girl she'd been, the child who had believed Jesus was with her always. Maybe this time she could feel it deeply and completely, the way she imagined it should be.

NINE

Marty had Red unsaddled, brushed off, and turned out in no time. Since he wasn't overheated she didn't have to cool him out. She practically ran from the barn to the house, bursting into the kitchen, out of breath.

The puppy jumped to his feet and wiggled over to greet her. She saw that the dirty dishes from the night before had been washed and left to dry in the drainer.

"My goodness, girl," Duke said, looking up from the Sunday paper. "Where in the world have you been? I thought you were still sleeping." Old Jake never even looked up from where he rested with his head on Duke's foot.

Marty smiled. Duke had to have done the dishes—an effort for him, she knew. "I was out for an early ride on Red," she said, hurrying to her father and kissing the top of his bald head.

Duke reached up and patted her cheek. "That's the girl I remember," he said.

She checked the kitchen clock—just a few minutes after nine. She poured herself a cup of coffee and sat next to her father. "Hey, I'm going to get the kids and go to church. Want to come with us?"

He looked up from his coffee mug, his watery blue eyes looking puzzled. "I haven't been to church since your mother died. Can't stand going alone."

"Well, you can go with us."

He ran his hands over his pajama-covered belly. "I've put on so much weight in the last six months, I don't think I've got a suit that fits me."

"'The Lord doesn't care what you wear as long as you go,' Grandma Stafford used to say. Just wear a white shirt and maybe a tie if you feel the need to dress up a bit."

"Can't do that either," Duke said, shaking his head. "Only have the one white shirt that still fits. Wore it to Dan's funeral and then spilled coffee all down the front."

"Coffee stains aren't too tough to get out, Dad."

"Well, I haven't really tried. It's still up in the closet. Tell you what. Maybe if you get my shirt clean this week, I'll go with you next Sunday. How's that?" Duke didn't wait for her answer; obviously satisfied that he'd solved the problem, he turned back to his paper. "Just be sure to pick me up for the picnic afterwards."

Marty's impulse was to argue further, but she caught herself. She was a fine one to lay guilt on someone about not going to church. She couldn't even remember the last time she'd been. She finished her coffee and went to wake the kids.

Since Jeff had hit puberty, he took a lot longer to get ready to go anywhere, so she called him first. "Jeff, wake up," she said, opening his door.

Jeff's head slowly came off the pillow. He brushed a long shock of straight brown hair off his face and turned half-opened eyes in her direction. "What'sa matter?" he mumbled.

"Nothing. I'm going to go to church, and I'd like you to go with me."

Jeff bolted upright. "Ahhh man! Now on top of everything else, I have to deal with you getting religion."

"Just because we don't usually go to church doesn't mean I haven't had any faith. I mean…" Marty frowned. She was barely convincing herself.

Jeff pulled himself up to sit cross-legged on the bed. "I don't believe this. Since we got here, you've been getting weird on me." He set his square jaw and his dark eyes glared. He crossed his arms over his still hairless chest.

"All right, Jeff. That's enough. I'm going, but you don't have to."

"Well, I guess this is something you need to work out yourself. Like Dad used to say, 'Religion is the opiate of the people.'" He flopped back against his pillows and closed his eyes.

Marty crossed the floor and stood above him, hands on her hips. "Actually, Mr. Intellectual, Karl Marx said that first and your father made his peace with God before he died."

Jeff turned away from her. "Do what you have to do, but you leave Dad out of this," he snapped.

Marty's hands fell to her side. What had she expected? Really she wasn't even angry that he didn't want to go to church. Why would he when it had never been part of his life? What infuriated her was his attitude. He was becoming negative and miserable, and she missed her joyful son, the one who played his music too loud and ran through the house with his friends. She laid her hand on his head and he flinched away from her.

"Jeff, it's okay. I really didn't mean to put pressure on you, but I am going to go and I think Annie will. Do you want us to pick you up for the picnic at Morgan's?"

Jeff flopped over and looked at her. "Are you going to be ticked off if I say no?"

"Probably a little. I want to show off my good-looking son to my old friends. Besides, Duke's coming and you'll have to cook for yourself if you stay. But then maybe you want to spend the day with your Uncle Kyle."

"No way. Even a picnic with your old farmer friends is better than that. Kyle keeps insisting that he's going to teach me how to rope a cow or asking if I'd like to take that she-devil dog of his and go gopher whopping. I won't even tell you what that is."

Marty smiled. "You don't have to. I know."

Jeff shook his head. "That's right, poor thing. You used to live here."

She pushed the silky hair from his forehead and kissed him. "Be ready by noon or a little after. Okay?"

Jeff just groaned and snuggled back into his pillow.

Annie was easier to convince. "Oh, good," she said. "Jennifer goes to church. She asked if I was going to go 'cause I'd be in her Sunday school class."

"Well, I'm afraid we can't make Sunday school this morning, but you can go next week," Marty said. "Come on now. We'd better hurry so we're not late."

Marty dressed in her good navy linen dress with the white trim, the one Dan had liked so much. For Annie she chose the flowered dress with the lace cape collar that her Grandma Harris had bought at a shop in Georgetown. Soon they were ready for church. As they passed through the kitchen, Duke whistled.

"Boy, oh boy," he said. "My girls are sure going to set that little country church on its ear."

Marty stopped, her hand on the door. "Oh, Dad, you're right. I forgot. Nobody around here dresses up for church in the summer. We better go change. Sometimes I'm still thinking like I'm in Washington—the capital, not the county."

Duke hauled himself to his feet and wobbled toward them. "Nonsense. Go. It makes me proud to think of you walking into church looking so beautiful. And we'll get me something just as nice to wear and next week I'll go with you. How's that?" He kissed them both before opening the door and ushering them out.

When Marty pulled her car up in front of the church, five or six cars had already parked at the edge of the hay field across the road. The beige fieldstone, darkened with age, looked gray but not much more than when Marty was a girl. The doors and the trim on the big double-hung windows and the eaves all sported a fresh coat of white paint. An historic marker proclaimed: Trinity Methodist Church—since 1817.

Marty looked around her while she waited for Annie to get out of the car. She'd forgotten how beautiful a summer morning could be on this hill, with green fields and forests rolling one after another toward the horizon.

Annie came around to Marty and took her hand. "The church is tiny," she whispered. "But it's so pretty here."

Marty squeezed Annie's hand and led her across the road and up the stone steps that over the years had been worn into hollows by the footsteps of worshipers. Inside, the men in jeans and short-sleeved shirts, the women in cotton skirts and blouses, and many of the children in shorts milled around and visited, calling to one anther, laughing and joking. Marty could feel her cheeks getting hot; she wished she had dressed more casually.

"Annie!" called Jennifer, running down the center aisle, the skirt of her checked sundress and her long dark braid flying behind her. "Come on. Come sit with us." Jennifer grabbed Annie's arm and led her to a pew near the front where the Patterson family sat. Marty had no choice but to follow. Darla stood and hugged her. "Marty, I'm so glad you came. All right, kids, push down and make room," she said, shooing the kids over. "Now save that seat by the window for your daddy."

Marty looked over her shoulder and saw Pudgy in the far aisle, talking to a bearded man. "Let me just slip in here behind you," Marty said. "Otherwise, Pudgy and your son will be crowded." Jennifer pulled Annie into the row with her.

Gayle and a woman Marty didn't recognize were arranging tall spikes of gladiolus, buttery yellow and deep red and red throated yellow, in two huge vases for the altar. "Gayle and Amy, the preacher's wife, always do the flowers," Darla said. "Nobody grows flowers like Gayle does."

Marty nodded and smiled, still uncomfortable speaking out loud in the church where Mama had taught her to sit quietly and pray, and where Aunt Bertie would pinch her and Renee on the soft underside of their arms if they stirred. She looked over her shoulder. When Bertie was in charge, the family always sat in the very center of the center row, halfway back. Bertie always arrived at exactly 10:55. Marty checked her watch; three minutes to go.

"Marty!"

She turned to see Gayle rushing toward her, followed by the other woman. Gayle hugged Marty and whispered, "I knew you'd come." She pulled back and introduced, "Marty Harris, this is Amy Cramer. Amy, this is my dear friend Marty."

Amy extended her hand, a surprisingly strong hand for such a small woman. "I've heard a lot about you, Marty. Gayle's had us all praying for you since the death of your husband. I'm so glad you could join us this morning." Amy turned to greet the Pattersons, smiling and calling them each by name.

"Amy's husband, Joel, is the pastor here," Gayle said. "They bought the old Randolf place, so they're neighbors as well."

Marty had passed the Randolf place and seen cattle and sheep in the fields that had for so many years been empty. So they had a pastor who was also a farmer.

"I'll see you after the services, Marty. I have to get Joel a pitcher of water. In this heat, he'll wilt if I don't." Amy went back across the altar and through a door.

"I'm going to sit here with you guys," Gayle said. "I'm all alone this morning. Chrissy's up at Penn State doing a summer scholar's program and Mac and Luke are at home with a sick cow." Gayle sat in the pew beside Marty. "Uh oh, it must be 10:55," Gayle said, nodding her head toward the center pews.

Marty glanced behind to see Aunt Bertie, Renee, her husband Fred, and their chubby teenaged twins filing into Aunt Bertie's pew. Renee and Aunt Bertie seemed to notice Marty at the same time, Renee with a prim, stiff-lipped nod and Aunt Bertie with an approving smile and small wave.

Marty knew she should probably walk over and greet them, that they expected her to, but Pudgy and the bearded man came toward them. "Oh, good," Gayle said. "I'm supposed to give Cam a report on that cow. He was at our place at eight this morning treating her."

Cam? Marty looked closely at the stocky man with the well-trimmed beard and the slightly receding hairline. Cam? Then he smiled and she recognized the dimples just above the beard and saw the laughter in his blue eyes. "Cam!" Marty called, before remembering to lower her voice, but no one seemed to notice except Cam, who laughed and hugged her.

"I was awfully glad when Gayle told me you were coming home," Cam said. A tiny girl peeked around his leg, and he tugged on her hand, coaxing her forward. "Kika, I want you to meet Marty. She's been a friend of mine since we were your age."

"Hello," said the little girl, not raising her eyes.

"Hello, Kika," Marty said, smiling at Cam, glad he had a child. She knew how he must treasure her.

"Kika, sit with us," Jennifer called.

"Now you girls are going to have to move up a row," Darla said, ushering the girls to the pew in front of them. Annie never even looked back. Jennifer was busy introducing her to Kika who was still looking terribly shy, but, at least, was smiling.

"Looks like we've been abandoned by our kids," Cam said, pushing in to sit next to Gayle.

Gayle stood and moved to the other side of Marty and pushed

her next to Cam. "There," she said. "Now we can share you."

The pastor stepped in front of the altar and everyone stopped talking. "Good morning," he said in a hearty voice, a big smile on his boyish face. "Members of our youth group will be leading the readings and hymns this morning." Four young people, all about Jeff's age, came and stood beside the pastor. They opened their hymnals and a young girl who looked so much like the pastor that she had to be his daughter, announced, "The opening hymn will be 310, 'Be Not Afraid.'"

Cam found the hymn and offered to share the book with Marty just as Gayle did the same. All three of them laughed softly. Marty slipped one arm through Gayle's and another through Cam's. She hugged their arms to her and began to sing, Cam in his clear tenor, Gayle in her lovely alto, and Marty quietly so not to throw anyone else off key. By the time they had finished the song, she didn't feel the least bit lonely or afraid. In fact, by the time the service was over, although she hadn't had felt the earth-shaking presence of the Lord she'd hoped for, she at least felt that she had come home, to a place as secure and loving as home was supposed to be.

T E N

After the service Marty spent a few minutes with Aunt Bertie and Renee before Gayle pulled her away to see yet another forgotten high school friend. The faces finally became a blur and Marty was glad to escape to the car with Annie. She needed to think about the service and Joel Cramer's sermon on the nature of faith. But Annie was excited about the picnic at Morgan's and, after being quiet for nearly an hour, she was not in the mood for silence.

When they arrived at the farm, Duke was waiting in the kitchen, drinking an iced tea and letting the window fan blow on him. Above them Marty heard the thump of bare feet hitting the floor. "Is Jeff just getting up?" Marty asked.

"I suspect he is," Duke answered.

"I told him to be ready," Marty said with a sigh.

"I guess I should have called him," Duke said. "Course on Sundays I don't see Kyle until dinnertime, unless he's got a roping somewhere. Didn't seem too strange to me that the boy was still sleeping."

"I'm going to get him, Mom," Annie said. "And he'd better hurry 'cause Jen and Kika will be waiting for me." Annie ran up the steps.

Marty could hear Annie banging on Jeff's door. "I better go up, or he'll roar out of there like a bear disturbed while hibernating." Marty hurried up the stairs. "Annie, you go and change. I'll see to your brother." Jeff threw open the door and stood with tousled hair and rumpled pajama bottoms in front of her. "I need a shower," he snarled and pushed past her toward the bathroom.

As if it had been waiting for the right moment to torture her, fear flooded back into her heart. Her son was in pain. She was the mom. She should be able to "make it all better," but she couldn't. She'd been a good enough mother with Dan there to back her up. Dan had been a great father—firm, decisive, and fair. She was okay at "fair," but the kids could always talk her out of "firm," and "decisive" was beyond her.

She pulled herself tall and knocked on the bathroom door her son had just slammed shut. "Jeff, take a five-minute shower and I'll give you ten minutes to dress. I am leaving here in fifteen minutes."

Jeff didn't answer, and Marty instantly regretted the hard edge she'd heard in her voice. She had to give him time.

Annie came bounding out of the bedroom wearing her shorts, tank top, and tennis shoes.

"Back in here, young lady, and hang up your dress," Marty said, careful to punctuate her order with a smile.

Annie bounced back into the room with a giggle and put her clothes away, but then, she always had been easier than Jeff. "Okay, kiddo, wait downstairs with Grandpap. I'll change clothes and be right down."

When she was alone, she kicked off her white pumps and slipped out of her dress. By the time she'd changed into pale blue shorts and a shirt, she heard the pipes squeal as Jeff turned off the shower. There was no way he'd be dressed in the five minutes left to him. Not wanting a scene, Marty stalled, picking up the church bulletin.

She had wanted time to think about the service anyway, perhaps to look up that quote from Peter that Joel Cramer had used. The quote was copied along the bottom of the paper as the "Thought for the Week." The Bible passage it came from actually dealt with belief in Christ as the Son of God, but, as the pastor had said, it should help with all issues of faith. It read:

When you doubt, remember the words of Peter: "Keep your attention closely fixed on (your faith), as you would on a lamp shining in a dark place until the first streaks of dawn appear and the morning star rises in your hearts."

Marty couldn't see the lamp shining, but since sitting among dear friends in her welcoming old church, she could feel the rays from that lamp warming her heart. That was all she had to fix on and maybe it was enough for now.

She remembered those debates over dinner between Dan and his friend Rabbi Langer who taught part time in the college's religion department. Rabbi Langer had once said, "God is infinite and humans are finite. We cannot hope to know Him completely with our limited minds, so we must have faith." That too was something to hold onto—she didn't have to be sure of anything. Faith didn't require proof.

She heard Jeff leaving his room and quickly slipped into her sandals. She followed him down the steps. He was dressed in khaki bermuda shorts, a starched white oxford cloth shirt rolled to just below the elbows and loafers without socks, the picture of D.C. preppie cool, but sure to be as out of place at a Morgan picnic as Marty's and Annie's fancy dresses were at church. Still, to say anything would only cause a scene. With luck, he'd be unaware of how out of place he looked.

In the kitchen, Marty grabbed the three-bean salad she'd made the day before and headed toward the car with the rest of her family in tow—Jeff sullen, Duke teasing, and Annie laughing. As she started down the farm lane, Cody ran out of the creek and chased the car. Marty slowed the Volvo.

"Don't worry about that crazy pup," Duke said. "He'll turn back when we get to the main road."

But instead of turning back, Cody made a sharp left just before the road and scaled the hillside.

"Do you think he knows we're going to Morgan's?" Annie asked.

"Yeah, right," mumbled Jeff.

"Who knows what that dog knows?" Marty said, with a smile over her shoulder at Annie.

When they arrived at the Morgan farm, several cars blocked the driveway by the house, so Marty pulled up by the barn. Cam, Pudgy, and Mac stood talking just inside the barn door. Mac took off at a run. He reached the car just as Marty stepped from it and threw his arms around her. "How in the world are you?"

Before she could answer, Cody came barreling down the hill, jumped sideways to avoid running into Marty and knocked Mac into the dirt.

"Ah, Cody, you darn fool," Mac snapped in the same rapid-fire, gravel-voiced way of talking Marty remembered. He tussled with the pup a minute before pulling himself back to his feet.

"I'm fine, but how are you?" Marty asked.

Mac grinned at Marty, scratched Cody behind the ear, and gave a high-pitched whistle. Around the back of the house charged another puppy, smaller than Cody but still long-legged and gangly. This pup, brown where Cody was gray but with the same black-and-white speckles, had to be the littermate Gayle had told her about. "Go on now," Mac said, giving Cody a shove. Cody took off at a run, and met his brother halfway across the lawn. The two dogs played and jumped and rolled until they were out of sight around the far side of the house.

Mac gave a chuckle and flung his arm around Marty's shoulder. "Now to answer your question, I couldn't be better," he said, his leprechaun face signaling mischief. "But what's this I hear about you and Derry Brady? I thought you'd learned your lesson where he was concerned when he left you at the prom to go off with old what's-her-name—you know, the one he married first."

"Marci," Marty said. "And I'm fine, thank you, and yes, I have learned my lesson where Derry Brady is concerned."

"Then how come you were out with him last night?" He squeezed her shoulder and brought his face close to hers.

Marty elbowed Mac playfully in the side, nearly dropping the bean salad. "It wasn't a date. We took Annie out for ice cream. Is that innocent enough for you?"

Mac gave her a big kiss on the cheek. "Just watching out for you, buddy. Remember, Derry is never innocent where women are concerned. Heck, I used to lock Gayle and Chrissy up whenever he came on the place."

"MacKenzie Morgan, behave yourself!" Gayle demanded, striding across the lawn, her wide smile softening the tone of her words.

"Me?" Mac said. "Hah! I'm just making sure this friend of yours is behaving herself." Pretending indignation, he took off toward the barn, linking his arm through Duke's and dragging him along. "You just can't please a woman, Duke. We might as well go back to hanging out in the barn."

"As you can see, he's still the same," Gayle said. She laughed as she watched her husband rejoin the men, who all laughed at some remark he made.

"I'd have been disappointed if either one of you had changed," Marty said. She looked over her shoulder. Annie had already run off to meet Jennifer and Kika who were with the rest of the Patterson kids down by the house. Jeff, however, stood awkwardly by the car, not seeming to know if he should go to the house with the kids or into the barn with the men.

"Hey, Jeff," Mac yelled, "you belong in here with us."

"Maybe Jeff would rather be with the young people, Mac," Gayle said.

"Luke and Walt Jr. are with us, too. Cam needs all the help he can get to figure out what's wrong with this cow."

Marty cringed, sure Jeff would not be pleased by the prospect of spending time in the barn seeing to a sick cow; but when she stole a glance at him, he looked amused and pleased.

She saw Cam come out of the barn, smiling. He shook Jeff's hand and clapped him on the back and then with Mac ushered her smiling city boy into the barn.

Gayle slipped an arm around Marty's shoulder. "He'll be fine."

"I hope so, Gayle. He's been so unhappy. I guess we all have been, but Annie seems to be able to contain it. She has her moments of sorrow and then moves on. Jeff can't. And he's been worse since we came home. He's spending most of every day in bed."

Marty looked down toward the house. Jennifer and Kika had each grabbed one of Annie's hands and were pulling her toward the back porch.

"There's a litter of new kittens on the porch," Gayle said. "When you're eight, even something as simple as kittens can distract you from pain, but it's not that easy for teenagers. Give him time, Marty. I've been praying especially hard for him. It's awfully difficult for a boy his age to lose a father."

"I hope God or someone will let me know when and if something more is needed."

"Just listen and he will."

Under the big maple tree behind Gayle's house the oldest Patterson girl and a girl about Jeff's age spread two long wooden tables with blue-and-red checked tablecloths. Darla and another woman came from the backdoor carrying bowls. It took Marty only a minute to recognize Gayle's older sister. "Karen," she called. She hurried toward the woman still resembling the high-school beauty and county-fair queen who had been Marty and Gayle's heroine.

Marty put her salad on the table and hugged Karen. Gayle hugged them both. "Isn't this great?" Gayle said.

"It certainly is," Karen answered. "It's been so long since I've seen you, Marty, I was beginning to think you'd fallen off the edge of the earth."

"Sometimes I thought I had, Karen," Marty answered. She noticed the young girl smiling in their direction bore an unmistakable resemblance to Karen, with light brown wavy hair, blue eyes, rosy round cheeks, and a shy smile.

"That's my youngest," said Karen. "Rachel. She's fifteen, the same age as your oldest, right?"

"Yes," Marty answered.

"Good. Then they'll both be sophomores at the high school next year. Rachel can show him around."

Rachel's smile widened, making her even prettier. Well, if they had to stay, Jeff might be more agreeable with a guide like Rachel. And if Gayle and the congregation had been praying for them, maybe those prayers had brought them home. Maybe they were meant to stay... or maybe not. At any rate, it was something she'd have to consider.

ELEVEN

When the time came for evening milking, Mac enlisted the help of the younger kids. Marty smiled, watching them scamper across the lawn as if they were following a circus train. Mac had that effect on kids. He'd make them believe he needed their help, even though all they'd be able to do was open and shut the gate and watch the cows file into their stanchions.

Duke rose from the table, patted his stomach and burped loudly, causing the heat to rush to Marty's cheeks. "Ladies, that was a delicious supper and I thank you," he said, making his way over to a hammock stretched between two maple trees.

Around the picnic tables, the rest of the men and the teenagers grabbed garbage bags and went to work picking up the debris. Marty and the women headed for the kitchen. They easily fell into a routine. Amy carried the dishes in from outside. Karen washed them and Marty dried. Darla put the dishes away and Gayle packed "take home" packages for everyone.

Happy talk and laughter filled the air. Although God was mentioned more than made Marty comfortable, she figured that was because the minister and his wife were present. Still, these were happy people, content in their lot. If their faith had much to do with that, Marty wished she could share in it.

Surprisingly, the only one who seemed a bit out of pace with the others was Amy, who silently placed another empty casserole dish in the sudsy water. Marty smiled at her and a smile briefly flashed across Amy's face and then disappeared. As Amy left to make yet another trip to the picnic area, Marty noticed Karen and Gayle exchange concerned looks.

Amy hadn't been gone long when her husband breezed through the door. "Thank you all for another wonderful afternoon," he said.

"Thank you, Joel, for another great sermon. It helped put us all in the mood for a wonderful afternoon," Gayle said.

He shook hands with all of them, coming last to Marty. "I'm

very pleased to have met you and hope to see you next week," he said before leaving them. Marty glanced out the window and saw that Amy was nowhere in sight. Just then, Casey, Joel, and Amy's daughter burst in. She ran to Gayle and gave her a hug. "Thanks," she said. And then she whispered, "Mom's got another one of her headaches."

Gayle gave the young girl a pat on the back and nodded. She pressed into Casey's hands a brown grocery bag and began to fill it with a foil-wrapped package of leftover chicken, margarine tubs of salads, and Amy's clean dishes.

"I'll be back after I feed our stock. The guys are going gopher whopping and I said I'd help." Casey charged out the back door as quickly as she'd entered.

"What a kid," Gayle said with a grin.

"What a mother," Karen said with a sniff. "I guess we're not good enough for her."

"Oh, Karen," Gayle said, "that's not fair. Amy just hasn't adjusted to country living yet. She misses Chicago, where she could walk around the corner to an art gallery or a play. And she left all of her family there. Give her time. As much as Joel and Casey love it here, I'm sure she will, too."

"And don't forget," Darla added, "it's been only a year since her miscarriage."

"All right, you two," Karen said. "I guess I'm not being charitable. I don't know her as well as you all do. After all, we usually go to church in town. I just can't stand mopey people."

Marty felt a wave of sadness. She tried not to let it show, but it must have, because Gayle patted her back.

"Oh, no, Marty, I'm so sorry," Karen said. "I wasn't thinking. I mean, you have a right to be sad. My goodness, you lost a husband."

Marty shook her head. "Karen, for goodness sake, you've known me too long to have to tiptoe around me, worrying about what you're saying. I never want any of you to do that."

"See what I mean?" Karen said. "Marty's had a major loss more recently than Amy has and she's not sulking around making everyone feel bad."

Gayle laughed and shook her head. "My big sister still has to have the last word."

Marty managed a smile, realizing how often her smiles were forced because she didn't want to appear the way Amy had, didn't want people fussing or feeling uncomfortable in the face of her sadness. Only she knew how often sadness, loneliness, and fear eroded her, just as something was wearing away at Amy.

"I think we should pray for Amy," Darla said. "And for Joel and Casey, because she can't always be there for them. And don't forget, there are extra pressures being a pastor's wife."

Seeing that the dishes were finished and wishing to escape what might soon become a spontaneous prayer meeting, Marty excused herself. She wasn't comfortable with that. She'd ask Amy to a play or a symphony. That she could handle.

Marty went looking for her family. The yard had pretty much cleared out. The men had probably gone to the barn with Mac. Duke still snored on the hammock with the two puppies stretched out beneath him. Luke, Rachel, Walt Jr., and Jeff were drinking pop at one of the tables. Jeff sat awkwardly away from the other three, looking uncomfortable, and Marty felt her chest get tight. They'd talk about him the way Karen had about Amy, believing he thought he was too good for them.

Jeff turned, caught her eye and waved, a look of relief on his face. He jogged across the lawn to her. "Tell me we're leaving, please. These savages are going gopher whopping and keep assuring me that they have enough baseball bats for me to come, too."

"Jeff, you don't understand. Around here gopher whopping is not as inhumane as it sounds. I mean I could never stomach it myself, but horses and cows can break a leg in groundhog holes, so they've got to be dealt with. Poisoning is not only a horrible prolonged death, but barn cats, dogs, and other animals can get into the poison. At a distance, a rifle can miss and only wound the groundhog—more prolonged pain. But a well-placed blow on the head with a baseball bat, awful as it seems, kills them instantly and so can actually be more humane."

"It's disgusting and so is anyone who approves of it," Jeff said. He set his jaw and glared at her.

"Jeff, don't be so quick to judge what you don't understand."

"Brutality deserves no understanding. I'm going home," he said, and took off walking toward the road.

Marty was about to call and tell him that if he cut through the pasture he was only about a third of a mile from home, when she saw Rachel hurrying to catch him and decided to let it go. Rachel might find him sweet and sensitive instead of stubborn and judgmental. Marty hoped so. Jeff needed a friend.

Coming toward Jeff in a cloud of dust, Kyle's truck screeched to a stop. Marty saw her brother lean out and say something to Jeff and saw Jeff fire something back before continuing down the road. Rachel waved at Kyle and continued to follow Jeff.

Kyle spun the truck into the driveway, over the bank and halfway up on the lawn. Luke and Walt Jr. whooped and laughed.

"Hey, wild man," yelled Luke, "what's happening?"

"Now what did you guys do to my city boy nephew?"

Kyle's words went through Marty like lightning. She couldn't hear what the boys answered, but she heard their laughter. Beyond them she could see the cows drifting back into the upper pasture. The kids streamed out of the barn door, Mac and the men following. Marty walked toward the group at the picnic table hoping to stop any fun they intended to have at her son's expense.

Mac ran around the group of kids, picking up Kika as he went. She squealed with laughter when he spun her around and put her back down. "Hey, Stafford, you bozo," Mac yelled. "What are you doing parking your sorry, beat-up truck on my lawn?" He ran up behind Kyle and after grabbing him in wrestling hold around the neck, clapped him on the back and plopped down on the bench next to him. "Hey, where's Joel and his family?" he asked.

"Went home," Walt Jr. said.

"And, Marty, where's your boy?" he continued.

Marty's throat was too tight for a quick answer. Luke gave a short laugh. "We're all going gopher whopping and I don't think he's too keen on it."

Mac looked over his shoulder at Marty and shrugged just as Gayle stepped up beside her. "I can't say that I blame him," Gayle said. "I know it has to be done, Luke Morgan, but you and your friends don't need to enjoy it as much as you seem to. That goes for you, too, Kyle Stafford."

"Ouch," Kyle said. "See, Marty, I've had Gayle making like the big sister, when you weren't around."

Gayle walked up behind him and pinched his ear lobe, giving it a gentle shake. "For all the good it's done. Now if you want something to eat, there are plenty of leftovers in the kitchen. Just be sure you clean up after yourself."

"Thanks, but I came to get Marty. There's a guy over at our place who wants to look at the barn. He needs to board a horse, and I thought that might be something Marty would want to do. I mean, you are the one taking care of the barn and I know you need to make some money," Kyle said.

Marty knew her cheeks were red, but she wasn't sure if it was from embarrassment or anger. Kyle had no sense at all, especially about when to talk and when to keep his mouth shut.

"Was the guy older, sixty-five or so?" Cam asked. Kyle nodded. "Probably Sam Marcus. I forgot to tell you that I suggested he try your place. He just bought an old quarter horse mare. He lives in Washington and needs somewhere close to keep her."

Marty had no idea how long Kyle had kept that poor man waiting, so she said her goodbyes. Duke and Annie decided to ride home later with Kyle. When she opened the car door, she turned to wave. "Gayle. Mac. Thanks for everything."

Cody charged around the side of the house, running right at her. She stepped out of the way just in time to keep from being knocked over as he jumped into the car. He sat upright on the passenger side, panting and drooling on the leather seat. Marty just put her forehead down on the rim of the roof and groaned.

"Looks like you got yourself a dog!" Mac yelled.

Marty slipped into the driver's seat. "Whether I want one or not," she called, starting the car and pulling out of the drive. So much of her life seemed to be foisted on her against her wishes. The pup flopped down and put his head in her lap, rolling his eyes to look at her adoringly. She patted his head.

Halfway down Morgan Road, Marty saw Jeff and Rachel sitting on the little stone bridge over the creek. She tooted the horn and waved, leaving Jeff in company he seemed to be enjoying.

When she pulled up to the farmhouse, she saw a lanky man sitting on the porch steps, stroking Bella's forehead. Dressed in tailored khaki pants, a carved western belt, and navy knit polo shirt, he looked like money from the top of his styled, gray hair to the tip of his bullhide boots. Old Jake lay with his head on the man's well-shined boots. "My goodness," Marty said, stepping from the car. "How did you do that? Bella hates everybody."

Bella thumped her tail on the porch.

"She wasn't very friendly until your brother introduced us. At least, I assume you are Marty and Kyle is your brother." The man smiled, one of those unselfconscious smiles that calls for a smile in return. He looked right at Marty with dark brown eyes that did nothing to discourage her first impression of him as someone easy to like.

She extended her hand and he grasped it firmly. "Yes, I'm Marty Harris and you must be Sam Marcus. Kyle tells me you are looking for someplace to board a horse."

"Right on both counts. I've already looked the place over. I hope you don't mind. If you'll have me, I'd love to keep Grandma here. It's obvious that someone's been working hard on that barn. Your brother tells me it's you and you're the one I need to speak to. I haven't ridden much in years. I'm retired—sold my business last year and moved here to the country. I got Grandma a couple of months ago and the two of us old folks are sick to death of being laughed at over at that fancy riding academy where I board her now. We want someplace where we can just be ourselves and have a good time. I took one look at that old pony in your barn and knew I'd found a place where we'd fit right in."

Marty didn't answer right away, but she liked this man and a little extra money over the summer wouldn't be a bad thing. And it would be nice to have someone to ride with. "All right," she said. "But I have to tell you, I'm not sure I'll be here much past this summer. I don't know how much my brother told you about my situation."

"I know you're recently widowed. I can understand that kind of sorrow. My wife is a patient in the Bellaire Convalescent Home. She has Alzheimer's and half the time she doesn't even know me. I've been losing her bit by bit for the past five years."

"I'm so sorry. I'd be happy to board your horse, Mr. Marcus, as long as you understand that if I can get a teaching job in Pittsburgh, I'll have to take it and my kids and I will be moving."

He shook her hand to close the deal. "Fair enough," he said. "But you know…" He stopped, shook her hand again and said nothing more.

He didn't need to. Marty already knew that finding a teaching position this late in the summer was very unlikely. Like much of the rest of her life, she didn't have as much say over her future as she wanted. Still, as Sam Marcus drove away, she was happy with the decision she'd made. A little extra money never hurt, especially if she didn't get a job.

Darla and Gayle would tell her to take it to God. Maybe that was the answer—give God the list of her needs and wait and see what happened.

Marty tried to pray, telling God how much she wanted to support her children without hardship, how much she wanted to get Jeff off this farm he hated, about all she wanted for Annie and Jeff and, yes, for herself, so they could live the kind of life she and Dan had planned.

She waited quietly for… something. She didn't really expect an answer, not yet; but, at least, she wanted to feel a presence.

Nothing.

How about a good feeling?

Only worry. She shook her head and ordered the anxiety away. It didn't retreat far, but she was able to get through feeding the horses and dogs and the rest of the evening without being totally miserable. Before she went up to bed, Duke stopped her.

"I left something by your bed," he said. "Your Mama would have wanted you to have it." He kissed her cheek and climbed the stairs to his own room.

When she went up to her room, Annie was already sound asleep. Marty turned on the bedside lamp and found Mama's Bible on the night stand. She ran her hands over the worn black cover. Mama had often turned to that Bible for comfort. She'd have to remember that. Maybe she would find peace there, too. She slipped into bed and turned off the light.

As she lay in bed trying to sleep, she realized that whatever this day had held, she did feel a bit better than she had yesterday. She had good friends, a place to stay, and some extra money coming in.

She looked over at Annie, her head nestled into her pillow, her lips curled into a smile as she slept.

A prayer seeped into Marty's heart and she thanked God for the gift of such an angel. She thought of Jeff and asked that he find peace. Finally, she felt the drowsiness that signaled sleep. Just before she drifted off, she thought maybe she had begun to feel something like peace in her heart, at least, part of the time—when she wasn't worrying.

TWELVE

At the top of the ridge, Marty reined Red to a stop. She looked over her shoulder.

"We're coming," Sam called, as he urged Grandma on up the hill. Grandma swung into a trot and Sam pulled her up beside Red. Marty smiled at the big gray mare. Grandma was what Sam called her, but her registered name was a lot fancier and beside it in the quarter horse record books were plenty of show points. The old mare was lucky; with Sam she'd retired to a good life. In spite of her seventeen years on the show circuit, Grandma was in excellent shape, with only a few windpuffs on her ankles and hocks that creaked a bit when she first stepped from her stall.

Sam gave Grandma a pat on the neck. "It's beautiful up here," he said, looking around him. "Thanks for taking us in."

"Thanks for asking me to," Marty said. She had come to look forward to their rides, this their fourth since Grandma had moved in five days ago. Sam treated her like a favorite niece. She certainly would have loved to have an uncle like him, one who could talk about books and ideas and what was happening in the world beyond the county. Active in his synagogue, Sam was comfortable discussing issues of religion and faith, even occasionally enjoying a good debate. Marty smiled at him. "All right, where to? The trail through the woods?"

"Sure, sounds good."

Marty led the way to the path and under the canopy of leafy branches into the woods. They followed the narrow trail, single-file, around the top of the ridge and had just begun to descend toward the clearing when Marty heard something moving quickly on the path above them. "Hey, Marty, where in the world are you!"

"Mac?" Marty called.

"Well, who else would it be?"

Marty laughed, pulling Red to a stop. "Straight ahead. Follow the trail," Marty called, turning in her saddle to signal Sam to hold up. "Wait until you meet this guy," Marty said.

Mac charged into view on a quarter horse, a mare much smaller than Grandma, but a beautiful dark bay with a large white star in the middle of her wide forehead. Mac reined the mare to a stop and she jumped sideways into the undergrowth. "Sass, you darn fool," Mac grumbled, guiding her back onto the path. He looked up at Sam and grinned. "Hi, I'm Mac Morgan. You must be the boarder I've been hearing about."

"Mac, I'd have introduced you if you'd have given me a minute. Grandma here is our boarder and her owner is Sam Marcus. Sam, this character grew up and lives on the neighboring farm. His chief redeeming feature happens to be that he's married to my best friend."

Sam nodded and smiled. Introductions made single file on horseback were awkward at best. "Well, Marty, let's push on to the clearing so I can tell you why I'm here," Mac called.

In the clearing Marty turned toward Mac, curious now.

He shook his head and gave Sam an amused look. "What do you think of this, Sam? A guy comes to give Marty a present and he has to chase her all over the countryside to find her first."

"Present? Come on, Mac," Marty said. "What did you bring me?"

"This mare, if you'll have her, but it's only temporary. She was born on my place and I'm pretty fond of her, but the truth is Luke's bringing home two more Belgians from the sale tomorrow. I don't have room for Sass. Of course, Gayle and Luke think I should sell her, but..." Mac reached down and stroked the mare's neck and then looked at Marty. "So, friend, what do you say? Could you use an extra horse? How about one to ride when Kyle's off at a roping?"

Marty rode Red around the small bay mare. "Mac, she's gorgeous. Is she quiet enough for Annie?"

"Well now, on the ground, even a baby could lead her. She's got a heart of gold. And at a walk and trot, she's fine for a little kid, acts like an old pleasure horse. But she gets a bit rambunctious at a canter."

"She's not a runaway, is she?"

"For Pete's sake, Marty, I wouldn't give you one you couldn't stop. No, she just won't lope slow. She goes to beat the band. I suppose if we'd had time to really work with her she'd be different, but, heck, she's five now and pretty set in her ways. And except for the fact that she hates puddles, she's great on the trail."

"Tell you what," Marty said, "I'd love to try her out. She reminds me a bit of Mama's old mare."

"Same old-time quarter horse breeding. Same type of good sense."

"Then, thanks," Marty said.

"Good deal. Now let's get back to your barn. I was pretty sure you'd take her and I have Gayle picking me up in a little bit." Mac headed toward the path on the other end of the clearing.

"You may think you know everything, but you don't. We can't go that way. A tree's down across the path," Marty said.

Mac trotted the mare over to have a look. "Ah, come on now, this is a pretty puny tree and that branch it's caught on doesn't look too strong either," he said, unwrapping a rope from the saddle. "Sass and I can pull this out of the way." He dismounted and tied the rope around the tree and pulled himself back on the mare, wrapping the other end of the rope around the saddle horn.

"Sam," Marty said, "I think we better get out of his way." They trotted their horses to the opposite end of the clearing as Mac kicked the mare forward. The rope pulled tight and as the small mare leaned into it, the tree came crashing down behind her. Grandma and Red both spooked sideways and then spun toward the noise with eyes widened and nostrils flared. The little bay mare stood quietly waiting for Mac to untie the rope. Marty smiled. She had a feeling she was going to like Sass just fine.

"There we go," Mac said. "Now it's nothing more than a small log to step over. A saw would take care of it in no time, but I'd just leave it. Give these stall babies you're riding some real trail experience."

Marty had forgotten how beautiful the rest of the trail was as it wound through the tall pine trees toward the farmhouse.

When they stepped from the trail, Gayle waved from the porch, but she wasn't alone. Marty saw Duke and Annie and Jeff, and someone else who was taking to Jeff.

Mac trotted up beside her. "Rachel's been hanging out at our place all week," he said with a wink.

They rode down to the house and Marty introduced Sam to Gayle and Rachel.

Sam greeted them warmly and then looked at Jeff. "And this must be Jeff," he said.

Marty felt her cheeks get warm. She'd been making excuses for Jeff's absences while he'd been hiding out in his room, barely talking to any of them. She shot a look at her son, but he was smiling at Sam.

"Hi, Mr. Marcus," he said.

"Jeff," said Mac, "boost Annie up here behind me. She might as well make Sassy's acquaintance since she's going to be staying here."

"Now, Marty," Gayle said, "you don't have to take her, you know. I told Mac, 'Keeping a horse is expensive these days and...'"

"Gayle, I think she's wonderful. With the amount of feed I'm buying now, one more won't make much difference. I'm delighted by Mac's offer. I may even give some beginner walk-trot lessons on her. Then she'd make me some money."

"For Pete's sake, Gayle," Mac said. "I hear she also gets a special deal from the blacksmith."

Marty felt her cheeks grow hot again, but no one was watching her as Mac reached down and pulled Annie up behind him.

"Oh, I nearly forgot," Duke said. "Derry called. He said he was going to stop by after his last call, probably before six."

This time Gayle joined Mac and Annie in a chorus of, "Owwwwww."

Marty's cheeks burned. "Come on, you guys, I'm too old for this silliness." She turned and headed toward the barn. "We'll be right back down. Jeff, will you get lemonade for everyone and cut some of that poundcake?"

In the barn they all went to work putting the horses away,

Annie giggling and helping Mac with Sass. Sam was the last one finished; he always spent extra time talking to Grandma.

Mac clapped Sam on the back when he joined them. "My daddy used to tell me the sign of a real horseman was a fella who liked the animal itself, not just riding it. I'm guessing that means you qualify."

"I really do like the old girl. No matter what happens in a day, I can always count on her to be happy to see me. I don't even care that it's because she's looking for carrots," Sam said.

"Now Marty here qualifies as a real horsewoman, and always did. I used to think there wasn't a better horsewoman in the county, unless it was her mama," Mac said. He scooped Annie up and lifted her to his shoulders.

Annie laughed and yelled, "Giddyup."

"Looks like we've got us another horsewoman in the making," Mac said. He whinnied and gave a playful jump. Annie squealed. "Come on now, girl, you've got to be able to stick with 'em." He charged down the hill with Annie laughing and squealing, her hands locked around his chin and her knees locked under his arms.

Sam patted Marty's shoulder. "It seems to me a person could make a very nice home here, especially one who already has such good friends."

Marty sighed and started down the hill. "I know… I just… well, I spent half my life trying to get away from here. It's not exactly a cultural center, you know."

"How long since you've been to Pittsburgh? It's only about forty-five minutes, you know."

"I haven't been there in years," Marty answered. "Of course, when I was a kid Pittsburgh might as well have been five hours away. I had no way to get there. But you're right, it really isn't so far now that I have my own wheels."

When they reached the house, Jeff and Rachel were nowhere in sight, but the sound of wild African drumming came from the living room. Annie and Mac were sipping lemonade on the porch steps with Duke, under two baskets of cascading lilac petunias hanging from the eaves. Gayle bent over a shovel, digging near the steps.

"Gayle, you had those baskets hanging on your porch," Marty said.

"I went by the nursery and got two more. You need some flowers here," Gayle said, turning from the hole she'd dug and heading for the truck. She reached in and pulled out a small bush, its roots wrapped in a burlap feed sack. "I had to thin my rhododendron. It's not the best time to do it, but I need the space. If this one doesn't make it, we'll get you another one in the spring."

"What do you two want to drink?" Duke asked.

"Iced tea would be wonderful," Sam said. "But let me get it. You look too comfortable to be getting up. How about you, Marty?"

"The same. Thanks, Sam," Marty said, aware that he seemed to have a need to be treated like family. Still, she was glad she'd cleaned the kitchen, since she wasn't sure anybody was ready for her family *au naturel.*

"What about some white climbing roses over the railing here?" Gayle asked.

"I'm sure that would be beautiful, but you know I don't exactly have a green thumb," Marty said.

"Mom kills house plants," Annie offered.

"I'll help you. Flowers make a place homey." Gayle tamped down the dirt around the rhododendron. "Annie, will you please get me a bucket of water from the kitchen?"

Annie jumped to her feet and disappeared. She returned with the water, followed by Sam with their beverages.

After watering the bush, Gayle sat on the step below Mac, her arm draped over his knee. Sam, Annie, and Marty took places on the steps. Easy conversation followed, with jazz from Jeff's CD player providing a backdrop. Marty looked around at her family and friends, and then relaxed against the step to enjoy the moment. The sun shone out of a deep blue sky and yet a mild breeze kept the heat from being oppressive.

The mellow mood was broken when Cody charged around the side of the house and leaped beside Marty, planting a big kiss on her cheek. "Down, you nuisance, you." The pup sat and cocked his head, looking at her. "Good boy," she said, giving him a pat on the shoulder. Immediately he lay down, his head on her thigh.

"Hey, you've taught him some manners," Mac said. "I'll have to let you work on his brother next."

The sound of wheels churning the gravel made them all look down the lane. Derry's truck barreled toward them in a cloud of dust, screeching to a stop just short of the porch.

"Hey, Brady," called Mac. "Your message said before six. It's only four. You—good grief, woman, you didn't need to pinch me!"

"Oh, yes, I did," Gayle said. "Now you behave yourself."

Derry came around the side of the truck carrying a cardboard box. "I'm on my way to another job, but I thought maybe Annie..." He looked into the box.

Annie jumped up. "What did you bring, Derry?"

Derry gave Marty a sheepish grin. "Annie, sit down a minute. I think I'd better ask your mom first."

Marty got to her feet and saw three tiny kittens in the box. "Derry, they're too young to be away from their mother."

"Well, their mother's dead, got hit on the road, and I'm not going to mention any names, but that yahoo who runs the hack stable in Finleyville was going to drown them. They are eating on their own, just barely but... well, I figured now that you have three horses in the barn you could use some barn cats."

Marty smiled at him. "Four."

"Four what?" Derry asked.

"Horses," Mac called. "I just brought Sass over for her to use."

"Oh, well, then..." Derry walked over and gave the box of kittens to Annie. "You really need barn cats, Marty."

"Derry, it will be a long time before they can perform any catly duties," Marty said.

"But, Mom, I love them," Annie wailed.

Everyone laughed, even Marty who sat down on the steps with a shrug. She was feeling encumbered. She took the box of kittens from Annie. Inside the three babies mewed and nosed each other, looking for food. The smallest, a tiny calico, looked up at Marty. She turned away from its sad eyes to find everyone staring at her, as if waiting for her to say something. "All right! All right! You win. I'm here. I'm running a boarding stable complete with barn cats. By fall I'll have roses climbing up over the porch railings! I'll stay as long as I can! Is that what you all want to hear?"

THIRTEEN

"**M**om, you look beautiful," Annie said.

"Thanks, honey," Marty said, smiling over her shoulder at her daughter who lay on the bed, watching her. She looked back at the mirror and wished she felt beautiful. She straightened the shoulders on the green silk blouse, Dan's favorite, the one he said matched her eyes. *Had* said, she corrected herself.

She still thought of herself as Dan's wife, and here she was getting ready to go out to dinner with Derry Brady. She felt unfaithful even though Derry had been appropriately playful about the invitation, insisting he was paying her back for allowing him to palm three kittens off on her.

She fastened the Celtic design pewter buckle on the black woven belt she wrapped around her skirt, her favorite with its paisley print in purple, gold, blue, and green, the same shade as her blouse. But how dressy was dinner at Angelina's? She remembered it as the nicest restaurant in town, but, after all, town was just Washington, Pennsylvania. She was probably over-dressed again, but it was too late to change. Derry was due any time now.

She dashed down the hall to the bathroom and knocked on the door.

"It's occupied," Jeff snapped.

"Jeff, I need my makeup bag. I left it on the back of the toilet."

"Yeah, I'm sure you do," he snarled. The door opened a few inches and he tossed the bag in a high arching throw that Marty barely caught.

"Jeff!" Marty swallowed her anger. "Gayle said she'd have you and Annie home by eleven-thirty. I should be back before that."

"Yeah, right!"

Marty bit her lip to keep from snapping back at him. Teen-agers! What had happened to that dear little boy she'd raised? It was obvious that Jeff liked Rachel, and she was the one who had talked her Aunt Gayle into taking them on this outing to the town pool. Marty was determined to cut him a little slack, at least for tonight.

As Marty walked back into her room, Annie was looking at her with big worried eyes. "Jeff's just afraid that you might like Derry better than Daddy," she said in a small voice.

Marty took Annie's face in her hands. "No, sweetie, and don't you worry either. Even if someday I do... well, if I do find someone else, I could never love anyone *more* than I loved your daddy." Annie gave her a smile. Marty didn't continue. Annie was too little to understand that Marty hoped someday—not now, but someday—to find someone to love. She needed that as much as she needed to be loved.

Downstairs the dogs started to bark and Marty heard her father moving across the entry hall toward the door. She swiped the mascara across her eyelashes and dabbed her mouth with lipstick.

"Marty! Derry's here," Duke hollered up the stairs.

"I'll be right there," she called.

Annie bounced off the bed, the straps of her swimming suit showing at the neckline of her T-shirt. She hugged her mother. "Have fun, Mom."

Marty wrapped her arms around Annie and hugged her tightly, kissing the top of her head. "You, too, sweetie. I love you." She grabbed her etched silver hoop earrings from the dresser and started down the steps, putting them through her earlobes as she went.

At the bottom of the stairs she stopped to finish putting on the last earring. With *Rodeo News* in his hand, Kyle stepped out of the living room and winked at her. "You look great, Sis," he said. He slipped an arm around her shoulder and kissed her cheek, walking with her toward the porch. "Hey, you're shaking. Come on, Marty, you're smoother than that."

"I don't feel very smooth," she whispered. "I feel awkward and foolish and half-sick to my stomach. Kyle, I'm a thirty-eight-year-old widow with two kids. This is ridiculous."

"Marty, Dan died. You didn't. He wouldn't expect you to

spend the rest of your life mourning. He'd want you to go out, to have fun."

She hugged her brother and patted his back. "Thanks, little brother." But she thought, *Dan would have wanted me to go out with some respectable widower, preferably a professor or professional man, not with the twice-married, twice-divorced Casanova of Washington County.*

She felt a growing tightness in her chest and took a deep breath.

"Gee, sighing already," Kyle teased.

Marty smacked him playfully on the back and opened the door, pasting her brightest smile on her lips. "Here I am," she said.

Derry looked at her, his own smile shining out of his eyes.

"Look here, Brady, do I need to give you a lecture on how to behave with my sister?" Kyle put up his fists and feigned a punch at Derry.

"No, Kyle, your dad already did," Derry said, reaching for Marty's hand and leading her off the porch toward his sporty car. She waved goodbye to her dad and brother as Derry opened the car door and handed her in.

"All right, you two," Derry called. "I promise to have her in before midnight."

They drove in uneasy silence to the end of the farm lane. Marty tried to think of something to say that wouldn't sound as silly as she felt. "I hope Duke wasn't too hard on you."

Derry put the car into park and turned toward her. He picked up her hand. "No, he wasn't. He was just looking out for you. He told me to be careful with you because you're fragile right now."

"Fragile? Duke actually said 'fragile'? I mean, I may be a bit stressed out or even feeling a little silly, but I have never been fragile!"

"Sorry, Marty. I think he's right, because you've never been nervous around me and right now the tension between us is so thick I can barely see you sitting on the other side of it."

He squeezed her hand, brought it to his face and pressed his lips firmly against it. "Marty, I'm not playing with you. I won't hurt you. I promise. Why, we're just two old friends going out for dinner tonight to catch up on each other's lives. All right?"

"Thanks, friend. That's exactly what I need."

He pinched her cheek. "Okay, my lady, you've got it. Now let's have a good time."

At Angelina's, waiters in white tuxedo shirts and black slacks bustled through an updated version of the restaurant Marty remembered. Instead of the starched white cloths, bamboo chairs, and plastic red roses in milk-glass vases, crisp mauve cloths draped the tables with white silk roses in crystal bud vases. The rest of the decor was in black and white with brass accents. She noticed from the menu that prices had gone up along with the tone of the place. Even though many of the diners were dressed casually, she didn't feel overdressed.

Derry seemed different in this setting. His classy silk sport coat and carefully pressed slacks contrasted sharply to his usual jeans and polo shirt, but it wasn't just that. He seemed somehow more sophisticated. As they read over the menu, he commented on the various dishes, recommending some, discouraging others. The hostess and waiters all seemed to know him by name.

After he ordered, Derry reached across the table and took Marty's hand. "Listen now, Marie," Derry said to the waitress, "I'm out with a special friend tonight, so tell whoever's cooking to make it good."

The waitress gave Marty a long look. "You poor girl."

Marty laughed a bit more loudly than she, intended. She felt the blood rush to her cheeks.

Derry squeezed her hand. "Don't pay any attention to her, she's been after me for years."

"Like I need another heartache," the woman said with a laugh as she headed toward the kitchen.

Derry launched into a story about how he had, years before between wives one and two, dated the waitress's sister who at the time was also dating a professional wrestler. Derry's slightly self-deprecatory chatter put Marty at ease. Here was a man who could laugh at himself, something Dan had never quite mastered. Maybe because Dan had never been quite as comfortable with himself as Derry seemed to be. Dan had always seemed to be struggling for something just out of reach, something he knew he'd never quite grasp.

"Anyway, after being bounced off the side of the restaurant a few times and having my neck twisted in a headlock, I decided that he liked her better than I did, so it only made sense to let him have her," Derry said.

Marty laughed, unrestrained, right out loud. Derry had always been able to make her laugh. She'd missed that.

Her laughter encouraged him, and he launched into another story of misadventure. By the time their dinners arrived Marty was relaxed, enjoying the excellent food and the company of her old friend, yet aware that a very pleasant tension stretched between them.

"There have certainly been a lot of women in your life, Mr. Brady," she teased.

"None of them mattered, Marty." He raised his glass to her and took a sip. "No one matched my memories of you."

"Derry, you had two wives. They had to mean something to you."

"Look, you know about Marci. I did the right thing; I married her. But after she lost the baby... well, we were done long before that."

Marty remembered the night he'd told her about Marci. They had both cried, and then she'd gotten angry—and so had he. He had tried to shift some of the guilt to her, telling her that if she had given him what he needed he wouldn't have had to look for it somewhere else. For a moment, just a moment, she'd felt guilty, as if it had somehow been her fault. Gayle and Mama had helped her through that, and her anger, resentment, and guilt had finally turned to acceptance. Acceptance, and relief that she hadn't made the same mistake Marci had.

"By the time Marci and I both gathered the courage to call it off, you were already married. So I went looking to replace you. I can't even tell you now what it was about wife number two that reminded me of you. Whatever it was, her bad disposition soon erased any comparison. In fairness, I wasn't the best husband in the world, but then I didn't love her. I had only loved something of you I saw in her."

She looked at him hard and long, knowing she was about to reveal more of herself than she intended, but needing to know. "You mean it, don't you?" He didn't answer, but she saw tears rise in the corners of his eyes.

"Marty, I've got to tell you right now that I've done a lot of things I shouldn't have, probably hurt a lot of people to boot, but I always believed if I found someone... well, I could be a better person." His voice was so low she could barely hear him. "I'm sorry. I promised to behave like a friend and here I am getting mushy on you."

Marty wanted to say something like, "I don't mind," or "that's okay," or "keep talking, you silver-tongued devil, you," but at the same time she thought of Dan and those uneasy feelings of betrayal rose to silence her.

"Forget what I said. I'm not going to ruin your evening by pressuring you. Let's get out of here and I'll give you a tour of the town. There have been a lot of changes here in the past few years."

At the door, Derry paid the check and then ushered Marty out to the car. They drove up one street and down another, all over Washington, which seemed to Marty much the same yet strangely different. Most of the change was more a sprucing up what had been instead of adding anything new. Marty found that somehow comforting, and felt a growing warmth with the man who had been a kid here with her. When Derry turned onto the college campus, the changes were more startling—there were many new buildings.

"That's the new theater," Derry said, pulling up beside a building of modern design. "They bring in all kinds of events— you know, symphony, opera, ballet, and of course plays. I think they have art shows and stuff like that."

"What's it like?"

"Never been there."

Marty turned to look at him. "But would you go if asked?"

He cocked an eyebrow and shot her a one-sided grin. "Depends. Are you the one doing the asking?"

"I might be." Marty's heart pounded. She hoped Derry knew how important his answer was. The world of theater and art and music, the world Dan had introduced her to, had become necessary to her.

"Lady, I'd go anywhere you asked me to go, but I can't lie to you. I mean, I am who I am, and Derry Brady will never be too keen on going to an opera or a ballet. But I could be persuaded to go to a play, as long as it had an understandable plot."

Marty jumped out of the car. "Wait here," she said, and ran into the theater. A poster listed the coming plays, one of them a two-week run of *Foxfire*. Excellent. And the box office was still open.

Marty ran back to the car where Derry stood leaning against the door, looking amused. She handed him two tickets for a Wednesday evening performance two weeks away. "The play is about country people. You'll love it," she said. "So, Mr. Brady, how about it?"

"Sure, but Marty…" he took both her hands in his. Marty could feel his hands tremble. "Are you… are you sure you…" He searched her face.

Marty took a deep breath to free the tightness in her throat. "Derry, I'm not sure of anything, but it looks like I'm going to stick around here for a while, so I guess I can take the time to find out." The tightness spread to her chest. She could feel, almost as if it were an anatomical reality, the gaping hole Dan's death had torn in her heart.

Derry took her face in his hands and he kissed her. But it felt all wrong. His weren't Dan's lips. His arms were more muscular than Dan's. He was shorter. Smelled different. At first she forced Dan from her mind and kissed Derry back. But Marty knew that kisses like this could warm her through a long winter, or burn her to ashes well before the autumn leaves fell. She pulled back.

A look of disappointment passed over Derry's face, but he let her go. "I know we said we'd take this slowly," Derry said, "but I don't think I can treat you like a casual friend."

Marty darted around to her side of the car. "How about a glass of iced tea? I have some at the farm. We can sit on the porch and wait for the kids." She grinned at him across the roof of the car and raised an eyebrow, questioning, hoping he understood.

Derry laughed and slipped behind the wheel. "All right, my lady. Back home it is." They rode in comfortable silence for a while, and then Derry reached across the seat and took her hand in a soft and tender hold. As they drove toward home she realized that she didn't feel lonely or afraid. Maybe, just maybe, he could make her stop hurting.

FOURTEEN

When Derry pulled up in front of the farmhouse, Duke sat on the porch step with Jake and Cody.

"It's not even eleven yet," Duke said. "You two fighting again?"

Marty and Derry both laughed. Derry slipped an arm around Marty's shoulder and walked her to the porch. Cody charged them, dancing around their legs, demanding attention. Derry flopped onto the second step and pulled Marty next to him. Marty let the pup squeeze in between her and the railing, determined that nothing—not even a gangling pup shedding all over good clothes and drooling on her lap— would mar her happiness.

They still sat there leaning against each other and sharing the soft moonlit evening with Duke when Gayle drove up the lane with the kids. Jeff jumped from the car, thanking Gayle for the ride. He turned toward the house, a look of cocky teenage contentment on his face, until he saw Derry.

"Uh, oh," Derry whispered.

Marty shifted slightly away from Derry. "Hi, did you guys have a good time?"

Annie crawled out of the backseat. "It was great, Mom. We met lots of kids, and guess what? Jeff likes Rachel."

Marty couldn't see Jeff's face clearly, but saw the angry snap of his head as he turned toward his sister. For a minute, Marty thought he was going to hit Annie. Instead, he snarled something and charged past them up the steps and into the house.

Marty leapt to her feet to follow him, but Derry grabbed her elbow. "Let him go," he said.

"Annie, you all right?" Marty asked.

"Sure," Annie said. "He'll be okay, Mom. Rachel likes him, too. I saw them holding hands."

Gayle threw her arms around Annie. "You are a big brother's nightmare."

Annie giggled.

Derry's beeper sounded. He jogged to the car phone, returning shortly with a frown. "I've got to go. A hunter-jumper threw a shoe and is shipping out tomorrow morning for a big show." He grabbed Marty's hand and pulled her with him to the car, calling his goodbyes to the others. Beside the car he kissed her quickly but firmly on the lips. "I love you," he whispered.

Still reeling from the kiss and the wonders of feeling that it shot threw her, Marty leaned against him. "Derry, I..."

He put a hand over her mouth. "Shhh. I don't want to pressure you. I'm just telling you how I feel. I love you. I always have." He kissed her cheek and released her. "I'll call you," he said before starting the car and tearing down the lane, leaving a trailing dust cloud behind.

Marty walked back to the porch, all of her nerve endings screaming. She eased herself back onto the step, only half-listening to Annie's chatter and Gayle's responses. The puppy gave her cheek a sloppy kiss. She pushed him away from her face, but kept an arm hugging his shoulders.

Duke pulled himself upright. "Well, since I don't imagine any of us will be getting much conversation from my daughter, I think I'll turn in."

"Night, Dad," Marty mumbled without turning around.

"How about you, Annie Banannie? Why don't you scoot up to bed and let your Mom and Gayle have some girl talk?"

"But I'm a girl, and I want to hear all about Mom's date," Annie said.

Marty laughed and pulled Annie onto her lap. "It wasn't a real date. I just went out to dinner with an old friend. We had a very good time." She gave a quick tickle to her daughter's sides, holding her close and kissing her cheek. Annie laughed and squirmed. The puppy bounced to his feet and gave the top of Annie's head a few licks.

"Oh, yuck," Annie said. "Now I'll have to wash the dog spit out of my hair."

"Well, scoot then," Marty said. "You need to rinse the pool chlorine off anyway."

Annie gave her a hug and kiss, then gave the same to Gayle. "Thanks for taking me to the pool. I really had a good time."

"You are certainly welcome, Annie," said Gayle. "We'll do it again soon."

Annie nodded and followed Duke into the house. "Ohhh, Gayle," groaned Marty.

"Okay, tell me all about it." Gayle slid down a step to sit next to Marty.

"Nobody kisses like Derry Brady. Those lips of his can certainly rev a girl's engine, but I think I need to idle for awhile longer. He's rushing things—telling me he loves me." Marty flopped back her head against the top step. "Gayle, what am I going to do?"

"No way, friend. Nobody can tell you what to do on this one. The thing about Derry is if he's telling you he loves you, he means it, at least while he's saying it. You just never know how long he's going to hold that thought."

"I know. I've been there before, but..." Marty couldn't go on, not even to Gayle, whom she had always trusted with her secrets. Even to her own ears, she'd sound like nothing more than a gullible schoolgirl if she were to admit Derry might be telling the truth: that he had never stopped loving her, that she was what he needed to turn his life around, and that he might be what she needed to start her life over again.

"There's nothing wrong with you going out with him, Marty. And he's never said anything to me to indicate that he doesn't completely respect you, so..."

"You mean, he won't try to seduce me?"

Gayle laughed. "No, I'm sure he'll try, but I'm also sure he'll respect your decisions."

She realized that Gayle just assumed she would say no to Derry. So had Marty, until his kiss had magnified her needs for closeness and affection, needs long satisfied by her loving relationship with Dan. Tonight they'd been eased with just a kiss, but how long would that be so? She looked at Gayle and shrugged her shoulders.

"Marty, don't jump in over your head."

"It was a lot easier when we were kids. I mean, good grief, Gayle, it's easier to say no when you don't know what you're turning down."

"Marty!"

"Don't worry," Marty reached over and patted Gayle's shoulder. "I always follow the rules, don't I? It's just... I'm so lonely, Gayle. And afraid that I'll never again have a man to love. Derry says he loves me. But he's nothing like Dan."

"No, he's not, and you've been burned by Derry once already, if you remember. And Marty, there are moral values involved that go beyond merely 'following the rules.'"

"I know that. I'm not going to rush off to bed with him, but I *am* going to go out with him again. I keep thinking maybe we're meant to be together now. Maybe not, but I won't know unless I open myself to the possibility. Maybe I can make a difference in his life. He thinks so."

"You've always had good sense," Gayle said.

"I still do. I'm not so desperate that I'd run off with the first guy who comes along. Actually, I wasn't even looking for anyone. Derry just sort of bulldozed his way into my life, but I'll be careful. I also have two kids to think of, and I won't do anything to jeopardize their respect for me. Although as far as Jeff is concerned, I already have—merely by going out with a man."

"Jeff will come around. Annie's right. He and Rachel do seem to like each other. Nothing can distract a teenager like a budding romance. And you don't even need to worry about *that* with them, because Rachel is a good kid, and unless my instincts have failed me completely, so is Jeff."

"Well, right now I feel like a little kid looking in a bakery window just before dinnertime. I know Mom has a good dinner prepared and I should go straight home, but, oh, boy, I can't tell you how much I want that chocolate cupcake in the window."

"Derry Brady as a cupcake? Now that's an interesting image. Just remember that cupcakes don't provide life-sustaining nourishment."

"But what's life without cupcakes?"

Gayle stood. "Sensible. And in order for me to be sensible, I need to get home. Morning comes early at our place."

Marty stood and hugged her friend. "Since I left here, I haven't had anyone to talk to the way I can talk to you. I love you, friend. You know that, don't you?"

"Yes, I do, best buddy. Love you, too. See you at church on Sunday?" Gayle looked at her expectantly.

"I told you I'd go. I even want to, but why the loaded question?"

"Well, all this stuff we've talked about—pray on it. Okay?" Gayle kissed her cheek and, without waiting for an answer, headed for her car.

"Maybe even God wants me with Derry."

Gayle stopped and turned back toward Marty. She seemed to be thinking. "Derry is a friend and I love him dearly, so I think that would be wonderful, if it's really so. Just please go slow and be careful. Remember that Derry may be the best friend in the world, but he's got a lousy track record as a husband."

Marty watched Gayle go. She was too charged to think about going to bed yet. The silvery moonlight provided enough guidance for Marty to make her way down to the creek with the pup sniffing along the ground after her. Cody caught a scent and took off down the lane at a lope. Behind the house, imbedded deep in the creek bed, she found the boulder that Mama had called her "sitting rock." Marty slipped off her shoes and hose. She climbed onto the rock and hung her feet into the cool, moving water. How many times she'd seen Mama sitting like this.

What would Mama say about her taking up with Derry again? The night Marty and Derry had broken up, Mama had rocked her in her arms. It was as though Marty was a little girl, not a young woman soon off to college. For the first time, she had a pain Mama couldn't make better. "It's you he loves, my darling," Mama had said. "But some men just can't seem to help blowing up what's dearest to them." Mama had held her until Marty nearly cried herself to sleep. Then Mama had whispered, "At least you're getting out of here. Go, and don't look back. Make yourself a happy life far away from this dead-end place."

That's what Marty had done, but she'd lost her happiness

when Dan died, and now her life had come full circle back to this place. And Derry Brady had been waiting right where she'd left him. Maybe in this part of her life, he was her happiness, just like Dan had been. She'd sometimes thought God had given Dan to her, to take care of her and teach her about a world she desperately wanted but was hopelessly ill-prepared to live in—a world of ideas, beauty, and culture. Maybe now God was giving her to Derry, to do for him what Dan had done for her. Dan was gone and Mama was gone. It was her turn now. She had to make a home and a life for her children, and Duke and Kyle and maybe Derry. She kicked a foot in the creek and watched the moonlight turn the spray to silver droplets. She smiled, sure that given enough time, she'd figure it all out.

FIFTEEN

By Friday of the next week Marty had sent for and received the kids' school records, advised the realtor in D.C. to drop the price on the house $5,000, authorized the moving company to transfer her furniture and the rest of their belongings from the storage facility to the farm, and had all of her accounts changed to area banks. Duke and Derry were ecstatic over her decision, offering to help in any way they could. Annie seemed sometimes pensive but mostly happy, playing with her pony and caring for the three kittens who now lived in a big box beside her bed. Jeff was downright hostile.

Kyle had been a whole other story. He'd seemed pleased until Marty had the dumpster dropped off. Then he became suspicious, especially when she threw away all the stained rugs and upholstered furniture, and insisted that the dogs went nowhere in the house until they were fully housebroken. When she and Derry hauled out the grimy couch, even Duke had protested. "But, Marty, where am I going to take my nap in the afternoon?"

"Dad, that old couch stinks. The dogs peed all over the skirt and there's been enough food spilled on it to feed a Third World country."

So out the couch went. The way Marty figured, Duke and Kyle had been alone so long without anyone to take care of them that they'd gotten stuck in their ways like two crotchety old bachelors. Well, once she got the house cleaned and redecorated, they would be happy.

Marty leaned against the doorjamb and surveyed her work. The living room did look pretty dismal stripped of furniture, even though Marty had spent the whole morning scrubbing down the walls and polishing the scarred wood floor. A good coat of paint would fix the walls. She'd pick up the paint when she went to fetch Annie from Patterson's later. Derry had promised to help her paint this weekend. By Tuesday or

Wednesday her furniture would arrive. Her navy and gold Chinese rug would cover the bad places on the floor and her other things would dress the place up a bit. Of course, they'd need new curtains, but they probably wouldn't be too expensive. Besides, now that she'd decided to stay, she wasn't nearly as tense about her financial situation and could even see where she had some extra money to play with. She also put out the word with Cam and Derry and all the other horse people she knew that she was taking in boarders and would be willing to give riding lessons.

She wiped the perspiration from her forehead with the hem of her T-shirt and then checked her watch. Nearly one-thirty. She dashed for the steps. They'd have to hurry to make their appointment to register Jeff at the high school.

Upstairs, she banged on his door. "Come on, Jeff. Fifteen minutes to departure." No answer came from the room, but she heard him lower the radio. She ran to the bathroom and leaped into the shower. A quick scrub and splash and she was out. "Bathroom's open," she yelled, as she flung her robe around her shoulders and dashed for her room.

Marty pulled a sleeveless summer dress from her closet and threw it over her head, gave her hair a quick brush, and sighed. She had an appointment at Chez Renee today. She just hoped her cousin was a better beautician now than she used to be.

"Okay, Jeff, let's go," she called. No answer, but the music coming from his room got louder. Marty banged on his door. Still no answer. She took a deep breath, squared her feet in preparation for a battle, and threw open the door.

Jeff was propped up on his pillows, his arms crossed over his chest. "I'm not going. I hate it here. If you really insist on doing this to us, I refuse to participate."

Marty glared at her firstborn who was far too big for her to haul from the bed, stuff into clothes, and drag to the car. "That's just fine, Jeff. But you will be signed up for school today, with or without your participation. And come fall, you will go." Marty slammed his bedroom door and stormed down the steps.

By the time she reached the high school, her breathing had

returned to normal. When she pulled open the heavy front door, she had even regained her calm. Inside, she saw that the old brick school hadn't changed much, except to look a lot more worn. It had that old school smell from years of chalk dust, cafeteria food, slightly damp paper, and the sweaty palms of thousands of teenagers.

In the office the young secretary invited Marty to sit and wait for the principal. When Dr. Bradley arrived, she looked vaguely familiar to Marty. The plump, gray-haired woman certainly wore a far more welcoming smile than Marty had ever seen under the bushy gray mustache of her old principal, Quincy Ford.

"How wonderful!" Dr. Bradley said. "So Mrs. Harris is really my old friend Marty Stafford." The woman extended her hand and shook Marty's heartily.

Recognition returned with the firm handshake. "Miss Starsky! Well, not anymore. I guess it's Dr. Bradley," Marty said.

She guided Marty into an office filled with photos. She pointed to a faded picture of some kids on the high school stage. Marty stepped closer to better see the photo shot during a curtain call of her senior class play directed by her English teacher, Miss Starsky. There she was right in the middle, with Cam as the tin man, Gayle as Glenda, and the rest of the cast, many of whose names she'd long forgotten.

"You were wonderful as Dorothy. Of course, you'd just gotten your acceptance at the university and knew you'd soon be off on your own yellow brick road. Did you ever find Oz?"

Marty had been wondering a lot about that lately. "Yes and no," she answered slowly. "My husband and I had a good life. We had two beautiful children and lived in a stimulating academic community but…" Marty hesitated and Dr. Bradley did not jump in to help her out. "I found that Oz wasn't paradise. And my husband—wonderful wizard he was—couldn't fulfill all my wishes."

Dr. Bradley patted Marty's shoulder and guided her to a chair. "No place is, and no one can. But now your ruby slippers have brought you home again, so let's see what we've got here." She took Jeff's records and sat down behind her big desk. After studying them a minute she looked up and smiled again. "Well, Marty, we've changed some since you were here, but I'm afraid we still don't have the kind of advanced placement or elective choices your son was offered at his private school."

Marty's stomach clenched. Jeff was bright. Maybe she'd made the wrong choice. He'd fare no better here than she had. Like her, he'd always be searching for more. Miss Starsky had provided caring guidance to her then and Marty knew she would again. She blurted out her fears, and the reasons she had decided to come home. "Maybe I should have tried harder to stay put and keep him in his school."

When she finished, Dr. Bradley leaned toward her. "But you can't afford to keep him in his old school. Somehow or other we do manage to raise kids here. Pretty nice kids, too, I might add. Just look at you and Gayle and Cam. And a good many of them go off to college these days, so I'll think he'll be fine. If we have to, we'll find ways to challenge him."

They went to work on Jeff's schedule. In addition to the mandatory academic classes, they signed him up for honors chemistry and English, the only honors options available. She knew he'd be disappointed that this school offered no Latin, since he'd planned to start that at his old school. Instead, she put him in Spanish 3 and hoped he'd go for it. She also signed him up for band, the only outlet available for his love of music. What he didn't like he could change.

Dr. Bradley walked Marty to the door. "I'm delighted you've come home, Marty. You know, I still count you as one of my favorite students. Have you decided yet what you're going to do?"

"Not yet. I mean, I was hoping to teach, but although I graduated and got my teaching certificate, I married Dan and never taught, so..."

"So you're not even getting called for interviews, right?"

Marty nodded.

"I know you'd be a wonderful teacher, but I'm afraid I can't help you. We've been losing population and have even had to let some tenured teachers go."

"I don't know what I'm going to do," Marty said. "Eventually, I'll need to find something. Right now I'm just trying to put the farm back in order. I have one man who boards a horse with me. I'm planning on taking in more and giving some lessons."

Dr. Bradley just looked at her, that same look that ate right into Marty's soul and seemed to ask, "Yes, and what else will you do?"

Marty shook her head and shrugged her shoulders. "I guess I still have a lot to work out."

Dr. Bradley patted her shoulder. "Understandable, but I can't imagine Marty Stafford slipping comfortably into the old life she fled without making some changes in it. Look around. This community needs people like you." Dr. Bradley turned back to her desk and rifled through some papers. "Yes, here it is," she said, pulling a pamphlet from the pile. She waved it in front of her "This may be something you'd want to consider. Therapeutic riding."

She handed Marty a pamphlet from the national licensing organization for therapeutic riding instructors. "What's this all about?" Marty asked.

"I don't really know much about it except that one of our special students, a boy with cerebral palsy, has been looking for a riding center. His doctors think he'd benefit from riding, not just psychologically but physically as well. I sent for some information but they tell me the only place near here with a year-round program is on the other side of Pittsburgh. Seems to me there's a need here that a person with your horse and teaching background could fill."

Marty left feeling challenged by Dr. Bradley, just as she always had. She'd wanted to find something significant to do. She could teach. She knew her horses. And therapeutic riding certainly was significant. For the first time she felt hopeful about her job prospects.

But it wasn't just her job prospects. Everything seemed to be falling into place. It was almost as if God was saying as Dan had, "Marty, you're stronger than you think you are. You will be fine."

S I X T E E N

Marty and Annie arrived back at the farm shortly before five. The trunk of the Volvo was loaded with paint, rollers, pans, and tape, everything Marty needed to get started on her redecorating. She'd also bought paint to finish the porch and then, on impulse, a wooden porch swing already painted white, a white wicker couch with two matching armchairs, and a table which Pudgy had promised to deliver after closing time. That all had been fine, fun even.

Her stop at Chez Renee was another story. Her hair had more poof on top than a dog-show poodle. Thank heaven it would grow.

She had decided to stay out of Jeff's way and respond to his questions when and if asked about the school or his schedule. He was nowhere to be seen and no angry drum rhythms sounded from upstairs. A note was tacked to the refrigerator.

> *Mom. Gone to Morgan's to help Gayle and Rachel make strawberry jam. Is that down home enough for you? Jeff.*

> *P.S. Grandpap is taking his nap in his room and he's not too happy about it.*

While Annie went to check on the kittens, Marty poured herself an iced tea, delighted at the reprieve from contention. Annie returned in no time with Duke in tow. "Grandpap was awake," Annie said.

Duke looked bleary eyed and rumpled. "Marty, I just can't take my nap without my old couch. My bed's for nighttime sleeping, not naps."

"You'll get used to it, Dad, really."

"The kittens are fine. Grandpap's taking me to the barn so I can check on Cocoa," Annie said.

"I might as well," Duke mumbled. "Sure can't sleep."

"I'll be along in a minute," Marty said. After they had gone,

107

she finished her tea, changed clothes, and headed for the barn. Derry had said he'd stop by after work and she wanted to be finished with her chores. She was halfway up the hill when she heard a car and turned to see Sam driving up to the house.

"Sam, hi." She went to meet him, glad to see this sensible man who was quickly becoming her sounding board and friend, like some wise old uncle on whom she increasingly depended. Sam pulled himself from the car and waved. After him bounced a little girl whose smile was so bright that it was all Marty saw at first, not noticing the squat body and blunted features until the child was right in front of her with arms stretched wide to hug her.

Marty immediately bent to return the child's hug. "Well, hello, who are you?"

"You're Marty and I'm Lisa and my grampy says you're gonna let me ride horses."

"I'm sure we can find a horse or two for you, Lisa." The child smiled so wide that her eyes squeezed shut. She rocked from side to side as she reached once more for a hug. Marty smiled at Sam over Lisa's head. What a remarkable man he was. Although he had told her a lot of "proud grandpa" stories about his beloved Lisa, he had never mentioned that she was a Down's syndrome child.

Lisa ran to her grandfather and took his hand. "Marty, if you're busy," Sam said, "Lisa and I will go up and play with Grandma."

"I was just going to the barn. I was thinking about giving Annie a lesson, so let's say we do a double—Annie on Sassy and Lisa on Grandma. How's that?"

"You have a girl like me?" Lisa said.

"Yes, I do. I have a little girl who is eight years old named Annie and she is smiley and bouncy and nice just like you," Marty said.

"I'm this many," Lisa said, holding all ten chubby fingers, stretched apart, up over her head.

In the barn Duke and Annie were brushing Cocoa. Without hesitation, Lisa ran up to the pony and hugged her hard around the neck. Fortunately, old Cocoa was used to such treatment and stood patiently until Lisa let her go.

"Lisa, you can't just hug any horse," Sam said. "Not all of them are as nice as Cocoa."

"And they're too big to hug. This one is just right." She again threw her arms around Cocoa's neck, rubbing her cheek against the pony's soft mane.

Marty handled the introductions and then asked, "Dad, will you keep an eye on the girls while Sam and I get the horses?"

Duke scooped up Lisa and tossed her onto the pony's back. "Now, Lisa, you sit real quiet and make Cocoa stand still while we finish brushing her, okay?"

"You bet I can do that," Lisa said, hunching forward and bending her legs at the knees, as if that would make the pony stand still.

Marty put her old kiddie saddle on Grandma and her own saddle with the stirrups as short as they'd go on Sass. Marty and Sam led the horses back to Duke and the girls. Lisa still sat in the same position they had left her in. Duke smiled and lifted her to the ground.

Lisa took off at a rolling run to Grandma. She reached as high as she could and stroked the mare's shoulder over and over. "I missed you, Grandma," she said.

Duke and Sam helped the girls into the saddles and Marty adjusted the stirrups for each of them. "Dad, will you walk beside Annie? And Sam, you beside Lisa? At least, until we see how this goes. Now, girls, both of these mares neck-rein." She walked over to Lisa and Grandma and took the reins in her hands. "That means if you want Grandma to go to the left—this way, you lay the reins against the right side of her neck—this side. Understand?"

"Got it, Mom," Annie answered.

"How about you, Lisa?" Sam asked.

Lisa nodded.

They led the horses to Kyle's makeshift arena, a large area leveled out of the hillside behind the barn.

"I like it here," said Lisa, looking out toward the valley below and the opposite hillside rising from the creek.

Marty tried to see through Lisa's eyes. For the moment she looked away from the sagging fences, the paint peeling from the house and barn, the moss growing on the barn roof, the shutters hanging askew on the back of the house. And when she did, she saw rising and falling hillsides covered in many shades of green, protected by woods ringing the ridges and reaching down into the valley. The lush green contrasted sharply with the starkness of the rock outcroppings on the opposite hillside, which from here looked like a cliff. Through breaks in the trees, she could see the Morgans' rich upper pasture rolling away from the top of the cliff, dotted with their black-and-white Holsteins.

A few coats of paint, some nails, and a little work could make this farm a showplace. And Marty saw no reason why, if she pushed everybody to help, it couldn't be.

She turned back to the girls who sat smiling on their horses. "Now we'll use the upper end of the ring and you walk in a circle around me." She called out instructions telling the girls how to hold the reins, as well as their feet and backs and heads. Annie sat straighter and much more quietly than Lisa. Grandma, God bless her, ignored the little girl who wiggled and bounced in the saddle with excitement. The old mare kept her head low, in spite of flapping reins, and walked steadily on.

After the girls had circled the arena several times, Marty had them walk in figure eights and serpentines, with Duke and Sam beside them.

"Let's giddyup," Lisa yelled.

"I don't think you're ready to go fast yet, Lisa," Sam said.

Lisa frowned and stopped bouncing.

Marty glanced at Annie who caught her eye and nodded. "Sam, it looks like you're outnumbered and I'm going to have to let these girls trot a little. Now here's how we'll do it—one at a time with you on one side and me on the other. Dad, you stay put. I'm not going to risk you having coronary by running around this arena."

"Now wait a minute here," Duke said with a cough. "I'm not that much older than Sam."

"Maybe not, but Sam jogs. This is the most exercise you've had in months."

"Grandpap, you'd better listen to Mom," Annie said. "You're puffing already."

"Don't worry, Duke, I'll be puffing before long," Sam said with a laugh.

Duke looked as if he were going to sulk, but Marty figured that was preferable to having him stretched out on the dirt. They started with Lisa. Marty clucked to Grandma who eased into a slow jog, not much faster than her walk. Lisa squealed and threw her head back, laughing and bouncing higher than Grandma's smooth jog could justify. Her uninhibited joy was contagious and Marty and Sam laughed right along with her.

Once around the arena and it was Annie's turn. Sassy jogged slowly and easily, and Marty was pleased to see Annie ride her like a natural. Annie even let the mare have her head, not falling into the beginner's hazard of pulling on the horse's mouth to balance herself with the reins.

And then it was Lisa's turn again. Then Annie's. By the third time around, Marty was puffing. "Sam, I'm dying and you're not even winded."

Sam shrugged. "Like you said, I jog."

"Looks like we've got a contender for walk-trot pleasure at the next county horse show," Gayle called from the barn door.

Marty stopped, grateful for the interruption. "Hey, I didn't hear you drive up."

"That's because I walked."

Marty handed Sassy over to Duke. "All right, girls, let's walk those horses for a while." Marty joined Gayle. "Tell Mac I love the mare and you can see for yourself that Annie does, too." Sam led Grandma by, with Lisa waving from the saddle. "You're a good rider, Lisa," Marty called.

Lisa grinned and nodded her head so hard that she almost lost her balance.

"And where did that little sweetheart come from?" Gayle asked.

"That's Sam's granddaughter."

"She's darling, and your teaching abilities are showing," Gayle said.

Later from the vantage point of the porch steps, Marty, Sam, and Gayle sipped iced tea and watched the girls playing down by the creek. Marty told her friends that she had signed the kids up for school, then asked what they knew about therapeutic riding.

"I don't know a lot about it, except what I've read," Gayle said. "But it seems like therapeutic riding centers for physically and mentally challenged riders have been cropping up all over the country lately. I've been hoping that someone would start one here in the county. The state 4-H horse and pony show offers special classes for challenged kids, but our fair board doesn't want to put money into the necessary mounting ramps and lifts until we can show them we have the kids to use it. Some of us feel that if we offer the classes, then the kids will come."

Sam edged forward, a look of excitement on his face. "I think you're right, Gayle. Lisa's mom checked into this a while back. Lisa's just plain animal crazy and my daughter-in-law thought she'd like riding. Besides, it's excellent therapy for muscle development and balance. Anyway, the closest year-round program is over an hour away. My son and daughter-in-law both work, so that was out of the question. Camp programs run only three or four weeks in the summer and are already full for this year, although they put Lisa on a waiting list."

Sam and Gayle both turned to look at Marty.

"Why don't you start a center here, with Lisa as your first student?" Sam asked.

"I need to know more about it, but Dr. Bradley, the school principal, suggested the same thing," Marty said. "I'm kind of excited about the idea, but I have to find out how I become licensed. And I'll have to talk to Dad and Kyle. It would be a serious commitment on all our parts."

"You'll need volunteers," Gayle said. "I'm sure we could get the local 4-H kids to help."

Sam listened as Marty and Gayle threw ideas around. When Marty turned to him, she saw a look of excitement on his face. "I hope you'll let me help," he said.

"Sure, Sam," Marty answered. "I'll need everyone's help."

"No, that's not what I meant," Sam said. "I mean, really help. You're going to need an indoor arena. And the insurance rates are bound to be high."

Marty hadn't even thought about insurance, but she was sure there was much she hadn't thought of. She needed time to sort it out, and Gayle and Sam were way ahead of her. "Sam, I couldn't accept that kind of financial help from anyone. I'll have to figure this…"

"Ever since I retired, Marty, I've been looking for something to throw myself into. This would be as much for me as for you. Give me a few days and let me see what I come up with."

"But, Sam—" Marty began.

Gayle clapped her hand over Marty's mouth. "Just say, 'All right, Sam.'"

"All right, Sam," Marty echoed, trying not to feel too hopeful, but without much success.

SEVENTEEN

Marty had just finished making the fruit salad when she heard Derry's car on the drive. The rest of the meal— fried chicken, potato salad, rolls, and pie from a local restaurant—waited in the refrigerator. No time to prepare a fancy meal tonight, not if they were going to get any painting done. She felt charged with new possibilities and a strong urge to get things started. She'd decided to begin with the house and had served notice to the whole family that she expected help. Annie was already taping the windows in the living room. Marty had no idea where the men were hiding.

Derry knocked and then opened the door, not waiting for her answer. Marty liked the easy way he'd slipped back into familiarity with her.

"Yikes!" he said. "What happened to your hair?"

Marty's hands shot up to her fluffy topknot. "Renee got me. Don't worry—my hair grows quickly."

"That's all right. I still love you," he said with a grin. "Are we alone tonight?" He threw his arms around her and nuzzled her neck.

Marty laughed and pushed him away. "We are not alone and we are not going to be. We're all painting tonight, remember?"

"Not in these clothes I'm not," Derry smoothed the front of his white knit polo.

Marty put her hands on her hips. "Then I'll find you old clothes of Kyle's."

Derry laughed. "Don't worry. I've got my painting clothes in the car."

Marty heard a giggle and turned to see Annie in the door. "All right, Miss," she said, holding out the bowl of fruit salad, "enough snickering behind my back and put this on the table, please."

Derry winked at Annie. "I guess I'd better help, or she'll get after me, too." He took the platter of chicken Marty handed him.

"Annie, you go and call everybody for dinner," Marty said. "I suspect they are all hiding in their rooms."

"Grandpap! Uncle Kyle! Jeff!" Annie yelled, as she charged up the steps.

Soon Marty heard her thumping back down. "Mom! Mom!" Annie hollered.

Marty turned to meet her. "What's the matter?"

"Jeff's gone."

"Annie, he's just hiding. Probably fooling around."

"No, Mom. He left you a note." She handed the sheet of paper to Marty.

Marty's breath caught in her throat. Jeff wasn't the runaway type. He liked his creature comforts too much. Marty's hand shook as she took the paper. On it he had scrawled in pencil:

> *A coat of paint isn't going to help this dump. Waste your own time if you want to, but I won't waste mine. I'll be home later.*

Now Marty's hands shook with anger. She bit her lip and took a deep breath.

Derry's face hardened as he reached for the paper. Marty crumpled it and threw it in the trash. "Marty?" Derry demanded.

"Never mind, Derry," she said. "Annie, are Grandpap and Uncle Kyle coming?" Even as she asked, she heard Kyle's quick step followed by Duke's lumbering thud on the stairs.

They all took their places at the table. "Where's the kid?" Kyle asked, nodding toward the empty chair.

Marty's hands trembled as she put the pitcher of lemonade on the table, sloshing some of it onto the cloth. She glared at her brother.

"I think he's taken off," Derry whispered loud enough for all to hear.

"Naw, Marty," Duke bellowed, "Jeff wouldn't run away."

"Oh, no, Grandpap, he didn't," Annie said, patting her grandfather's arm. "He's just hiding out until we're done painting."

Kyle shook his head. "Marty, that kid needs a good swift kick in the…"

"Kyle," Marty warned, sitting down abruptly. "I will handle my son."

"You better, Sis, 'cause he's out of line. If you don't, I might not be able to help myself."

"Please," Duke said, "let's eat this nice dinner Marty's set for us and not ruin it with fighting. Annie, you say the blessing."

Before Marty could jump in and protest that Annie might not know a grace, her daughter folded her hands and bowed her head. "For this day and all we are about to receive, Lord, make us truly grateful and please make my brother behave. Amen," she said. "I learned that first part at Jennifer's house. The rest I made up."

"Good job, Annie," Derry said. "We're sending you back to Washington D.C. They need you in the diplomatic corps."

"Huh?" Annie asked.

"Never mind, Annie," Marty said with a smile. "Please pass the fruit salad."

Duke and Kyle poked through dinner, stalling coffee and dessert as long as Marty would let them. She finally lost patience. "All right, everyone, listen up! Here are your assignments. Duke and Kyle, you take the cans of forest green and start on the porch floor while there's still some light. You should be able to get the first coat on." She picked up Kyle's coffee cup and started toward the sink.

"Hey, I was thinking about having another cup," he said.

"After you paint awhile." She raised an eyebrow and gave him a look. "Derry and I will start in the dining room and then we'll all move into the living room when Annie's done taping in there. Annie, you'll also be errand girl, all right?"

Annie nodded her approval, grabbed her masking tape, and headed back toward the living room. Marty set to work stirring the paint, white for the ceiling and moldings and dove gray for the walls. Derry came in, dressed in an old T-shirt and jeans with a few ragged holes in the knees. "Derry, you start on the ceiling and I'll do the walls. I've taped the edges of the molding, so I can work on that tomorrow."

"How about one kiss for encouragement?" He stepped up behind her where she bent pouring the paint into the roller pan.

"Derry, don't get silly on me. I'll spill the paint."

"No, you won't. Put it down," he said, as he pulled her to her feet. He slipped his arms around her waist and kissed her.

She put her hands on his shoulders and pushed him back. "If you don't stop, we'll never get the painting finished," she said.

"Would that be so awful?"

Marty laughed. "Yes! This place is a mess and I've promised myself I'd do this."

"The problem, my dear, is that you also promised yourself the rest of us would do it, too. And I can think of many other things I'd rather be doing with you." He reached for her again, but she spun away from him and grabbed his bucket of white paint, the pan, and the roller. "Here you go, Brady—to work!"

Their old friendship made the talk flow easily between them as they painted. Romance gave their work a crisp edge. Duke ambled by on his way to the refrigerator for an iced tea and stuck his head in the room to check their progress. "Whoa, we'd better get a move on. You two are further along than we are," he said. Marty was hardly surprised, given the number of times she'd heard Kyle head to the basement refrigerator for beer.

A few minutes later Marty heard Kyle talking to Annie in the kitchen and the porch door slam. Annie came to the dining room carrying a can of beer. "Derry, Uncle Kyle said to tell you this is the last one and it's for you. He's going into town to get more."

Outside Marty heard Kyle's truck start up. She threw down her roller and ran through the kitchen to the porch, but she was too late to stop him. "Why'd you let him go, Dad?"

"It's all right, Marty," Duke said from where he knelt painting the porch. "We've gotten a good bit done."

"He drinks too much and you know it."

"He's like me. When I was a young man, I drank, too. God bless your Mama for putting up with me, but I quit when I couldn't handle it anymore, and so will Kyle."

Marty looked at her father, the alcoholic who'd quit drinking years ago, but had never really changed the addictive behaviors that had prompted the drinking. Even Mama had denied he was an alcoholic. "Your father has never laid a hand on me or said a mean word because of drink. He doesn't miss work because he's hung over, either, and he hands his paycheck over as soon as he gets it, so don't you be calling him a drunk, Missy," she had scolded.

Marty looked at her father kneeling there all innocent and sure of himself. He'd be a dry drunk until the day he died.

The light was fading from the western sky and only about half of the porch had been painted. "Aw, Dad," Marty groaned, "what have you two been doing for the last hour or so?" Duke rocked back on his heels and then plopped into a sitting position. He gave Marty an apologetic smile and shrugged. He was breathing hard, and his fringe of hair stuck out in wisps around his head. Marty sighed. He could look so pitiful.

"It's all right, Daddy," she said. "We'll finish it together." She picked up the broad brush Kyle had left to dry on the edge of the paint can and dipped it into the paint. She knelt beside her father and went to work. "Annie," she called, "turn on the porch lights and then tell Derry to keep on painting the ceiling. I'll be in as soon as we get the porch done."

Marty began to slap the paint onto the porch floor. After bumping into Duke for the fourth time, she ordered him off the porch and put him to work on the steps. "Now don't paint them clean across. Give me a path to walk down, you hear?"

Duke grumbled something about not being born yesterday and then Marty heard again the slow swish-swash of his brush. She slapped the porch with her wet brush. She'd probably have to finish the steps, too.

When it was too dark to work outside, Marty said, "All right, Daddy, let's move inside."

"And just how are we going to get in?"

"The old front door which is now the back door," Marty said.

"We nailed that shut when the steps started to rot."

"Dad, why didn't you tell me? How were you planning on getting in?"

"I wasn't. Kyle said it was quick drying paint, so I figured I'd just sit out here and wait for it to dry."

Marty walked a few steps away from her father. The temper that was rising rapidly in her chest was sure to shoot out of her mouth if she didn't get control of it. When she was certain that she could speak without shouting, she said, "Why don't you just relax out here awhile. I'll try to climb through a window. I really want to get the first coat on the living room and dining room tonight."

"That's too much for one night, Marty," Duke warned.

No, it wasn't, not if she had to stay up all night. She had no sooner climbed through the living room window when she heard a truck driving up the lane. She ran into the kitchen and threw open a window. Pudgy had arrived with the new porch furniture. "Dad, tell him to just hold on. We'll be right there."

She hurried into the dining room. Annie had taken over where she had left off, painting the lower half of one wall and doing a pretty good job of it. Derry was climbing down from the stepladder. The first coat of white sparkled from the ceiling. "You're both wonderful!" she said.

"Derry told me what to do and I just went slow and careful," Annie said.

"You did a beautiful job," she said to Annie, smiling at Derry. "Pudgy is here with the porch furniture. We'd better help him unload it."

After cleaning their hands enough to avoid marking the new furniture, they crawled back through the living-room window. Pudgy already had the swing and the two armchairs on the lawn. Derry jumped up into the truck and handed down the wicker couch to Pudgy and then the table to Marty. Duke immediately squeezed himself into one of the armchairs. "Marty, you bought this for us?"

"Yes, I did," she answered, proud of her purchases.

Suddenly they were all caught in the headlights of another truck as it bumped down the lane. Kyle slammed to a gravel-spraying stop and jumped from the truck. "What did you do? Start the party without me?" he said. He reached into the bed of the truck and hoisted a case of beer onto his shoulder. "I bought 'em already cold, guys."

Marty wanted to grab him by the ear and drag him into the house, tie a paintbrush to his hand, and make him do his share of the work, but Pudgy and Derry were laughing.

"He's right, Marty," Derry said. "We could use a break and old Pudge deserves a cold one for bringing this stuff out here."

Marty bit her lip. "Fine. I'll clean up in the dining room." She forced a smile for Pudgy. After all, he had just done her a favor. "Thanks, Pudge, I really appreciate it."

"Hey, Marty, I appreciate the business," he said.

She held out her hand. "Annie, come with me," she said, motioning her daughter forward. When they had climbed back into the house, she could still hear the men laughing on the lawn. "Let's finish the dining room, Annie," said Marty.

"All right, Mom. It will be our special project."

"Hey, Marty, throw Pudgy and me a couple of soda pops before you start working," Duke called.

Marty went to the refrigerator and grabbed two cans of pop. She opened one of the kitchen windows and hurled them toward her father. She heard them hit the ground and roll, and then more laughter.

"You better stay clear of her for a while, Derry," Kyle said. "Big sister is steamin'." More laughter.

In the dining room, Annie went right to work. Marty picked up the extra roller and joined her. She set her jaw and rolled the paint onto the wall, fast and hard. Derry probably wouldn't even miss her. And Kyle and Duke would just think she was doing what she was supposed to do—what Mama had always done— most of the work while the men played.

EIGHTEEN

Marty and Annie had finished the first coat on the dining room when Pudgy's truck drove off. Soon she heard Derry in the kitchen. "Is it safe to come in?" She didn't answer. With a silly grin on his face, he stuck his head into the room where she was tapping the top back onto a can of paint. She gave him a stare with one eyebrow raised.

He rushed into the room and kissed the back of her neck. "Forgive me! Forgive me! But I couldn't let Pudge sit out there and drink alone."

She smelled the beer on his breath. "He wouldn't have been alone. My father and brother were there and, furthermore, Pudge wasn't drinking." She knew there was a sharp edge in her voice, but she couldn't help it. She looked at Annie who stared warily back at her. "Up to bed, Annie. You were a wonderful help to me, but it's way past your bedtime."

"Will you walk me up, Mom?" she asked.

"Go ahead, Marty," Derry blurted. "I'll finish cleaning up in here and then get started in the living room. Even though it's already eleven, I assume you're still planning to paint the living room?"

"Yes, I am," she said sharply, hating how she must sound to him. She turned and gave him a feeble smile. "I'm sorry. You didn't have to help with any of this. I'm just tired. Don't start on the living room. Wait for me. Okay?"

Derry winked at Marty. "Good night, Miss Annie. You're quite the painter," he called, as Annie headed for the hall.

Annie ran back to Derry and gave him a quick hug. "Thanks, Derry. See you tomorrow." She looked rapidly from Derry to Marty and back again. "I mean, I guess I'll see you tomorrow."

"You'll see me tomorrow, sweetheart. Count on it."

After Annie washed a few smudges of paint off and slipped into her sleeveless pink nightgown, she ran to tend her kittens, who mewed for attention the minute they heard her voice. She got them fresh water from the bathroom faucet.

Marty looked into the box at the three kittens. They had grown considerably in the last week. The calico batted at the head of the tiny spotted one who jumped back into the one Marty called the orange marmalade cat. "Another week, Annie, and they'll be big enough to move outside."

Annie stopped patting the calico. "Do they have to go to the barn?"

"Yes, they do, Missy. That was the deal." Marty scooped Annie up and dropped her into bed. She pulled back the covers. "Just the sheet tonight?" Marty asked.

"Mom, we didn't say prayers."

"You're right. I..." She watched Annie climb from the bed and kneel beside it. Marty knelt beside her. "What do you want to say? How about 'Our Father...'?"

"Yes, and 'Now I Lay Me Down to Sleep.' Grandpap taught me that one."

Marty mouthed the words, feeling grateful for the child who seemed more open to letting God into her life than her mother was. As Annie went right from the Lord's Prayer into the prayer her Grandpap had taught her, Marty prayed silently, "Lord Jesus, please help me to accomplish all the tasks now set before me. I need to make a living and a home for my children. And Duke and Kyle seem to need me to give shape and stability to their lives. As for Derry, I know I can make a difference in his life. Help me with all these things, please."

"And, Dear Lord, please bring Jeff home," Annie ended.

"He will, honey. I'm sure," Marty whispered, and kissed Annie on the head.

"And don't let Mom be mad at Derry."

"I'm not, not really."

"And bless Cocoa and my kittens and the dogs, especially Cody, and everyone here. Amen."

"Amen and goodnight," Marty said, as she again scooped Annie into bed. "Sleep well."

With Annie safely tucked in, Marty joined Derry in the kitchen. She poured herself a tall glass of lemonade. "How about you?"

"Not after beer, but how about some coffee? Two beers are about my limit and I've had three."

"Coffee won't make you feel better."

"Yes, it will, and since I doubt you're going to let me spend the night, it will get me home. Just microwave what's left in the pot."

Marty poured the coffee into a mug and popped it into the microwave. Just as the bell went off, Marty heard angry voices outside. She listened to Kyle let loose with a long line of curses and then heard a thump as something hit the side of the house. She ran out the kitchen door and across the porch toward the noise, not remembering the fresh paint until it was too late.

The other voices were angry and garbled, but she heard Duke yell, "Now you two cut it out!"

Derry was right behind her. As they rounded the corner of the house, she saw that Kyle had one hand on Jeff's throat, pressing him flat against the house. Kyle's other hand was drawn back to level a punch right at Jeff's face.

"Kyle, no!" she screamed, as Derry dashed past her and tackled her brother. Derry, Kyle, and Jeff all fell into the yew bushes beside the house. Jeff jumped up and ran toward her. Derry rolled off Kyle and leaped to his feet. Kyle was slower to rise. Marty stood over him. "Don't you ever raise a hand to my son. You could have killed him, Kyle. He's only fifteen."

Kyle pulled himself to his feet. "Yeah... well, for fifteen, he has a nasty mouth on him. If he ever calls me again what he called me tonight, I guarantee I'll kill him."

"Kyle, you're drunk. You don't mean this. Jeff, in the house this minute."

"You can't tell me what to do anymore," Jeff said, his words sharp and cutting. "You're not my mother. My mother wouldn't be running around after some... some... lowlife like him." Jeff pointed a trembling finger in Derry's face.

"Jeff!" Marty screamed.

"Boy, you've just pushed past my boiling point." Derry pushed past Marty, his voice sounding harder and colder than any Marty had yet heard. Before Jeff could move, Derry grabbed

him by the back of the T-shirt and spun him around. Withou'
letting go, he also grabbed the waist of the boy's jeans and half
pushed, half-carried a struggling Jeff toward the house.

Marty ran alongside. "Derry, don't hurt him!"

"Marty," Derry said between clenched teeth, "I'm not gonna
hurt your baby boy. Not as long as he keeps moving."

Jeff planted his feet and wrenched his shoulders, trying to
break free. Marty heard the T-shirt rip. Derry picked Jeff up so
that only his toes hit the ground as Derry ran him toward the
porch steps. When they reached the porch, Jeff grabbed a post.
Derry jerked him free. Jeff yelled in pain.

"Derry! Please!" Marty begged.

"Marty, open this door," Derry said.

Marty pushed the door open and held it as Derry dragged Jeff
through and up the stairs.

"Cut it out," Jeff yelled, "You're hurting me, you stinkin'…"

Halfway up the steps, Derry pinned Jeff to the wall. "Stinkin'
what, little boy?"

Marty's breath came hard and fast. "Please, Jeff," she whispered. "Just shut up and go to your room."

"He's hurting me, Mom," Jeff whined, now sounding like a
little boy.

"Go to your room and stay there until morning and no one's
gonna hurt you, kid," Derry said. He pushed Jeff in front of him
the rest of the way up the steps. "Marty, show me where his
room is."

Marty ran past them and turned the corner to open the door
to Jeff's room. Derry pushed him through the opening and then
rushed into the room to stand over Jeff where he had fallen onto
the floor. "Get something straight, kid. Nobody will ever talk
like that to your mother as long as I'm around. Got it?"

Jeff glared right back at Derry and then his lips began to
tremble.

"I asked if you got it?" Derry roared.

"Yeah, I got it," Jeff said, choking on his words. He turned
onto his stomach and buried his face in his arms. "Get out of
here! Leave me alone!"

"Jeff..." Marty reached toward him, but Derry took her arm.

"You heard him, Marty. He needs to be alone." Derry pulled her from the room.

"Derry," Marty protested.

"Downstairs, Marty."

In the kitchen, Derry went right to the table and sat down, his face hard. Marty heard Kyle's truck start and then tear off down the lane.

Duke stood at the sink munching a cold chicken leg. "There goes another one having a temper tantrum. Sure gets noisy around here sometimes." Still chewing, he threw the bare bone into the sink. "Now, if things are calmed down, I'll be going to bed." He waved at Derry and patted Marty on the back on his way out of the kitchen.

Marty glared at Derry. "You could have hurt Jeff. He's not used to being mauled. Dan and I don't believe in corporal—"

"Not 'Dan and I don't,' Marty. It's 'Dan and I didn't.' He's dead, remember? And maybe if you two had been a little tougher, you wouldn't be having problems with that kid now."

A sharp retort formed in her brain. She took a deep breath before speaking. "Derry, it's not up to you to decide what Jeff needs."

"Well, excuse me!" Derry said, his eyes hard. "I thought I was becoming part of your life."

"Yes, but..." Marty choked on the words. Derry was probably feeling noble because he had just defended her. But she didn't need to be defended against her son who lay on the floor upstairs, miserable and needing her. Annie had probably heard all the screaming. And Kyle was too drunk to be driving. She and Derry should go and try to find him. Couldn't Derry see that she was only trying to do what was best for everyone?

Derry kicked the chair next to him out from the table. "Sit, lady," he said. "We need to talk."

Marty went toward the chair, but before she could sit in it, Derry grabbed her hand. "On second thought..." He pulled her onto his lap.

She resisted only a moment and then folded into the comfort

of his arms, her tears wetting his shirt.

Derry kissed her forehead, rocking her in his arms. "What's the matter with you?" he said.

Marty sniffed and ordered the tears away. "When I was a kid, I knew what I was supposed to do. There were rules... I followed them and they worked for me. With Dan... with Dan..." She took several deep breaths, squeezing her eyes shut to stop the tears. "With Dan, I tried to follow his rules or, at least, the rules he followed. But what do I do now? Just when I think I've got a hold on it all, everything goes haywire. How am I going to raise these kids? Take care of Daddy and Kyle?" She sniffed and wiped her eyes. "I know they should be able to take care of themselves, but they are helpless."

Derry put a hand under her chin and lifted her face to his. "What about taking care of Marty?" he whispered. "And what about me? I need you." Derry wiped a tear from her cheek and kissed her lips softly. "Come home with me," he pleaded.

She pulled away from him. "Derry, I can't..."

"Duke will keep an eye on the kids." He pulled her closer.

Gasping for breath, Marty sat straight and took both of his hands in hers. "Derry, please, I can't think."

"Then don't," he said, kissing her again.

"Derry, please!" Marty pulled away from him, standing. She took a glass from the cupboard and poured herself a glass of water. She took a deep breath and drank, her heart still feeling too large for her chest, her legs rubbery.

Derry came up behind her and put his arms around her. "Marty, quit worrying about rules; there are no more rules. If you want to come with me, you can."

She spun around to face him. "No. There have to be rules. Life makes no sense without rules," she said.

"That's right, sweetheart. Life makes no sense. We're adults. We make our own rules by doing what's right for us. That's the only way life ever makes sense."

This time when she pulled back from him, she stepped to the other side of the table. She needed to think. She heard the toilet flush upstairs. Duke? What would he think if he heard what was going on in his kitchen. He had become such a shadow of a person, he'd probably look the other way. Or pretend he didn't hear.

The footsteps overhead weren't as heavy as Duke's. They went toward Jeff's room. She straightened her shoulders and looked at Derry, hoping that all she was feeling, not just for him but for everyone, showed in her eyes. "Derry, I'm sorry. I can't."

Derry set his jaw. His violet eyes turned hard. "Not now? Or not ever?"

"Not now. I don't know about ever. I… I still believe in rules."

Derry strode from the kitchen, letting the kitchen door slam shut behind him. Marty stood where he'd left her, until she heard his car roar down the lane. Then she put out the rest of the lights. The empty place in her heart ached. Her hand heavy on the banister, she pulled herself up the stairs.

N I N E T E E N

As she climbed the steps Marty tried to ignore the sliver of light under Jeff's door, but it glared at her like a reproach. She knocked softly on the door. "Jeff?"

"Look, I know I was awful, but I can't talk to you," came his hoarse reply. "Just please let me go to sleep."

Marty pushed the door open. "We need to talk, Jeff."

He looked away and shifted deeper into the pillows he'd piled behind his head. Marty sat on the foot of the bed.

Jeff turned on his side away from her. "All right. I'm sorry I ran off, but I'm not sorry I called your brother a drunk. And your boyfriend is a total jerk."

"Jeff, Kyle wouldn't have gone that ballistic if you'd just called him a drunk."

"I guess the word I put in front of it wasn't too nice."

"Jeff, that kind of language is never acceptable. Remember what your dad used to say, 'Foul language is a sign of a limited vocabulary and a failed intellect.'"

"You leave my dad out of this," Jeff said, burying his face in his pillow.

Marty patted his foot where it rested under the sheet. "Jeff, talk to me."

"I've been talking to you. I keep telling you I hate it here and you don't pay any attention."

"I'm sorry, Jeff, but I don't see any other options for us right now. We've been all through this—before we left D.C. and four or five times last week. What is it you want from me?"

"If you hated this place as much as I do, you'd do whatever you had to to get us out."

"I'm not saying we're staying here forever. I'll still try to get a teaching job, but right now we have to stay, and I need your help."

"If Dad hadn't died, none of this would be happening."

"No kidding, Jeff," Marty said, her words drenched in

sarcasm. "Do you think this is easy for me?"

"Ever since that Brady guy started coming around, you act like you don't even care that Dad died."

"No, Jeff, no!" Marty reached for Jeff, needing to hold on to him, to reassure him, realizing that she hadn't hugged him in weeks, that he hadn't let her.

Jeff threw himself away from her. "Don't touch me!" he cried. Muffled sobs came from the pillow where he buried his face.

Marty's chest ached and her throat squeezed tight. Tears ran silently down her cheeks, even though she felt as if she were screaming inside.

The door hinges creaked. Marty turned to see Annie, her sleepy eyes peering through the crack.

"Is Jeff crying again, Mom?"

"I guess we both are, Annie." Marty said, wiping her eyes with the hem of her T-shirt. "But we're all right."

Annie shuffled across the floor and climbed on the bed beside her brother. "Everything will be all right, Jeff. Don't cry," she said, patting his back.

Jeff didn't pull away from Annie. He turned toward her and forced a smile. "Annie, I get sad sometimes, but I'm all right. You have to stop worrying about me."

Annie crawled down to the foot of the bed and onto her mother's lap. "Jeff's okay, Mom. Take me back to bed."

"In a minute, Annie," Marty said, realizing how desperately ready for sleep she was. "Jeff, I love you and Annie with all my heart. I loved your father very much. You kids and he were my whole world. But—"

"But he's not here anymore," Jeff snapped.

"Jeff, you're wrong. He'll always be here in our hearts, as long as we remember him."

"Then help us remember, Mom," he said. "Annie and I talk about him all the time when we're alone. You never do. Sometimes it seems like you've just erased him. That's even worse than him dying."

Marty reached a hand toward Jeff and he took it. For her, talking about Dan sharpened the edges of the void he'd left, but maybe the children needed to know that. "I will never, ever forget your father. He was the finest man I've ever known. I guess I was afraid that if I talked about him, it would make us all sadder than we already are," Marty said, her throat tightening. She coughed and banished the tears pushing at the corners of her eyes, then scooted up with her back against the pillows and the wooden headboard. Annie snuggled in on one side and Jeff, still holding Marty's hand, leaned toward her on the other side. "This still isn't easy me for me, so who wants to go first?"

"I remember that time at the beach," Annie said, "when the pelican pooped on his shoulder and we all laughed and laughed. Except Daddy, who said real loud, 'Aw man.'"

She said it just the way Dan had, but in her own tiny voice. Marty and Jeff both laughed. Marty squeezed Jeff's hand. "Jeff says that a lot, too, doesn't he?"

"And remember," Jeff added, "how he jumped in the ocean to clean off and then chased Annie and me up the beach? We were laughing so hard we could hardly run, but so was he."

"I love how Daddy laughed," Annie said.

"Me, too," Marty said. And Jeff jumped in with another story and then Annie, until Marty felt comfortable telling stories of her own, some the kids had never heard about when she and Dan were young and in school.

Marty was about to launch into another remembrance when she heard the front door open. "Come on, dogs," Kyle said. She heard the dogs rush across the linoleum and then down the cellar steps. "Cody, you fool. Get down there!" Kyle said, slamming the cellar door. As his footsteps sounded on the stairs, Jeff tensed beside her. Marty squeezed his hand.

Just as Marty had known he would, Kyle knocked on Jeff's door. Jeff whispered an unidentifiable curse. "Come in," Marty called.

Kyle looked sheepish and sober when he stuck his head through the door opening. "What's this? A family party and I wasn't invited?"

"You weren't home, buster," Marty answered. "In fact, the way you left here, I supposed we'd see you sometime tomorrow."

Kyle nodded. "Probably would have, but I ran the truck into a ditch down by Morgan's. The walk home sobered me up some. I've been sitting outside thinking." He came into the room and sank onto the end of the bed. "Look, kid," he said, slapping Jeff's knee, "I was a jerk."

"Yeah, you were," snarled Jeff, but not too ferociously.

"Well, all right, so what can I say? I was drunk, but believe me, no one's nominating you for sainthood either!"

Jeff looked away. "Guess I was a jerk, too."

"What happened?" Annie whispered.

"Nothing that's not mendable," Marty said.

"So how about it, kid?" Kyle stuck out his hand.

"My name's not 'kid.'"

"All right then... Jeffrey."

Jeff took his hand. "Just 'Jeff' will do."

Kyle clapped Jeff on the shoulder as he shook his hand. "The thing is, Jeff, your mom needs your help. It really ticked me off when you ducked out on her tonight. Then I got to thinking, she needs mine, too, and I haven't been here much either. So, Sis, what's on the schedule for tomorrow? I have a roping tomorrow evening, but I'm yours until then."

"How about painting the living room and touching up the mess on the porch steps?" Marty said. "We charged out over wet paint when you two were going at it."

Kyle stood and walked to the head of the bed. He leaned over and kissed Marty on the forehead. "You got it." He scooped Annie up and kissed both her cheeks, "Goodnight, princess," he said, softly. "Jeff, we're going to get along just fine. Aren't we, buddy?"

"I guess so," Jeff muttered.

"That's right. Now, Marty, not too early in the morning, all right?"

"I doubt if I'll be up at dawn myself," Marty said. "But what about your truck?"

"I'll worry about that tomorrow. Luke or Mac will pull it out with the tractor." He shook his head and started for the door. "The problem with sobering up before you go to bed is that it gives you time to feel hung over." He shut the door softly behind him.

Marty slipped her arms around her children and hugged them to her. "I love you guys with all my heart."

"Hey, Annie, why don't you say your prayer for Mom," Jeff said.

"You mean the shepherd song?" she asked.

"Yeah, nobody says it quite like you do," Jeff said, smiling at Marty.

"If you went to church, Jeff, you'd know it, because that's where I heard it," Annie said. She took a deep breath and dramatically folded her hands and bowed her head. "The Lord is a shepherd and he'll give me what I want. He makes the green pastures and the beautiful streams for his sheep and me. He keeps me healthy so I won't die and he will always protect me from evil, so I shouldn't be afraid."

"The Twenty-Third Psalm," Marty said. "You got the gist of it, Annie. Maybe Jeff will go to church with us on Sunday."

"Don't push it, Mom," Jeff said. He looked at Annie. "Maybe I will. I don't know."

Marty kissed his cheek and wished him goodnight. Then she led Annie to their room. After they were both tucked into bed, Marty asked, "Annie, does Jeff cry a lot?"

"Only sometimes, Mom. Sometimes you cry, too—in your sleep."

"Annie, I'm sorry. I didn't know you were taking all of this on yourself." Marty heard Annie throw back the sheets and then felt her crawl into bed beside her. She threw her small arms around Marty's neck and hugged her.

"Don't be sad, Mom. I'll be good. I promise."

Marty sat up and pulled Annie onto her lap. She flipped on the lamp beside her bed. "Annie, you are good. You are the best little girl in the world. I'm sad sometimes and so is Jeff, because Daddy died. It's not your fault when we're sad, and it's not your responsibility to make us happy."

"I get sad sometimes, too, Mom. After Daddy died, every time I cried, you cried too, and that made me feel worse. So now

I try not to show it if I feel sad. And when I get scared, I just say the shepherd song... I mean psalm... and I feel better."

"That's good, Annie, but you know you can tell me when you feel bad. I promise to pay more attention."

Annie hugged her tight. Marty picked Annie up and put her back into her own bed, pulling up the sheet and kissing her on both cheeks.

"Mom, will you lie here with me for a while? Till I fall asleep?"

"Sure," Marty said. She turned off the light and snuggled in with Annie until she breathed the deep sighs of sound sleep. Marty slipped back to her own bed, fear and loneliness flooding her. "The Lord is my shepherd. I shall not want," she whispered. But she did want. She wanted Dan back. She wanted to be free from all her worries. And her children had been wanting more than she knew. She forced her mind back to the psalm, but she didn't remember all of it. "Yea, though I walk through the valley of the shadow of death, I will fear no evil, for thou art with me." She wished it were that simple. She did believe it to be abstractly true, but she didn't feel it. "Lord," she prayed from somewhere in past memory, "give me the faith of a small child." She shut her eyes and tried to join Annie in sleep.

TWENTY

The next morning Marty felt better. She woke determined to exert all of her will for the good of her family. Where that left Derry Brady she wasn't sure, but then maybe she didn't need to be. Maybe he wasn't coming back. The thought brought pain and a feeling of aching incompleteness. She pushed it from her mind.

Stick to the job at hand, she ordered herself. Right now that job was getting this house in shape, making it a home where the kids wouldn't be ashamed to bring their friends.

She looked at the clock beside her bed—eight o'clock and late for her; but, after the events of last night, too early to wake everyone else. After slipping into her paint-stained clothes from the night before, she fed the kittens so their mewing wouldn't wake Annie and tiptoed from the room.

She put on the coffee, let the dogs out, and headed to the barn where she fed the horses. While they ate and Cody chased barn swallows, she swept the aisle and straightened the tack room. Sam was busy with family today and none of her crew would be riding, so she turned Sass, Grandma, and Cocoa out into the pasture with Red. As usual, Sass tried to bully Red, who ran from her, and Grandma, who gave her a good swift kick in the hip. Cocoa headed for the shade of the nearest tree. When they all settled down, Marty called Cody. He charged from the barn and raced ahead of her toward the house.

By ten o'clock she had everyone fed and ready to paint. Marty, Annie and Duke headed for the living room. Jeff and Kyle promised to tend to the porch after they got Kyle's truck out of the ditch. No more than ninety minutes had passed after they returned when Marty heard Kyle head for the basement and then go back outside again. She could hear Jeff and Kyle moving around the house and an occasional thump or prying sound, but couldn't stop what she was doing, although curiosity was plaguing her. As she finished a long wall, she heard Kyle's truck drive off.

"There he goes again," Duke said with a sigh. He slowly stroked the paint on the short wall that faced the front of the house with Annie helping by carefully following him to touch up the drips.

Marty put her roller down and went to the window. Outside on the lawn, window shutters surrounded Jeff who had already painted one the same deep green he'd used on the porch. Marty threw open a window. "And what's going on out here?"

"Kyle's gone for more paint. We decided that the fresh paint on the porch made the rest of the house look really tacky. Besides some of these shutters need to be rehung anyway." Jeff smiled at Marty.

Marty swallowed hard to rid herself of the lump forming in her throat. "Jeff, that's wonderful! Thank you."

Marty went back to her work but hadn't been long at it when the phone rang. She dropped her roller and ran to answer it, hoping it was Derry. The lump returned to her throat when she heard Kyle's voice.

"Hey, Sis, I'm calling from Pattersons. I didn't think to ask what color you want to paint the house. I just thought we'd go with the same old white, but Darla says a tan would be nice, especially with the green trim. Casey is here and she agrees. Now Jennifer thinks pink would be wonderful, but I kind of nixed that."

"I hadn't even thought about it," Marty said. "Tan might work. What do you think?"

"I like it. Darla's picked out one that's not too dark, so it won't startle us with the change. Should we go with it?" Marty heard Darla say something in the background and then Kyle continued, "Darla says we can return any unopened cans if we don't like it, so what do you say?"

"Great! Let's do it."

Kyle hung up and Marty returned to the living room where Duke and Annie had made little progress. "That was Kyle," she said. "Looks like we're getting the whole house painted."

Duke mopped his forehead with the back of his hand. "Now Marty, I'm too old to be crawling around on ladders."

135

"That's all right, Dad. You won't need to. Kyle, Jeff, and I will do it." *Yeah,* she thought, *until Kyle gets bored and Jeff rebels again.* Still, she smiled as much to reassure herself as her father. Besides, maybe Derry would be back to help her.

Kyle returned, followed soon after by Casey, who had picked up Rachel and come to help. Marty loved the color Darla had picked—it would look wonderful with the deep green trim. The girls were each assigned a scraper and a window while Kyle and Jeff went to work with the electric sanders Kyle had rented.

By early afternoon, the first coat was on the living room and nearly half of the house front was sanded and scraped. Duke climbed the stairs to his room for a nap and Annie went to care for her kittens and phone Jennifer. Duke was still sleeping when Marty called a late lunch break. Because the porch was not quite dry, she and Annie climbed out through a dining room window to take ham sandwiches, apples, and lemonade out to the lawn for a picnic.

The kids all waded right into the creek to rinse their hands and splash water on their faces and at each other. Even though Annie had washed in the house, she joined them. Marty looked at her partially scraped house and had to fight the impulse to order everyone to eat quickly and get back to work. Kyle had already settled onto the grass for what looked like a long slump.

"Hey, Sis," he said, around bites of a sandwich, "where's that lazy boyfriend of yours? I thought he'd signed on for work duty all weekend."

Marty didn't look at Kyle when she answered. "I guess something must have come up."

"Uh, oh, trouble in Loveland," Kyle said.

"For Pete's sake, Kyle," Marty said. "I've been having a good time with Derry, but I'm certainly not in love." Not yet, anyway, but she knew she was getting dangerously close.

"I'm glad," Kyle said. "I mean, I like Derry, he's a friend, but he's not very good to women. Or, maybe it's that he's too good with too many women. At any rate, the guy's a walking heartache and I don't want it to be your heart aching."

As touched as she was by Kyle's concern, Marty didn't want

to hear the criticism of Derry. Besides, she really thought he'd call to explain his absence. So why hadn't he? She frowned and looked toward the kids who were now engaged in a full-scale water battle. "Everybody ashore," Marty yelled. "Eat first, then take a play break and then back to work."

By four o'clock Marty had done most of the trim in the dining room. Duke had not reappeared. She heard the faint squeak of his bedsprings and the sound of his television in the room above her. Annie had stayed outside to play gopher for the group there. That was fine with Marty. At her dad's age she didn't really expect him to work as hard as she and Kyle, as long as he didn't opt out altogether. As for Annie, she'd already been doing more than Marty expected.

Marty surveyed the dining room. It looked gorgeous, and would be even more so when she put up some of her paintings. Grandma Stafford's lace cloth and her own big blue-and-white English fruit bowl would look wonderful on the table. Marty put her paint and brushes away and went outside, across the now dry green porch. She met Kyle coming around from the rear of the house. Sunburned and sweating, he handed her the electric sander. "I've had it and so have the kids. I need to get a shower and I think they're planning a trip to the town pool," he said.

Marty looked at the untouched side of the house. Her completion urge ran rampant, but maybe everyone had had enough for one day. She'd been working inside all afternoon, where it was relatively cool. "Quitting time," she yelled.

Hoots and hollers were followed by splashes and laughter. Kyle smiled. "They're good kids, Marty. It was a good day." He started to walk away and then stopped. "Tomorrow we'll get more of this done and I'll hang your porch swing. How's that?"

"That's great, Kyle. Thanks," she said. She watched the kids playing in the creek, remembering how good the cold water felt on a hot day. While she watched, Cody ran around the back of the house and took a flying leap into the middle of the stream. Jeff jumped out of Cody's way and up onto the bank. He looked happy. Marty smiled and waved at him, as he jogged toward her. "Jeff, thanks for all your help today."

Jeff nodded. "No problem, Mom. Hey, Casey says she'll drive us into town to go swimming. What do you say?"

"That's fine with me. In fact, let me give you money and you treat the girls to dinner somewhere."

"Cool. We'll probably go for pizza."

When Marty passed through the kitchen to get her purse, the phone rang. She lunged for it, believing it had to be Derry, but Darla was on the other end asking if Annie could join them for a swim and a picnic at the pool.

While Jeff and Annie were getting their swimming suits, Kyle loaded Red into the trailer and took off for the roping. The kids followed him down the lane, leaving Marty alone with Duke who still hid in his room, no doubt worried that Marty was going to try to get more work out of him.

Since feeding time was close, Marty trudged up the hill which seemed much steeper than it had that morning. She quickly picked out the stalls, filled the water buckets and put grain in the feed pails. Then she let the animals in for their dinner. When she returned to the house, Duke was waiting on the porch.

"Derry called," he said.

"Dad, why didn't you call me?"

"He was calling from the mountains up in Somerset. Said to tell you he'd be there all weekend, but would call you when he got back."

Marty frowned. Was that a good or a bad omen? She didn't know. She plugged in the sander and started on the side of the house, hoping the work and the noise would distract her from worrying.

TWENTY-ONE

The next morning Marty rose stiff, sore, and worried. Kyle hadn't come home. Duke said he'd probably won enough to pay his entry fees at the jackpot roping in Ohio that evening. As much as she hated to admit it, she fretted over Derry. She thought she'd been going slow and easy, protecting herself. Ha! It felt like high school all over again.

Upstairs she heard the squeal of old pipes as Jeff turned the shower off. Even though Marty had been unsuccessful at coaxing Jeff to go to church for the last two weeks, he'd agreed when Casey and Rachel asked him. After Jeff had declared his reluctance to start school only knowing a bunch of girls, they'd tempted him to church with the promise of meeting some of the guys there. Annie bounced down the steps, pretty and fresh in her flowered sundress. Since that first Sunday, both Marty and Annie had dressed down a bit to be less conspicuous. As warm as it was this morning, they'd appreciate the cooler clothing. Jeff joined them in khaki trousers and a green knit polo shirt. Marty smiled her approval and, with her two children, headed for the old church. Next week she'd work on Duke.

While Annie and Jeff attended Sunday school, Marty walked through the graveyard. She went right to the Stafford plot where Mama and her grandparents and all the preceding generations of Staffords were at rest. The earliest stone, barely legible now, belonged to Hepzibah Stafford, wife of Joshua (1786—1835). Most of the early ancestors had not lived long, but then neither had Mama or Dan. Marty knelt to pull the weeds around her mother's headstone. "You'd never put up with this kind of untidiness, would you, Mama," Marty said, promising herself to bring a trowel next time, and maybe some flowers to plant. "I miss you, Mama," she said, before moving on to weed Grandma Stafford's grave. When Gayle found her, she had nearly finished weeding around Grandpa Stafford's headstone.

"Amy's home with a headache," Gayle said. "How about giving me some help with the altar?"

The church was empty and because of the thick stone walls it felt surprisingly cool. "The windows let in enough sunlight. Maybe if we leave the lights off and turn on the fans, we can keep this place cool for the service," Gayle said.

On each end of the altar, they arranged pink, blue, and white delphinium with delicate sprigs of fern in tall etched crystal vases. Gayle moved with such surety, her face content, but more than that—radiant. Marty felt disturbing stirrings of envy. She wanted that peace Gayle seemed to have found; yet, maybe it was the luck of Gayle's happy life.

"What's the matter?" Gayle asked.

Marty smiled at her friend. "Nothing really. Just a bit pensive."

Gayle moved from the altar and began to arrange some pink and purple flowers in a rounded vase. "I started these lisianthus last year and I love them. They last wonderfully after they're cut." She carried the small vase of flowers back to the table at the entrance to the church. Marty followed her. "Does your mood have anything to do with Derry who nearly ran me off the road Friday night, tearing away from your place?" Gayle asked.

"Probably a little. I don't know. Where did you see him? I assumed he went home."

"He was headed into town when I saw him. He took the turn a bit wide and fast and came into my lane."

"He called yesterday and told Dad he'd gone to a friend's place near Somerset; but if he'd gone right there, wouldn't he have been turning toward the highway and away from town?"

Gayle frowned and looked away from Marty to study the flowers she was arranging. "Yes, he would have... if he wasn't stopping somewhere else first."

"Like where, Gayle?"

"Anything I said would only be gossip and guessing, Marty. That's not fair to Derry or you. You just be careful, you hear? Don't give your heart away until you're sure."

After church Marty drove home in silence, not really listening to the kids except to note that Jeff sounded happier than he had in a long time. Throughout the service and even now, all she could think about was Derry. If she hadn't already given her heart away, she sure had been preparing it for the trip. She rounded the curve before the farm and almost didn't see Cody tearing off the bank and into the road. She spun the wheel and heard a sickening thud, but it wasn't Cody she'd hit. The pup leaped back toward the bank and then ran around the front of the car.

Marty threw the car into park, ignoring the kids' questions. She jumped out and followed Cody to where a red fox lay on the side of the road. Marty grabbed Cody by the collar.

"Did we kill it?" Jeff asked, joining her.

"I don't know. Jeff, put Cody in the car." Marty handed the pup over to Jeff and crouched for a closer look at the fox. The orange fur on its flanks rose and fell in jerky spasms. "Jeff, it's breathing. You and Annie run back to the turnoff and try to flag down Dr. Brady. I'm sure he was still at the church when we left and he'll have to come that way." The kids took off at a run and Marty bent back over the fox. Inside the car, Cody barked and clawed at the door. Marty opened the trunk and found some rope left from their move. She took Cody out and tied him to a tree. "Now sit and stay, you rascal," she scolded.

He cocked his head and looked at her with the white rings showing around his eyes, and she couldn't help but be glad that she hadn't hit him. She hugged him and kissed the white triangle on his forehead.

Returning to the fox, she looked more closely and saw small swollen nipples protruding from the light fur. She was feeding babies. "Please don't die, mama fox," Marty whispered. She wanted to stroke the soft orange fur to offer some kind of comfort, but she knew for a wild creature that would provide only terror.

She heard a truck approaching and looked up to see Cam in the cab with Kika, Jeff, and Annie squeezed in with him.

"So, let's see what we've got here," Cam said, patting Marty's shoulder and giving her a reassuring smile as he pushed past her to the fox.

"That fool pup of ours ran her off the bank. I was so busy trying to miss him that I never saw her," Marty said.

"I better get her back to the clinic and see what I can do," Cam said. He tossed Jeff his truck keys. "Jeff, the middle key unlocks the back. Please reach in there and get me the plastic pet carrier. You'll see it just inside. And grab us each a pair of leather gloves. She's not conscious now, but she could come to."

While Jeff ran to get the carrier, Marty asked, "Is she going to make it?"

Cam shrugged his shoulders. "Don't know yet. Sure hope so." Cam ran his fingers over the fox's swollen teats.

"I noticed," Marty said. "She's got babies in the woods, doesn't she?"

"Most likely," he said. "But we're getting into midsummer. They'll be fine and chances are her mate is still helping hunt for them." Jeff returned with the carrier and Cam slipped on the heavy gloves before lifting the limp fox and sliding her into it. "Jeff, I may have to operate and could use your help, if you're up to it."

"Cool," Jeff said, taking the carrier from Cam and starting back to the truck with it.

Marty smiled at her old friend. Had Cam known how much Jeff needed to feel important and capable?

Cam winked. "Marty, why doesn't Kika ride with you and Annie. You'll need to take that pup back up to your farm first. You know how to find my place?"

"Sure. Turn right this side of town onto McMahan Road."

"You've got it. My place is about a mile and a half down the road on the left." Cam put a hand on Kika's dark cropped hair. "You go with Mrs. Harris and Annie and help them get that puppy home, all right?"

Kika's big eyes looked frightened, but she nodded. Annie clapped and took Kika's hand, leading her toward the car.

"Don't hurry," Cam whispered. "This doesn't look real good."

Marty untied Cody and shoved him into the backseat with the girls who squealed and laughed as he rolled all over their laps, licking first one and then the other. By the time Marty pulled up in front of the farmhouse, Cody had calmed down. She led him to the cellar; if she turned him loose, he'd head straight for the woods and the baby foxes.

"Annie, why don't you change your clothes. I'll make some lunch for you and Kika before we take her home." Annie dragged Kika by the hand toward the stairs. Her infectious enthusiasm seemed to be having an effect on Kika who actually laughed and chased Annie up the stairs.

Duke sat at the kitchen table drinking coffee. Marty explained about the fox and what had happened.

"The other night when I was sitting on the porch steps, I thought I saw a fox and some kits cross the lane heading toward the creek," Duke said. "They were all the way down by the bend and it was dark enough that I wasn't real sure."

Marty made sandwiches and poured iced tea. She put a bowl of apples and a plate of cookies in the center of the table before calling the girls. Kika and Annie came down dressed alike, in Annie's last season's soccer shorts and National Zoo T-shirts.

"Well, aren't you two something," Duke said with a smile.

Marty looked at her father. She'd forgotten how he loved little kids, any little kids, not just his family.

"Can we take our lunch and have a picnic by the creek?" Annie asked.

"Sure," Marty said. She reached into the cupboard and took down two round wicker bread baskets. She lined each with a blue-and-white checkered napkin. "Here," she said, handing each girl a basket. "The food's on the table. Take what you want."

"What about me?" Duke said. "Can't I come on your picnic?"

Annie giggled. "Sure you can, Grandpap."

Marty found a square plastic food container and draped it with a napkin so that it looked like the girls' baskets. "Here you go, Dad," she said. He looked at her with such innocent delight that she had to hug him. "You are something else, Duke Stafford."

The picnickers hadn't been long out of the house when the

143

phone rang. Marty answered to find Cam on the line.

"Good. I caught you before you left," he said. "She didn't even make it into the clinic. We were carrying the case in and she convulsed and died. Probably internal bleeding."

"I feel like a murderer," Marty said, "but I never saw her come off the bank."

"I know. Jeff's feeling the same way, so I'll tell you what I told him, 'Just be glad you saw Cody.' Think how you'd feel if it had been him."

"I know, but—"

"No buts. We all did everything we could. I'm going to show Jeff around the place and then I'll bring him home. How's that?"

"Fine. I have lunch made. I'll save some for you."

When Cam and Jeff arrived, Jeff was the first into the kitchen. "Mom, you wouldn't believe his place. He's got all kinds of animals there—hawks, a golden eagle with a broken wing, a coyote that got its leg mangled in a trap. I didn't even know there were coyotes around here."

Cam came into the kitchen behind Jeff and laughed. "There aren't too many. This is the first one I've treated, and he's nearly ready to release."

"Gee," Marty said. "And I thought you were a horse vet."

Cam grinned, his dimples deepening at the edge of his beard. "Actually, the horses, cows, and all my other patients pay for my charity work—treating injured wildlife."

"Do the animals just find you? Are you like St. Francis?" Marty teased.

"No, most of them are brought in by the game warden or people who call because they've heard I do this kind of work. The goal is always to treat and release."

"And I'm going to help," Jeff said. "After lunch we're going to find the fox's den. I'm going to watch the den for Cam and make sure her mate is taking care of the babies."

Marty wanted to ask if she could go along, but she held back. This was the first time she'd seen Jeff enthusiastic about anything since they'd left D.C., and he didn't need his mother marching in his parade. She remembered Dan saying, "Marty, our job as parents is to make ourselves unnecessary—and to make them independent." She looked at her son who was nearly a man and felt that empty place in her heart grow bigger. "You'll change out of your good pants and shirt first, Mister," she said. When the time was right she'd be willing to let him go, but not without instructions. Not yet, anyway.

TWENTY-TWO

Cam and Jeff were gone about an hour looking for the fox den. Marty saw them coming up the lane from where she stood on the creek bank, watching the girls splash and play in the creek.

Jeff broke into a run. "You should have seen them, Mom. Five babies. Well, five that we saw and they look pretty big. But I'll have to keep an eye on them and make sure they're being taken care of. And it didn't look like Cody had found the den, so they're probably safe."

Cam came up behind them. "This kid's all right," he said, clapping Jeff on the back. "Not only does he move silently through the woods, but he's also got good eyes. He spotted the kits before I did."

"Jeff, come on in," yelled Annie.

Jeff slipped off his tennis shoes and pulled his T-shirt over his head. He took off running and leaped, cannonball-style, into the water, thoroughly splashing the girls and his grandfather who sat on a nearby rock watching them.

"Thanks, Cam," Marty said.

"For what?"

"For trying to save the fox, but more than that for... well, for Jeff. He's been having a hard time and he seems happy today."

"That may have more to do with Rachel than with me," Cam said. "How about some more of that iced tea?"

Marty and Cam walked back to the house, got themselves each a glass of iced tea and then went back to the porch where they could watch the kids.

"Marty, this place is really shaping up," Cam said, easing himself into a wicker armchair. "You have to be proud of yourself."

"I've had help, although sometimes I feel like nothing would get done if I didn't keep pushing everybody."

"You must be pushing hard if you got Derry to paint. That's not one of his favorite pastimes."

Marty forced a smile. She wanted to talk to Cam about Derry, but it felt too juvenile.

"Jeff doesn't seem very fond of my brother. He sounded absolutely pleased when he told me that you and Derry had a fight the other night."

"Not a fight exactly. A disagreement. He took off for a friend's place in Somerset, but he called and left a message that he'd talk to me on Monday."

Cam frowned and looked away. When he finally spoke he said, "Well, anyway the place is really looking good. I'm glad. I always liked it here."

"Cam, is there something you're not telling me?"

"Hey, he's my brother. You're my friend. I really hope you can work it out. Derry needs someone like you. But don't kid yourself—he rarely recognizes what's good for him."

"I've always had trouble believing that you two are really brothers."

Cam laughed. "We are. Derry's more like Dad, and I guess I'm more like my mother."

Marty remembered their father as a hard, uncompromising man with none of Derry's sense of fun. "I don't think Derry's like your dad."

"In many ways, he's not. But in stubbornness and in not always thinking before he acts, he's Tom Brady all over again. With Derry I guess it's more like impulsiveness, but with our old man it was explosive anger. I learned early on to stay out of Dad's way. Derry was too bullheaded and often took the brunt of the outbursts. All those bumps and bruises Derry sported when we were kids weren't from tussles on the playground, Marty."

She stared at Cam. How could she not have known? Because she'd been a kid and didn't suspect violence. Before she could respond Duke came walking toward them, the front of his shirt soaked. "Those kids are getting too rambunctious. I'm going to get me an iced tea and stay here on the porch where it's safe."

When Duke had gone into the house Cam began again, talking in a rush of words, like he had something Marty needed to know. "I think that's why Derry never goes to church, because Dad never missed a Sunday and a lot of the beatings he gave Derry were given in the name of God to 'drive the devil out of the little heathen,' as Dad used to say. Derry didn't deserve that, Marty, but he took it. Dad's been dead years now, but sometimes I think Derry's still living the way he does just to get back at him."

Duke opened the screen door. "Do I hear you talking about your dad? He was a good man, a regular churchgoer and a good provider. But he sure had a temper, Cam. Everybody down at the mine knew to stay away from Tom Brady if he was having a bad day. But, when he was having a good day, no one was more fun. Now in that way, I think Derry is a lot like your Dad. That boy sure knows how to have fun."

"Derry and Dad didn't get along too well, Duke. Better not tell him he reminds you of Dad," Cam said.

"You know, Cam, you're right," Duke said, as if the thought had just occurred to him. "Old Tom never had a good word for Derry. Now you... you were the golden boy."

"I know and that didn't help matters any," Cam said. He stood and called Kika. "We've got to get going. I promised to take Mom and Kika shopping this afternoon and I'll never hear the end of it if I don't."

The girls ran upstairs to change. Jeff stayed in the creek's one deep pool floating on his back. Marty smiled at him, but inside she ached for Derry. He had made jokes about how tough his dad was on him, but he'd never told her his father had *beaten* him, not once in all the years they'd known each other.

"Well, don't you worry about Derry," Duke said to Cam. "He's like I was. In my day, I raised a bit of a ruckus now and then, but I met Marty's mama and she settled me right down." Duke slammed an arm around Marty's shoulder and hugged her tight, nearly knocking her off her feet. "The love of a good woman is about the only thing I know of to settle the wild blood in a man."

"Dad!" Marty said.

Cam laughed. "It sure would be wonderful if it happened,

but that's a heck of a job to lay on Marty."

"But it's one she'd sure enjoy, hey, Cam?" Duke said and then chortled.

"That's it! Enough! Both of you," Marty demanded, this time laughing in spite of her efforts to sound fierce. In her heart she knew she could help heal Derry's wounds, if only he would let her.

When Kika and Annie came out on the porch, Cam held out his hand and Kika ran to grasp it, waving at Annie as she went. Cam turned her toward Marty and Duke and gently nudged her. "Oh, thank you very much for lunch and everything," she said, her voice barely above a whisper, her face serious.

"You are certainly welcome, Kika. Come back anytime," Marty said.

The little girl's lips curved into a shy smile and this time she pulled Cam toward the truck.

"Marty, I told Jeff clinic hours are every Monday, Wednesday, and Friday morning. If he'd like to come by and give me a hand, I'd be real pleased to have him anytime," Cam said.

She waved goodbye and watched them leave. She hoped Dad was right and she was what Derry needed. She'd been bombarding heaven with prayers for their relationship. If God was listening, then she and Cam would really be brother and sister. She'd like a family that was growing, not shrinking. And she'd be Kika's aunt. That little girl definitely needed a woman to help pick her clothes and fix her hair; then maybe she'd feel more sure of herself. Marty scolded herself. That was certainly a shallow thought, worthy of her cousin Renee. Well, maybe she could shower little Kika with enough love to bring her out of her shyness and then she'd work on her clothes and hair.

Marty heard a creak as Duke threw himself onto the wicker sofa. She winced.

"I sure hope you don't have another day of painting planned," Duke said, pulling Annie onto his lap, "because yesterday plumb wore us out."

"Dad, we have to get this finished. If we hit a rainy spell, we'll be in trouble. Annie doesn't look at all worn out."

Annie flopped back against her grandfather. "Grandpap's right. I'm ashausted."

"You mean exhausted and you weren't too tired to play with Kika," Marty said.

"You're getting to be as bossy as your Aunt Bertie," Duke said. "I'm sorry, but I don't work on the Sabbath."

Marty put her hands on her hips, knowing and not caring that the gesture would only cement the comparison to Aunt Bertie. This place needed someone to take charge. "Your argument would be more convincing if you'd also gone to church this morning," she said.

"Next Sunday, sweetheart. I promise," Duke said, looking pitiful.

Marty patted his shoulder. "I have to get some of this work done today. How about Jeff and I paint, and you and Annie take care of dinner?"

"You got yourself a deal, but the cook picks the menu," Duke said.

"And the cook's helper gets to pick dessert. Right, Grandpap?"

Marty was halfway into the house when she realized that yesterday Annie would have stoically taken up her paintbrush. She smiled. This was better, more natural, even if it was somewhat irritating.

When a tired, hot, and paint-flecked Marty came to the dinner table, she shook her head in amusement. Duke had cooked hamburgers and baked beans straight from the can, the only dinner Marty ever remembered him cooking. Fresh sliced tomatoes were a new addition. "All those years you've been alone and you never learned to cook anything else?" she asked.

"This is what I do best," he said.

"There's something to be said for knowing what you do best," Marty said. She wasn't at all sure what that would be for her, but she had begun to feel the world held possibilities. Even the trauma of Friday night had served to bring her closer to her children. That was important, because mothering was what she'd always thought she'd done best, the role that had most suited her. As she looked around the table at Jeff and Annie, she knew it still did.

T W E N T Y - T H R E E

After dinner Annie announced that she and her Grandpap were taking them to the ice cream parlor in town for dessert. Duke insisted on driving, so they all piled into his old Buick. Duke took out his handkerchief and dusted the thickly coated dashboard. Marty stifled a cough and closed her nose to the smells of rotten food and dirty dog that rose all around her. Miraculously, with only one or two backfires and one very odd engine cough, they made it into town.

The ice cream parlor was busy, but mostly with young families, nobody Marty knew by name. A waitress came and took their order.

As the girl turned to leave a woman at the next table called to her, "Where's Ceci today?"

"She needed a weekend off. She's at her place in Somerset."

Ceci had gone to Somerset, where Derry was. Who had followed whom? Or had they gone together? Maybe it was just a coincidence. Marty didn't even taste her ice cream when it came. She gulped it down, wishing the others would hurry. The sooner she got home and found something to distract her, the sooner she could stop torturing herself with speculation.

When they finally arrived home, Duke and Annie went to clean the kitchen. Marty took up her scraper and started for the side yard, but Jeff stopped her.

"I was going to go and check on the kits," he said. "Want to come?"

She put down the scraper. Being with Jeff was more important than stewing over Derry Brady, especially if he was two-timing her. "Sure," she said, and called to Duke and Annie to tell them where they were going.

They walked to the end of the lane, crossed the creek and climbed into the woods. "Try not to make any noise, Mom," Jeff said. "When I hold my hand up, stop."

Marty pushed through the underbrush and stumbled over

fallen branches, trying to keep up with Jeff who moved quickly ahead of her, crouched and silent. Positive she sounded like an approaching army, she stopped even before Jeff held up his hand. He froze beside a big locust tree, staring down a worn deer path to his left. Marty tried to see what he saw, but no movement or flash of color indicated anything but empty woods.

She looked at Jeff. He stood exactly as she'd last seen him, so still he barely seemed to breathe. Suddenly, a ring-neck pheasant burst from the underbrush near Marty's foot, cackling and crashing through bushes and dead leaves. Far ahead of her beside the path, a doe with her white tail fanned bolted from the undergrowth. A spotted fawn leapt behind her.

Marty turned to Jeff. He was looking happier than he had in months. He put a finger to his lips and held out a hand to her. She crept toward him. He took her hand and pulled her up the hill toward the path. He gestured ahead to where the path curved toward the Morgan place and then again held a finger to his lips. He glided ahead of her, ducking under overhanging branches, holding them back until she passed and then easing them back into place.

The path turned to the right and then made an easy climb back to the left toward the ridge. Halfway up the rise the land on their right began to slope away toward the road. A sofa-sized rock jutted out over a shallow ravine below. Jeff eased himself onto the ledge and held out a hand to help Marty. He pointed toward the opposite hill.

The evening sun shot shafts of light into the woods, but the bottom of the ravine lay in shadow. As she watched, shapes became evident—a few outcroppings of rock, a fallen tree and more underbrush—all possible dens for young foxes. Marty sat beside her son without talking, scanning the valley and hillside for any movement, any flash of color. They sat long enough to watch the sun arc downward. Overhead a squirrel scolded them. In a nearby tree some crows squawked. The only other sound was the rippling of the creek far below and the song of birds returning to their roosts for the night.

Marty felt the fatigue and tension of the day slip away. How she loved this son of hers, especially with the return of his quiet thoughtful ways. She respected the intensity with which he approached everything. In some ways, she even admired his attitude of indignation over the death of his father and the changes in their life.

Guilt rose to the surface, marring her peace. She had not given Jeff what he needed. She had not been there for simple and beautiful moments like these, private moments to assure him he could still count on her.

She'd missed all Annie's signals, too. Annie had always been a good kid, but not the constantly accommodating angel she'd become since Dan's death. If Marty had been at all discerning, she would have seen that Annie's perfect behavior just wasn't normal for an eight year old. She fought off the descent into sadness with a silent prayer, "Lord Jesus, please let me always be aware of my children's needs and be able to fulfill them."

Beside her she felt Jeff stiffen slightly. He nudged her arm and pointed off to the left where a narrow path dipped over the hill from Morgans' pasture into the ravine. At the very crest of the hill was a full-grown fox, one foot raised, a rabbit hanging from his jaws. He stood motionless as if sculpted from the woods around him, the bright stare of his golden eyes the only clue to his vitality.

Jeff eased backward off the rock and motioned for Marty to follow. He turned and started back down the path toward home, not making any sudden or loud movements, but not bothering to creep. Marty followed his example, knowing Jeff was telling the fox not to worry because they were leaving.

Their descent was much faster than the climb had been. When they emerged from the woods, Jeff turned toward Marty. "Aw, man, was that cool or what?"

Marty laughed. "That was definitely cool."

"You know what it means, don't you?" he asked. "Foxes are territorial, so that had to be the male. He was heading toward the den, so he'll keep on feeding the babies. They're going to be all right, Mom."

"I'm glad, Jeff. I've felt so guilty. The sick sound of my wheels hitting the mother fox has stayed with me all day."

Jeff put an arm around her shoulders. "Mom, you couldn't help hitting her. I was sitting right beside you and I didn't see her come off the bank, either."

"Thanks, Jeff," Marty said, giving him a hug. "I love you, kiddo."

"Yeah, me too, to you," he said. They walked a few steps before he continued. "Mom, I really don't hate it here. It's just that I hate... I don't know... I hate that Dad died... and everything. Do you know what I mean?"

"Yes, Jeff, I do."

Jeff nodded and then smiled. "Let's go tell Annie and Grandpap about the fox."

That night Marty sat with Annie on the edge of Jeff's bed, saying goodnight.

"Annie, tell Mom what you told me... you know, about the fox family," Jeff said.

Annie wrinkled her forehead as if she were thinking hard. "I think we're like that fox family, only we lost our dad, not our mom. But you can take care of us just like that fox dad is taking care of his babies, huh?" Annie snuggled closer to Marty's side.

"You bet I can," she answered.

"And just like those foxes, Mom," Jeff added, "we're going to be okay."

"You bet we are!" Marty said, vowing that she'd do whatever was necessary to make it so.

TWENTY-FOUR

Derry did call on Monday, but late in the afternoon and only to act as if nothing had happened. He made a date with her for the next night. "I'd come over tonight, but I'm behind with work. I had a couple of calls I was supposed to make early Saturday."

Marty forced her voice to sound cheerful. "That's fine. I have a lot of work to do around here, so don't worry about it."

"Listen. Uh... about the play Wednesday night... I've got to go to a farm north of Pittsburgh on Wednesday afternoon. Some guy with a six-horse hitch of Percherons has decided to take - them to an exhibition and they all need shoes. I might not make it back in time."

"That's all right. I'm sure Jeff or Gayle or someone can use the other ticket." She bit a corner of her lip and hoped she'd said that in her best "I couldn't care less" voice. Derry Brady managed to find time for anything he wanted to do. If he wanted to go with her to the play, he'd be sure to be home in time. He was up to his old games again, but she knew he kept score by the amount of irritation he created. "I'll be looking forward to tomorrow night then," she said in a voice so sweet it could cause a diabetic coma. She was determined to play this out, but not with him thinking he had the upper hand. She'd known a relationship with him wouldn't be easy. Now she had some tough questions for him and he'd better have some right answers.

After she hung up, she stomped outside to continue painting. Cody charged her with his tail wagging. "What are you so happy about?" she snapped but still bent to scratch behind his ears. She hadn't gotten far when she again heard the phone ringing. Hah, she'd won. She'd worried him, so he was calling to say he would see her tonight. She dashed up the steps and into the kitchen, grabbing the phone just as Duke reached for it.

She took a deep breath and said hello as evenly and casually as she could.

"Marty, is that you?" asked Sam. "You don't sound like yourself."

She let out her breath and hoped he didn't hear her disappointment. "It's me, Sam. Did you have a nice weekend?"

"Sure did. Listen, are you free tonight? I saw something this weekend that I've got to show you."

"I'm free, but aren't you going to tell me what's up?"

"Not now. I'd rather tell you in person. Pick you up a bit before six, all right?"

Sam arrived early just as Marty was dishing up spaghetti for the kids, Duke, and Kyle who had arrived home sometime near morning after losing in the jackpot nearly all his earnings from Saturday. By the looks of him, he'd kept just enough to drown his sorrows in a barrel of beer and put him in bed all day.

"Sam, do you want some dinner before we go?" Marty asked. "There's plenty."

"No, I ate," he said. "Have you fed the horses?"

"I was going to as soon as I ate," she said.

"I'll feed. I brought some carrots for Grandma anyway. You eat and I'll be right back," he said, eagerness showing on his face and in his quick movements toward the door.

"Now what's he up to?" Duke asked.

"I couldn't tell you," Marty said, her curiosity finally overriding her day-long indignation with Derry Brady's casual treatment of her.

Soon she was in Sam's car crossing the old iron bridge. "So where are we going?" she asked.

"North of Pittsburgh. It will take us a little more than an hour to get there, but what I want to show you will start at seven."

Marty kept questioning him even though it was obvious he wanted to surprise her. Finally, he said, "Marty, I saw miracles this weekend and I want you to see them, too. Look in that briefcase on the backseat." Sam turned onto the highway toward Pittsburgh.

Marty reached over the seat and took the leather briefcase. She snapped it open, taking out the pamphlet on top—*Therapeutic Riding at McFarland.*

"Marty, I took Lisa and went up there to observe on Saturday. I saw kids in wheelchairs—one of them completely rigid with cerebral palsy—who were able to ride. You've got to see it to believe it."

Sam sure was true to his word. Give him a few days and here he was back with information and an excitement that Marty found contagious.

"Now I don't want to tell you any more until we get there and you can see for yourself." Sam maneuvered his car around a slower moving van. "So, tell me about your weekend."

Marty gave Sam the edited version—the painting, the new porch furniture, the foxes—leaving out Jeff's episodes with Kyle and Derry, and certainly not talking about the problems she was having with Derry.

They arrived at the farm with plenty of time to spare before the first lesson. This gave them a chance to talk to Joanne McFarland, the riding instructor, and for her to show them around.

Marty immediately liked Joanne with her matter-of-fact manner and easy sense of humor. She spoke in a husky but soft voice and had quiet, reassuring ways.

"All of my horses are donated," Joanne said. She stopped in front of a stall in which a bony paint stood, its head over the door. "Some of them, like this old girl, are rescue cases. Believe it or not, she's been here about a month and has already put on considerable weight." She stroked the horse's forehead between its sunken eyes. "She was about two inches from dead when she first came in."

Marty looked around at the barn setup. She didn't know what she had expected, but the barn was really very ordinary, not nearly as nice or large as their barn at home.

She listened to Joanne, taking more in with her eyes than through her ears. She saw what had to be the mounting ramps, large enough to push a wheelchair as high as a horse's back, and an arena smaller than Marty had expected, with large numbers posted on the sides and cones of various colors positioned around the arena floor.

"With autistic kids or even with Down's syndrome riders, part of what we work for is improved ability to follow directions. That's when we use the colored cones and the numbers. For instance, I might tell a rider to turn at the purple cone and ride to the yellow or stop by the number ten. The kids think they're playing a game, but it has hidden benefits," Joanne said.

She led them through the whole barn and arena and then settled with them into chairs in the office. "The killer in this business is the paperwork. That and juggling the schedules of your volunteers. You'll need volunteers, you know."

"Yes, I figured we would," Sam said.

"As I told Sam, Marty, the licensing isn't difficult. It's demanding and you have to know your stuff, but when you realize what the therapy does for these people—intellectually, physically, and emotionally—and how great the need is... well, any extra time or effort is worth every minute of it. Normally, you'd come and work with me for a couple of years and then you'd be eligible for your license. Sam doesn't want to wait that long to open your facility, and since he's a hard man to say no to, I'm willing to come to you a couple of nights a week and get you started. Of course, I realize you'll need time to build your indoor arena. The weather around here is too unpredictable to try to operate effectively without one. And I'd still like you to come and work with me at least one day a week."

Marty looked at Sam. How much of this had he already set in motion? She raised an eyebrow and he laughed.

"Actually, Joanne, I think we're a bit ahead of Marty here. I've sort of surprised her with this."

The barn door slammed and Joanne stood. "In that case, I'm going to just shut my mouth and let her watch this lesson."

Through the window in the office door, Marty saw a wheelchair being pushed up the barn aisle. A small, twisted body sat stiffly amid much padding. The little boy's bird-bright eyes fixed on Joanne and he grinned.

Joanne waved at him and turned to Marty. "Tim is fourteen years old and has cerebral palsy. Notice the rigidity of his joints. But wait until you see him ride. That should convince you more than anything I can say."

While Joanne and her assistant got the horse ready, Marty watched Tim. His arms and legs bent stiffly at his elbows and wrists and knees and ankles. His head twisted toward the left and his jaw toward the right, yet he managed a smile, excessive in its brilliance, which she tried to return, feeling somehow less adequate than this tiny teenager locked in his distorted body.

When the big bay gelding was led forward, a sheepskin cinched across his back instead of saddle, Tim bounced in his wheelchair, his arms and legs flailing wildly. His father snapped a safety helmet on Tim's head and wheeled his chair up the ramp as Joanne led the bay into place. Tim's father lifted him from the chair, a woman who had been introduced as Tim's home therapist waited on the opposite side of the horse, and Joanne stood at the horse's head. The gelding never moved a muscle—not even to twitch off a fly or swish his tail—as Tim was laid stomach down, arms on one side, legs on the other across the horse's back. Joanne urged the big horse forward with the command, "Walk on." With Tim's father on one side and the therapist on the other each massaging his limbs, Marty could see Tim's muscles begin to relax. After only two or three times around the arena, his body hung limply over the horse's broad back.

"We're ready," the therapist announced.

Joanne led the horse back over to the ramp. A volunteer took the reins from her and she mounted the ramp. Tim's father lifted him from the horse until Joanne straddled the bay's back and then placed Tim in front of her. With Joanne holding him, Tim rode around the arena, his arms, legs, and back as loose as a rag doll, a huge grin on his small face.

When Sam patted her back, Marty realized she was crying. But miracles demanded some response, and the one she'd seen—a child of stone turned to flesh and blood—had been spectacular. She wiped her eyes so Tim wouldn't see or, for that matter, Joanne who might then believe Marty too emotional for this kind of work.

She saw other miracles that night—a class of premature stroke victims all in their forties and fifties, two Down's syndrome children and an autistic child—but none quite as spectacular as Tim.

It was late when the lessons were over. She and Sam had a long drive ahead of them, so they left before Joanne could answer all of Marty's questions.

As they drove away from McFarland Farms, Sam excitedly related what he had seen there over the weekend, but Marty's head was reeling with the images she'd just witnessed and she couldn't fully attend to him. When they pulled off the highway near home, Sam pulled into Malone's.

"I love their homemade pie," Sam said. "And you look like you could use a cup of coffee and a piece of pie to bring you back to earth."

As Marty followed him into the restaurant, a medley of delicious smells met them. They ordered pie—caramel apple walnut for Sam and raspberry-apple for Marty—and coffee. She looked around, hoping to see Patsy Malone; but like all the other times Marty had been in the place, Patsy was nowhere to be seen.

While they waited for their orders, Sam opened his briefcase. "Now before I show you these papers, you have to know that I made a great deal of money over my working life and I inherited a good bit from my parents. Since I've retired I've been looking for something worthwhile... important even... to do with it." He handed her some papers.

The heading read, "The Lisa Center at Stafford Farms, Funded by the Marcus Foundation." A lot of copy followed and then some sketches of her barn with an indoor arena attached, and an office and spacious waiting or observation room.

"I worked on this all day yesterday. I even got my lawyer off the golf course to see if it was feasible and then this morning I talked to my son who's a banker. It can be done, Marty. With very little additional fund-raising and a core of responsible volunteers, we can swing this as a self-sufficient operation. It will pay you a salary and eventually hire you some help to run the barn. Joanne says she turns down potential clients every day because she simply doesn't have any more time. She assures me that the need is there and we shouldn't have any trouble filling our schedule. What do you think?"

Marty had been thinking and feeling and hoping, ever since

she'd seen Tim's lesson. She had so much she wanted to say, but it was all garbled and jumbled in her mind. "Sam, I... I..."

"If Gayle were here, she'd tell you just to say, 'All right, Sam.'"

Marty laughed right out loud and from deep in the center of her joy. "All right, Sam. And bless you, you dear man."

TWENTY-FIVE

Tuesday night Derry showed up at eight, only a half-hour later than he'd promised. Marty was sitting at the kitchen table playing Hearts with Jeff and Annie when she heard his car on the lane.

Jeff put down his cards and with a sour expression headed out of the room toward the stairs. "I think I'll sit this one out. Besides, I promised to call Rachel."

Annie ran to greet Derry. Marty met them on the porch which was now completely painted with the swing hanging and furniture in place, as well as a few new flower baskets.

Derry looked surprised, glancing from the porch to the stripped but unpainted front of the house and finally to the shutters, newly green, lined up on the lawn.

"Pretty impressive, isn't it?" Marty said.

"Yeah, amazing. And to think, you got this far without me."

Marty leveled a look at him. "Yes, we did and I'm pretty proud of us."

"And guess what?" Annie said.

Derry swung her up to sit on his shoulder. "What?" he asked.

"Sam is opening a big place here to teach handicapped kids to ride and Mom is going to run it."

Derry deposited Annie on the swing and took a seat on the couch. "What's this?" he asked Marty.

Marty explained about the workings of the foundation Sam wanted to establish and about her part in it.

"It sounds too good to be true, Marty. I mean, I can see what's in it for you, but what about Sam? What's he getting out of it? Has the old guy gone sweet on you or what?"

Marty looked away from him to Annie, a ploy to keep her expression pleasant. She took a deep breath before she answered. "Charity, Derry. And the chance to still do something important, not just for himself but for his granddaughter. Sam's at that age where he's looking to what he'll be leaving behind him. He's like that." She knew she had spoken harshly, but at least she stopped herself from adding, "which is something you could probably never understand." Marty thought she saw Derry smirk. That did it.

"Annie, I need to talk to Derry. Why don't you go and take care of your kittens? When we're finished, I'll bring him in to see them, all right?"

Annie left with a minimum of protest. Marty turned to Derry. "We have to talk, Derry."

"I thought that's what we were doing."

"No, we were playing the old game of 'Who's going to win this round?'. We promised no games, remember?"

Derry rose from the couch and took her hand, leading her to the porch swing. He put his arm around her and pushed off with his foot causing the swing to rock. "You're right. We need to talk this out," he said, his voice as smooth as Mama's custard. "Let's kiss and make up first. I hate being mad at you."

He was mad at her? More games, this one being "the best defense is a good offense." She let him gather her into his arms and kiss her. Once more she clearly felt the outlines of the empty place inside her, but now she doubted if Derry was the one to fill it, not the way she needed to have it filled. She pulled back.

"Don't tell me you didn't like me kissing you, Marty. Your innocent act worked in high school, but come on... you've had two children. You know how two people can need each other."

"I know I want you. But I'm not sure that's the same as a need. Food, water, clothing, shelter—those are needs."

"And between two mature people who care about each other, so is sex," Derry said. "If you really did save it for your husband, like a good girl, well... fine. He was a lucky man. But now, what are you going to do with the rest of your life?"

"I don't know, but it's important to me that I do what's right. Yes, I remained a virgin until my wedding night. It was the right thing to do, and I've never regretted it. Doing what's right is especially important to me now. I'm raising children, and it's what I expect from them."

Derry jumped to his feet and began to pace the porch. "If

there is such a thing as right and wrong, then there must be a rule book to explain all this. I've never seen one. Have you?" He stood in front of her, an arm on each side of the swing holding it still, his eyes boring into hers. "Produce this rule book, Marty, because if you can't or if you're going to give me some obsolete garbage about conscience, then you're making up the rules. Come on, Marty, for God's sake…"

Marty put her hands on his arms. "That's right, Derry… for God's sake. His are the only rules that make sense, and I'm trying to follow them. I don't think I ever really realized that before, but it's the truth."

"You mean, then, that I'd have to marry you first! Well, sister, I've got news for you—"

Marty jumped to her feet. "No. I've got news for you! You're rushing me. You're the one talking about love and marriage and all this stuff. I've been widowed now less than a year. Yes, I've started to care for you, but I'm not ready for any of this. It's too soon. When I wake up in the middle of the night, I still imagine I feel Dan lying next to me. It surprises me that he's not there. I'm not saying I can't ever love you the way I loved him, but—"

Derry grabbed her roughly by the shoulders. "Look, you know where to find me. I've always been crazy about you, and I'm sure I'm probably enough of a fool to come when you call. But I'm not promising anything. Like you've said, I've never been wanting for female company. You'd best remember that while you're trying to forget Dan and figure out what you want." His expression was deadpan, his voice deadly serious. "It'd be a real shame if you decided it was me… and I was gone."

Marty braced herself, afraid he was going to shove her. Instead, he dropped his hands to his side and turned away. "Derry," she called. He turned back toward her. She didn't know how to phrase it but she had to know. "How 'gone' do you mean? Gone for good, or just gone to the mountains with Ceci Collins?"

"Yeah, well… if you're asking about last weekend, it was to the mountains with Ceci. But from what I hear, you shouldn't be throwing stones, running around like you were with your sugar daddy."

"Sugar daddy? What sugar daddy?" Marty sputtered.

"You know who... Sam Marcus. Is that the real dilemma, Marty? Deciding between me and Sam's money? Remember, Ceci chose an old man who died and left her all his money and I still got her. It's no sweat off my nose if you do the same."

"You're wrong about Sam. He's a good man and a dependable friend."

"Wake up, sweetheart. There are no free rides. No guy's going to give you all that and not want something in return. And this guy was some kind of hot-shot businessman, wasn't he? They never invest without a big payoff."

"Get off my porch, Derry, and out of my life. If, indeed, you had ever managed to be faithful to me, I might have been able to eventually forgive you this weekend with Ceci. I might even have been able to tolerate your skewed views, hoping that someday I might change them, believing that if I loved you enough I could make a difference in your life. But you're just plain hateful." She realized that she was yelling, but she didn't care.

Derry sneered and backed off the porch. "What's the matter, Marty? Did I hit a nerve about your friend Sam?"

"Just go, Derry." Marty sank down on the porch swing and watched him strut off, like a boxer who'd just won another round.

How could she ever have believed Derry Brady could fill the void inside her? Because she was so lonely she had wanted him to, and because Derry changed shape so easily he made her believe he could. Once again she'd discovered what she'd always known—Derry had too many edges to fit smoothly into anyone's life, and each one of those edges cut like broken glass.

TWENTY-SIX

As Marty and Cody took their ritual morning stroll to fetch the paper, she realized that today she'd have to call Derry. She simply couldn't put it off any longer. It had been four weeks since he'd stormed out of her life, and all of the horses were in desperate need of having their shoes reset. Not that there weren't other blacksmiths, but he was the best. She'd seen him from a distance at the fireworks display on the Fourth of July, and had planned to at least say, "Hello." Nothing overly friendly, just a simple "no hard feelings" greeting between old friends. But he had disappeared before she got the chance.

She took the newspaper from its holder under the new mailbox she'd found at a craft sale last week. Covered with painted fruits and vines, it was a bit fancy for a farm mailbox, but she liked it. As she walked back to the house, Cody followed splashing through the creek, periodically charging and circling her before again leaping into the water.

She rounded the corner and the sight of the house, freshly painted with all the newly hung shutters in place, made her catch her breath. It had turned out so much nicer than she had even dreamed, a clapboard charmer in tan and dark green, nestled on a small rise above where the creek bent toward the woods.

She'd been using her free time well—mostly being with the kids, reassuring them and shoring herself up in the process. They'd all cooperated to get the house painted, even Duke and Kyle, laughing and working and squabbling together like a real family.

Red nickered to her from the fence line as if thanking her for breakfast. Not to be outdone, Cocoa trotted up behind him and nipped his flank. Red took off at a run and Cocoa replaced him at the fence line, whinnying for Marty's attention. She walked over and scratched the pony's neck. Cocoa hardly bore any resemblance to the broken-down animal she'd been at the beginning of the summer; luster had returned to her coat and eyes and she walked with the cocky confidence of age and position.

"You're a good girl, aren't you?" Marty cooed. The pony stuck her nose between the wires of the fence and Marty kissed her, getting a whiff of the warm, sweet smell of oats on the pony's breath.

Jeff met her on the porch. "Mom, can you run me over to Cam's? He just got a call. Some lady's cat caught a squirrel and mauled it. She brought it to Cam and he wants me to help, since he's got a bunch of farm calls this morning."

"Sure," Marty said. "I'll get my keys."

In the kitchen, Kyle was hanging up the phone. "Hey, Sis, I called Derry to reset the horses. He'll fit us in before the end of the week." He grinned at her. "I figured better me than you."

Marty gave him a hug. "I love you." She hurried by and grabbed her car keys from the hook behind the door.

"You don't need to drop off Jeff. I go right by there on my way to that job we're working on. Just let me get my boots on. Pour my coffee into my travel mug and we'll be off."

Marty poured herself a cup of coffee and filled Kyle's travel mug. She went out onto the porch with the newspaper. As Kyle charged by, he caught Jeff in a headlock and dragged him toward the truck.

"Kyle, cut it out!" Jeff yelled, when he was unable to wiggle out of his uncle's tight hold. "Man, you know I hate—"

Kyle ruffled Jeff's hair with his knuckles. "What's the matter, sissy boy? Can't even beat your old uncle?"

Jeff locked a leg behind Kyle's and threw his weight against him, knocking him to the grass. Jeff gave a hoot and flung himself on Kyle's chest, pinning him. "What did you call me?"

"City boy! Didn't I call you city boy?" Kyle said, laughing and struggling to get free.

Cody jumped off the porch, circling them and taking playful nips at their legs. "Cody! Get back here," Marty called, and the pup came to her. "Now, would you two behave and get going?"

Kyle surrendered, but as Jeff backed away, he kicked his legs out from under him. Dashing around to the driver's side of the truck, Kyle jumped in and started the engine. As he took off down the lane, Jeff jumped on the running board, opened the door, and swung into the truck.

Marty shook her head. What had she called them? A real family? She curled up on the porch sofa with her coffee and the paper. Cody dropped down on the floor beside her. She kicked off her shoe and ran her bare toes over his back, enjoying the cool softness of his wet coat.

Annie joined her, still in her pajamas, munching on a bagel and carrying a glass of juice.

"Good morning, sunshine," Marty said.

Annie crawled over Cody who thumped his tail but didn't move. She snuggled in next to her mother on the couch. "What are we doing today?" she asked around a mouthful of bagel.

Marty slipped an arm around her little one's shoulders. "Well, early this afternoon Sam is coming over with the final plans for the center. He's bringing some lady who has volunteered to help us with fund-raising. He may bring Lisa so you two can play while we talk, all right?"

"Sure. We'll brush Cocoa and Grandma and play with the kittens, and then you can give us a riding lesson, and then we'll take a swim in the creek to cool off. How's that."

Marty chuckled. "That sounds like a very full afternoon, but definitely doable."

"Mom, I like it here. It's a good place for us to be now, don't you think?"

"Yeah, I do."

"And next month when I start school, I'll already know lots of kids from church and from going to the pool. And Jen says our teacher is real nice."

Marty took a drink of her coffee. "That's right," she said.

"Is it bad that I don't miss our old house? I mean... I still miss Daddy, but I don't miss where we used to live, and except for a couple of kids, I don't really miss my friends there. I'd like to see them again sometime, but I don't feel awful that I'm not with them."

"I'm glad, Annie. It makes being here easier."

"I still miss Grammy."

"Well, then, I think we should call her more often. I'm sure she misses you, too." Marty had to be more thoughtful about Dan's mother. She wasn't an easy woman to talk to, sure as she was that she knew better than anyone what was best for her son's family, but Marty did care about her and the kids loved her. "Let's call her later. She said she'd like us to come up over Christmas. How about if we go between Christmas and New Year's? You can see some of your old friends and we can visit the Smithsonian."

"Can we take Jen?"

"Maybe. I'll have to talk to her parents."

"She's never been to Washington, D.C."

Marty kissed the top of Annie's brown hair. "We'll see." Annie had been the first to settle in, but Marty was also feeling more content. She'd teamed up with Amy and every week or two they went to Pittsburgh for the symphony or to an art gallery or play. Marty found this was as necessary for Amy as for herself.

Amy was a gifted artist and had volunteered to design the logo for the new riding center. She seemed happier, and Marty hoped that their friendship played a part in that.

Duke shuffled out on the porch, dressed in jeans and one of his few going-out-to-see-the-world shirts. To qualify, a shirt only had to cover his belly, have no more than one rip or snag, and be fairly clean. Well, at least, he wasn't in the one good pair of slacks and shirt Marty had bought him and that he'd been wearing to church.

Marty glanced at her watch. Not yet nine o'clock. "Where are you going so early?"

"I've been hungry for duck eggs. Thought I'd head over to the auction off of eighty-four and see if they have any. Would my princess like to come along?" he asked.

Annie jumped off the couch and over Cody. "Is that the place you were telling me about that sells animals and eggs and all kinds of farm stuff?"

"Sure is," Duke said.

That was all Annie needed to know. She dashed off to get dressed.

After Duke and Annie left, Marty grabbed a dust cloth and tore through the house, touching up where it needed and marveling again at how good her furniture looked in the old place. Even Kyle and Duke seemed to like the changes. In the hall, she nudged Jake out of the way to climb over the gate she installed to keep the beasts out of the living and dining rooms. She hadn't won her war over the dogs in the house, but at least Cam had put them all on oral flea medicine. She'd also discovered that when they were let outside with any regularity, they really were housebroken. That and bathing them regularly made living with the dogs tolerable. Besides, she kind of liked that Cody had taken to sleeping on the rug between her bed and Annie's.

She straightened a watercolor of an Amish farmer plowing his field with a pair of Belgians. She'd bought the painting at a craft fair in Maryland years ago, intending to give it to Gayle and Mac for Christmas; but it made her feel so close to them that she'd never been able to give it up. All of her paintings looked even better here than in her old home, perhaps because she had always chosen pastoral subjects over city scapes. Never able to afford oil paintings, she had a nice collection of watercolors.

She filled a small watering can and sprinkled the hanging plants on the porch; she loved these cascades of heavy-headed petunias. She was making plans to plant perennial bulbs and mums in the fall and even had visions of what her garden would look like come spring.

Marty poured herself another cup of coffee and then went back out onto the porch, settling on the couch with one of the books Joanne had given her. Before she could be licensed as a therapeutic riding instructor, she had a lot of studying to do, but learning had always invigorated her. She loved the increased sense of purpose and the feeling of involvement with a world beyond her own boundaries.

She was so absorbed in her reading that she didn't hear Cam's truck until it pulled up by the house. Her coffee sat untouched on the table beside her.

"Mom," Jeff called, "just say yes!"

Marty laughed. "Not until I know what I'm agreeing to."

"You'll love it, Mom. Come on. Say it's okay."

Cam got out of the truck. "I told him to call you first, but that's what he said—you'd love it."

Jeff came toward her carrying a wire cage. Marty couldn't quite make out the fluffy lump in the corner. "It's the squirrel, Mom. He's young and pretty torn up. Cam says he can be my first patient."

"If..." Cam prompted tapping Jeff on the shoulder.

"I mean... if it's all right with you."

"And..." Cam again urged.

"And, it's not like I'm asking to keep him forever, because the idea behind rehabilitating wildlife is to release it back into the wild. If I do a good job with him, Cam will give me other animals to care for."

"Whoa there, Noah," Marty said. "You better let me check out this critter before you start building your ark." She peered into the cage at the small gray animal. Patches of fur and part of its tail were missing, puncture wounds glared red by his shoulders, and a jagged railroad of stitches crossed his back. "I don't know... this poor little guy looks like he's on the way out. Jeff, how are you going to feel about that?"

"Mom, I know he might not make it, like the fox didn't, but he doesn't have any chance at all if we don't help him."

"Wonderful technique, Jeff—bring up the fox to appeal to Mom's guilt feelings." Marty leveled one of those "mother" looks at Jeff, trying not to smile. "Cam, you've told him what to do here, I assume."

"You bet. All instructions have been given and also we'll stay in touch."

"Then I'd be a real villain if I said no, wouldn't I?"

"See, Cam, she's a softy," Jeff said, heading for the house. "I'm going to put him in my room for now."

Cam took off for his next farm call, promising to check back at the end of his day. Marty had barely gotten her concentration back when Duke and Annie drove up the lane.

"Wait until you see what we got!" Annie yelled.

"Oh, no," Marty said, as Duke pulled a huge cardboard box from the backseat. Something in the box bleated. "Dad!"

"Now, Marty, the poor little thing was just going for dog meat, being crippled like she is. There was this guy from the packing plant bidding on her. I told him I wanted her for my granddaughter and he backed right down. I got her for almost nothing. Given a little time, I'm sure her leg will heal."

Marty looked into the box at a small brown-and-white goat. One white-stockinged leg jutted stiffly in front of her. The little thing lifted her triangular head and fixed Marty with her moist eyes. "She stays in the barn. Understood?"

Annie hugged her mother. "Of course, she will. Goats don't live in the house."

"We'll have Cam look at her leg when he comes back to check on your brother's squirrel," Marty said, as Duke and Annie started up the hill to the barn. They stopped and turned back to her, puzzled looks on their faces. "Don't ask. It's a long story and every bit as convincing as yours."

Marty left her books on the couch and sat on the swing, shoving off gently to let it rock her. She smiled. Maybe it was time to build an ark. Contentment flooded her. Six months ago she never would have believed she could be this happy. It was as if she'd finally been able to integrate into one life everything that she was—art enthusiast, culture hound, nature and animal lover, daughter, sister, mother... No, not wife, not anymore. But for now, even that was all right. There was less empty space inside so it hurt less. In fact, sometimes she hardly noticed that space at all. And she wouldn't complain, because God had been taking good care of them all, answering every one of her prayers—except about Derry, but that wasn't God's fault. She shut her eyes and rocked, thanking God for all He'd done for her, begging Him to keep the good times coming.

T W E N T Y - S E V E N

Sam knocked on the door shortly after two o'clock, accompanied by an attractive young woman. "Marty, this is Kristen Baker. She's going to help us with the fund-raising for the Center."

Marty shook the slender manicured hand the woman offered, aware of how work-roughened her own had become. But there was strength in that slim hand and in the way the woman looked Marty right in the eye when she spoke.

"Marty, Sam's told me so much about you," Kristen said.

"And he's talked a lot about you—how good you are at what you do. It's wonderful to have our first volunteer be someone with your experience."

"Well, my work won't exactly be free. I've always wanted to learn to ride, so I figured I'd trade for lessons. How's that?"

"Sounds good to me," Marty said. She led them into the dining room where she'd laid out her china cups and some sugar cookies on a crystal tray. The breeze from the creek wafted through the window, making it one of the coolest rooms in the house.

"First, I want to show you the plans," Sam said, excitement in his voice and on his face making him look younger than his years.

Marty watched as he spread the architect's drawings out over her lace tablecloth. They were fabulous, so much more than Marty had expected after seeing the setup at McFarland. Essentially, the architect had used the barn as it currently stood, a twenty-stall pole barn with feed and tack rooms and a wash rack, and had added an indoor arena behind the barn where Kyle had already leveled the ground and cut into the hillside. But there was also a glass-fronted observation area and an office. "Sam, it's wonderful!" Marty said. "But it's going to cost a fortune."

"No, it's not. The barn's already there and that would be the big expense. Honestly, the exterior treatment almost costs more than all the rest." Sam turned over another paper.

The color drawing showed an exterior view of the entire complex from several angles, complete with landscaping. New siding had been added to the barn so that it matched the arena. "Sam, it's unbelievable, but how can we afford this?"

Kristen spoke up. "I've already contacted some local lumberyards. Two turned me down flat, but the third has promised some of the materials free and the rest at cost. The landscaper is my brother. He'll just charge us an hourly rate for his work crew."

"Now, Marty," Sam said, "do you think Kyle and his partner could get a crew together to do the work?"

Marty didn't answer at first, not only because she was overwhelmed but also because she didn't know how to answer. She didn't want to be disloyal, but she had to be honest and the truth was Kyle wasn't the most responsible worker she'd ever seen.

Sam reached across and patted her hand. "Look, I know most weekends he runs off to play cowboy and I know he parties pretty hard when he does; but I've also been asking around and his work is first-rate. I figure with you here to keep after him, the work will get done; and, more than some outside contractor, he has a stake in how it turns out."

"I'm certain he'll give us a good price," Marty said. "In fact, if you let him build a roping chute at one end of that huge arena, he'll give you a great price."

"Great," Kristen said. "Have him look at the plans tonight and give us a bid on the job without materials."

"Sam," Marty asked, "how much of your own money is going into this? Shouldn't you be safeguarded in some way? I mean, I don't own this place; my dad does. When he dies—God willing many years from now—Kyle and I will inherit, but what if we have to sell?"

"Actually, not as much of my money is going into this as I originally thought, thanks to Kristen. I've had my lawyers draw up some papers to protect you and your family as well as the

Foundation I'm starting. Basically, we get first option to buy the farm or part of it whenever you sell, for a price established by fair market value and agreeable to all parties. It also involves some complicated formulas that I frankly don't understand, based on a current assessment and future expectations." Sam handed Marty a file.

"I'll have to read these after my brain clears, Sam, but it seems overwhelmingly generous on your part." Marty thought of Derry's words—"There are no free rides." She also thought about the exciting possibility of making a living at something so worthwhile, so suited to her talents.

"It's going to cost both of us a lot of hard work and dedication, Marty," Sam said. "But I think we're up to it. As for me, it's already been worth whatever it will cost. I haven't felt this enthusiastic and vital in years. I'm at an age where most of my friends are concerned with nothing more than improving their golf game. And here God has given me something of importance to do. How can I not heed his call?"

Marty covered the hand he'd placed on her arm with one of her own. That was pretty much how she felt. Derry didn't understand people like Sam, who made decisions not based on personal gain but on faith and giving. Marty tried to be one of those people; only recently she'd redefined her decision-making in terms of faith instead of "following the rules." That more than anything else was why it would never work with Derry.

Kristen drew out papers of her own and outlined some of her plans—articles about the center to be placed in all the area newspapers, a booth at Community Day at the mall to enlist volunteers, and a splashy dinner dance and silent auction to be held at the local country club in the fall. Marty liked Kristen's intensity and frankness. She was bright, articulate, and savvy.

Kyle came in around four o'clock and Marty could tell he was smitten with Kristen. And no wonder. With her dimpled smile, clear gray eyes and long honey-colored hair, she was a lovely woman.

After Kyle looked at the plans, he promised a bid within a few days. "If everything goes well, we'll finish up the jobs we've promised, and start on the Center in a few weeks. We should be done by late September. How about a grand opening the first part of October?"

"All right," Kristen said. "When do I get my first lesson?"

"You want to ride?" Kyle asked, a combination of disbelief and eagerness in his voice.

"Ever since I was ten, but when I was a kid I had awful allergies and my parents wouldn't let me. So, you see, I never got to naturally dispel that horse thing most young girls go through and it's stayed with me," Kristen said, her dimples deepening and her cheeks coloring slightly.

"Give me a minute to get out of my work clothes and into my jeans and boots and I'll take you riding right now," Kyle said. He leaned on the table flashing his best boyish grin and looking right into her eyes.

Marty watched with amusement. These two were definitely sparking each other. Is this how she'd been with Derry? If it was this blatant, no wonder Jeff had felt like gagging. Kristen said something about not wanting to ruin her linen pants and Marty heard Kyle offer some of her clothes. "Sure," Marty said. "I'm sure I can find you a pair of jeans. You'll have to cinch them in and roll them up, but they should do."

"Go ahead," Sam said. "Marty and I still have some details to talk over. You can ride Grandma."

"Is he trustworthy?" Kristen teased, nodding toward Kyle.

"No," Marty answered, "but he'll make sure you don't have trouble with the horse. Sam or I should probably go along to make sure *Kyle* doesn't give you trouble."

"Now, Marty," Sam interrupted, "I think Kristen can handle herself. Besides, I'll stand as a character reference for Kyle."

Within minutes Kristen and Kyle, oblivious to Marty and Sam waving from the porch, headed up the hill toward the barn.

"Let's sit on the porch for a while," Sam said, settling onto the swing. "It's so peaceful out here."

Marty sat on the couch across from him. They talked about the Center, sharing ideas and dreams. Marty searched for something to say to express her gratitude, but found mere words inadequate.

"Marty, you're beaming at me like I'm your Santa Claus," Sam said. "We have to get all this straight between us or it will never work out. As far as I'm concerned, we're partners here."

"Sam, I just—"

"Let me get this out first. Ever since I saw the miracles Joanne performed with those kids, I've wanted to be part of it. Not just because of Lisa, although for me she's certainly a driving force. It's all tied up with how I believe we're supposed to live—helping each other when we can. My wife based her whole life on that belief. Nobody did more charity work than my Barbara when she was well." Sam looked past Marty and pointed up the hill.

Marty looked and saw Kyle and Kristen cresting the ridge and heading toward the path through the woods.

"That's nice. They'll have a good ride," Sam said softly. "She's quite a girl."

"Sam, does it still hurt as much... about Barbara's illness, I mean?"

"Sometimes, but I guess I've accepted it as well as I can. I still miss her horribly... or, rather, miss the way she used to be." Sam smiled at her. "Why are you asking me? You know about loss."

"I know. I miss Dan. So much has happened that I want to tell him about. I feel guilty because I've started to like my life here better than I liked it in D.C. For the first time, I feel as if I'm in charge of my own destiny and that of my family. I'm more together as a person. I just wish Dan were here to share that."

"I understand. At least, I still have a shadow of what was Barbara and sometimes the old Barbara shows me a glimpse of herself. Like the other day, I was telling her all about our plans and how I felt God wanted me to keep up all the good work she'd done the whole time we were together. While I was still with the company, my main contribution to her work was financial. She'd hit me for a donation and I'd give, but she was the one in the trenches—visiting the hospitals, tutoring the 'at risk' kids, dishing up lunch at the soup kitchen." He shook his head, his eyes misted with remembering.

Marty squirmed slightly in her seat. "Sam, you don't have to..."

"No, Marty, I want to tell you what happened. A few days ago I sat holding her hand, telling her about our plans, and suddenly she looked at me, her eyes clear, her face untroubled and beautiful again. She smiled and squeezed my hand. Then, just as quickly, she was gone again. The next day she didn't even know who I was."

"I'm so sorry, Sam."

"That's not why I'm telling you this, Marty. I think God gave Barbara and me that moment so she'd be proud of me and know that I was going on with the kind of life we believe in. That's why you mustn't think I'm doing you a favor with the Center. No, it's bigger than that."

"Sam, I want to be just like you when I grow up," Marty said. She squeezed in next to him on the swing and took his hand. "We're going to make this thing fly. We'll make it the best darn therapeutic center the world's ever seen."

Sam raised her hand to his lips and kissed it. "Let's just hope we can do as the Lord wishes, my young friend."

Sam was right, of course, but Marty couldn't help it—her imagination continued to build grand designs for their success.

TWENTY-EIGHT

The first donated horse arrived five days later. Marty had run to the store and wasn't there when Cam called about it. Duke told Cam to have the man bring the horse on over. Up the lane bounced a battered station wagon pulling a rusted one-horse trailer. By then Marty had heard they were coming, but was still surprised when she saw what backed off the trailer. One look at the jug-headed, rack-ribbed standardbred mare and Marty was ready to shoot her father and Cam. With The Meadows, the harness-racing track just a few miles away, she could end up running an old age home for retired racehorses, if she didn't stop them.

The grizzled old man who led the mare toward her kept wiping his eyes with a gnarled hand. "I'm real ashamed, Ma'am, at the shape Glory's in. Last few years have been hard. The Missus and I have barely had enough money for food for ourselves, let alone the horses. Sold off the rest and just couldn't bear to part with Glory here. She sure took care of us in her time. Got a trotting record of 1:58 flat. And that was twenty years ago, when most horses weren't going that fast."

Marty looked at the mare more closely. She wasn't really as thin as she'd first seemed, but her aged flesh had shriveled against the bones. With a solid bay coat unrelieved by white markings and her large angular head, she'd never been pretty, but she had a calm, intelligent look to her eye. "How old is she and does she ride?"

"She's only twenty-four and, of course, she rides. Always trained mine to both harness and saddle, but Glory here will just walk and trot. She never broke stride on the track and you can't make her canter under saddle either. But Dr. Brady said that was fine, 'cause you're going to be training little kids with handicaps."

Annie and Duke came out of the house. "Harry!" Duke called, and hurried to greet the man. "Cam didn't tell me you were the one bringing a horse out."

"Duke, good to see you. I was told to see a Marty Harris, so I figured you'd died or sold off or something."

"Marty's my daughter and this little one is my granddaughter, Annie. Marty and Annie, this is Harry Simms, one of the finest harness-horse trainers ever worked in these parts."

"That was a long time ago, Duke. Now I'm fixing to move to Arizona for my health, so I've sold my place. Glory's the only horse I got left. Knowing you, I'm feeling better already about leaving her here. You know... with someone who knew her when she was the best."

Duke stroked the bony head and the old mare leaned into his hand. "Glory Girl sure gave me a thrill or two watching her race.... She'd come from behind and fly past the rest. Whew! She could turn it on. And had more heart than is usually given to five horses." Duke grabbed Annie under her arms and swung her up onto the mare's back.

"Just hand the little girl the lead rope, Duke. Glory will take care of her," said Harry.

Annie nudged the mare with her heels and they moved slowly off before Marty could protest. Harry hadn't lied; the quiet old mare would probably take care of whoever was on her back. And, she was sound, not a trace of lameness. "We'll be proud to have her, Harry," Marty said, before she could stop herself. She thought of the old paint horse at McFarland and sighed. It seemed that this whole business was built on salvaged horses.

By the time Derry arrived an hour later, Marty already liked the old mare enough to defend her. "What do you mean, bag of bones? I'll have you know this was once a famous trotter."

"If she didn't make any of that purse money for you, you shouldn't be the one retiring her. You better get tougher, Marty, or you'll never make it in this business," he said, an edge of condescension in his tone.

Marty chose to ignore it, preferring to keep this first confrontation as smooth as possible. "Let's do Red first. He's going to a roping tonight." Marty turned to get Red from his pasture before Derry could respond. She could hear Annie talking brightly to him when she came back into the barn leading Red.

Good, Annie would help dispel the tension.

In fact, Derry kept talking to Annie and ignoring Marty. Glad for the reprieve, Marty went about her barn work. She saw Annie show Derry the kittens he'd given her and could hear her gaily describing their antics. Marty moved her wheelbarrow to the goat's stall and began to clean it. The goat bleated a greeting and Marty stopped to scratch her behind the ear. She wanted to show Derry the goat and tell him how annoyed she'd been when Duke had brought her home. And he didn't know about Stumpy either, the squirrel that was making such a fast recovery under Jeff's care.

Finished with the stall, she pushed the wheelbarrow out into the aisle, letting the goat hobble after her. Annie saw the goat and called, "Here, Daisy! Come and meet Derry."

Marty headed out to the manure pile with the full wheelbarrow. When Marty came back into the barn, she saw Derry laughing with Annie and patting Daisy. She put her hands on her hips and stared down the barn aisle. She felt left out, not jealous, not with any romantic urgings, just left out.

"Annie," she called, "will you take Daisy out and let her eat grass? I want to talk to Derry for a minute."

Derry turned and gave her a smug look, like he expected that sooner or later she'd come crawling back. But he also seemed uneasy.

As Annie passed her, looking like *she* now felt displaced, Marty whispered, "Just a few minutes, sweetie, all right?"

"Don't take too long, Mom," Annie said. "I have lots to tell him."

Marty squared her shoulders and walked up to Derry with her hand extended. "Truce?"

Derry took her hand in both of his. "Depends. Are we talking a cease-fire or a reconciliation?"

Marty gently pulled her hand away. "Cease-fire."

He nodded and stepped back from her, his violet eyes wrinkling at the corners, his dimples deepening, but the smile never quite curving his lips. He took her hand again and pulled her next to him, so they were standing side by side, his arm encircling her shoulders. "No matter how right it feels, we just don't fit, do we?"

Unable to give voice to her answer, Marty bit her lip and shook her head. When her throat relaxed she said, "We don't believe in the same things, Derry."

"Doesn't feel like that should matter so much... but it does," Derry said, dropping his arm from her shoulders.

"I guess at our age we have to go on more than feelings," Marty said, holding out her hand. "Please stay my friend."

Derry squeezed her hand and bumped her shoulder. "Heck, I'll settle for having you as my friend. Truth is... the whole time I was telling you I loved you—and please believe me that I meant it—I was telling Ceci the same thing, and meaning that. I'm not sure I can give her up. I came here with the idea of being honest with you. I'd have hurt you, Marty, even though that's the last thing I'd ever want to do."

"I know," Marty said, bumping him back. "Now let's get shoes on these horses."

Annie came back in with Daisy as if on cue. Marty smiled at her and waved her over. Together they filled him in on all he'd missed in his absence from their lives.

Marty could hear herself laughing and chatting, but she was not all that happy. For the first time in their long friendship, she really understood Derry and felt sorry for him. Sooner or later he'd end up in marriage number three followed by a third divorce. His relationships ran on pure feeling, divorced from any real commitment or spiritual bond, so they were doomed from the start. Marty guessed that was what Gayle had been trying to tell her weeks ago.

But Derry seemed totally at ease. By the time he put his equipment back into his truck, he was teasing her and joking again. "Hey, you want some advice from an old friend?" he called, leaning out the truck window.

"Sure, friend," Marty said.

"Find someone you can depend on."

"I need to be able to depend on myself before I let anyone else in. And, you know what? I think I'm getting there."

After he'd gone, she stood on the hill and surveyed the farm. In just under two months, she had transformed the place. Mama would have been proud of the freshly painted house filled with nice furniture, the groomed lawn, the repaired fences, and the clean and tidy barn. Nestled in their own small valley surrounded by woods, it was once again a fine place, a good home for her and her children. Marty did credit God for the setting, but she was especially pleased with the transformation she'd brought to the man-made structures. She hoped God would forgive her this moment of hubris, but doggone it, she had a right to be proud. What she hadn't been able to complete with her own two hands, she'd managed to get done by pushing the others.

TWENTY-NINE

After she finished her barn chores, Marty left Annie at the barn playing with her kittens and started for the house to make supper. Before she even opened the kitchen door, she could hear Jeff yelling for her. She took the steps two at a time, and charged around the upstairs banister to his room. "Be careful opening the door, Mom. Stumpy's loose."

Marty slipped in and shut the door quickly after her. "What do you mean, he's loose?"

Jeff crouched with his arms outstretched, facing a corner of the room. "He jumped out when I went to feed him. Help me catch him."

Marty picked up the wastebasket and dumped the few papers in it on the floor. She passed it to Jeff over his shoulder. "Don't try to catch him with your hands. He could bite you."

Jeff held up a red, angry looking finger. "No kidding!"

Jeff lunged forward and in the next instant Marty felt something hit her leg. The maddest-looking squirrel she'd ever seen—eyes glaring, ears laid back, all four feet splayed and digging in—was on its way up the leg of her jeans. It had already reached her hip when she screamed, startling the animal, which jumped from her to the bed. Jeff leaped after it, but this time it jumped to the windowsill and clung to the screen. Quickly, Jeff lowered the window, trapping Stumpy between the window and the screen.

"Aw, man! If I open the window, he'll just take off again," Jeff said. "Gloves! Mom, where did you put the winter gloves?"

"Oh, goodness, I don't know," Marty said. Stumpy started to chew on the screen. "Jeff, distract him. Slip some food under the window or something."

Jeff pushed the window up a tiny crack and put some nuts and seeds under. He tapped on the glass until Stumpy turned and saw the food, but he had already gnawed a tiny hole in the screen. Stumpy looked from the hole to the food several times before making a dash for the food. "Hurry, Mom," Jeff said.

Marty took off at a run for the downstairs coat closet, where she thought she'd stashed the gloves and winter hats. She was in luck. She grabbed a pair of thick leather gloves and was on her way upstairs when she heard Jeff roar, "Nooooooo!"

Marty ran into the room in time to see the last of Stumpy's tail vanish through the screen just as Jeff threw open the window and leaped for him. Jeff's hand punched through the screen, widening the hole.

Marty stood beside Jeff and watched. Stumpy had jumped to the porch roof a few feet below. From there he scurried to the far end and leaped, landing on a branch of the big maple. Once on the maple, he went up instead of down, stopping on a level with Jeff's window and peering at them.

"I think he's laughing at us," Jeff said.

"He certainly seems well enough to be on his own."

The ringing of the phone sent Marty dashing downstairs to the kitchen, wondering why her dad didn't answer the phone in his room. Surely, all the noise had wakened him from his nap.

"Hello," Marty said breathlessly into the receiver.

"Bertie, here. Who's this?"

"Hi, Aunt Bertie, it's Marty," she said, snagging a chair with her toe and pulling it over near the wall phone. She flopped onto the chair. She stopped herself from asking, "What's the matter?" even though the only time Bertie called anyone was when she had something to complain about.

"I might as well just come right out with it, Marty. No sense in beating around the bush." Marty heard her suck in her breath and could imagine the frown on her face and the furrows in her brow. "Renee is terribly hurt that you went all the way into the mall to get your hair cut. I mean, she's your kin, Marty, and if you don't trust her enough to do your hair, then why should other people?"

Marty ran a hand through the hair that had just been cut the day before. The county hot line was obviously operating at full speed. As Aunt Bertie continued to babble on about the deep levels of disappointment and betrayal felt by her only child, Marty soaked up the guilt her aunt was dishing. Still, after the last disaster Renee had wrought on her head, why should she give her another chance? Mama used to say that a 'less than perfect haircut' was a small price to pay for family peace, but Marty didn't see it that way.

"Now you know Renee would just die if she knew I called you, so mum's the word."

Marty could see Annie coming down the hill from the barn. Annie was due for a trim; she thought about making an appointment for her, but then decided she couldn't do that to a kid about to start a new school. "I'm sorry, Aunt Bertie. I'll make it up to her. I never thought..." Then anger hit. "Listen, Aunt Bertie, I have to be honest. Renee gave me a really lousy haircut last time."

Only silence came across the receiver until Marty heard Aunt Bertie suck in another noisy lungful of air and then laugh. "I know," Aunt Bertie said, chuckling. "Look, Renee does fine if you tell her exactly how you want your hair. Just be real clear with her and for my sake, give her one more chance, all right? I don't want my daughter hurt, but neither do I want my niece prancing around town looking like some silly French poodle."

"Oh, Aunt Bertie, you're something else," Marty said.

"And you've always been a good girl, Marty, so I know you'll do this. Family has to stick together, miss. And just to show that I practice what I preach, I want to be your first volunteer in this new enterprise of yours."

"Do you mean the Therapeutic Riding Center?" Marty had trouble imagining Bertie helping out with the horses.

"Yes, I do. Everyone in town is talking about what a wonderful thing this is and how lucky you are to have a backer like Mr. Marcus. I was a bit surprised to hear you'd taken a booth to sign up volunteers on Community Day and didn't call me first. I may be retired, but I still do the books for Renee's salon and I certainly can do them for your Center."

"Thank you, Aunt Bertie," Marty said, for once meaning it. She'd been worried about how she'd handle the mountains of paperwork. "But you know what this will mean—you'll have to see my father once in a while."

"Now if I can tolerate that for the sake of family, you can survive an occasional bad haircut."

Marty heard the distinct rumble of Duke's car engine and saw him pull up to the porch. Aunt Bertie was giving her advice about keeping Duke's paws off the profits and about how to most efficiently run a business, any business. But Marty was preoccupied, wondering just what Duke had been up to this time. He had definitely sneaked away, leaving her to think he was still napping.

She saw Annie run to greet her grandfather just as he pulled a large cage from the car. When Marty saw what it contained, at least four white Peking ducks, she was glad Bertie was still running a monologue and she didn't have to answer. Complaining to her aunt about her father would only have added fuel to Bertie's fire.

When she managed to get her aunt off the phone, Marty hurried out to the creek where Duke was freeing the ducks. There were two downy yellow ducklings that she hadn't seen from the house. "Dad, you're turning this place into a zoo." The ducks, with their noisy quacks and frantic wing flapping, seemed to be scolding him, too.

"I told you I was hungry for duck eggs. Remember the ducks we used to have when your mother was alive—enough for all the eggs we wanted and an occasional roaster for the oven?" Duke beamed at the latest additions to their growing menagerie.

Marty just shook her head. Of course, she remembered. She remembered all the fights over who was going to slaughter the roaster ducks. Duke never could make himself do it and the job always fell to Mama. Marty shivered remembering how Mama had wrung their thin necks with a swift jerk of her strong hands. Like Mama, Marty usually managed to do what she had to do. The difference was that Marty didn't have to wring a duck's neck to eat, so she knew she couldn't do it. And Duke had only an occasional hankering for duck eggs; they were too gritty for everyday use. If the foxes didn't carry off some of the hatchlings, they could very well be up to their kneecaps in feathers and duck manure within a few years.

She had a vision of hundreds of ducks bobbing on the creek and eating along the banks; in the background, dozens of sway-backed, crippled horses grazing in the fields. Derry was right. She had to get tougher.

Kyle arrived as she was putting dinner on the table and announced that they had finished the renovation job early and would be able to start on her indoor arena on Monday. Marty gave him a hug and an extra helping of meatloaf and mashed potatoes.

"What time are you leaving for the roping?" she asked.

"I'm not going," he said around a mouthful of food. "It's supposed to rain and..." He took a big drink of milk. "And, anyway, I'm taking Kristen to Pittsburgh. We're going to the Wild West Dance Hall and Saloon, so I can teach her the two-step."

"Yeah, right," Jeff laughed. "She looks like she could teach you a step or two."

"Hey, preppy boy, you could learn something from your old uncle. Women love cowboys," Kyle said with a wink.

"Kyle, you behave yourself with her. She's a nice girl," Marty scolded.

"For Pete's sake, Marty, I'm not Jack the Ripper. I'm not even much of a Don Juan. Lately, I've been as celibate as a hermit monk on a mountaintop," Kyle complained. "I know how to behave around a lady."

Later, cleaned up in a freshly starched shirt and sharp creased jeans, his silver trophy buckle gleaming from his belt, Kyle looked like the gentleman cowboy as he drove off to pick up Kristen. "Lord, don't let him mess this up," Marty prayed, not just because she liked Kristen and thought she would be good for Kyle, but because Kristen, at this point, was the creative drive behind the Center.

After she'd done the dishes, Marty sat with Duke on the porch, Cody and Jake by their chairs. Annie perched on the steps with Bella, who had become quite attached to her. The ducks quacked and grumbled as they searched for shelter for the night. Inside, Jeff was talking to Cam on the phone, explaining about the escaped Stumpy. She looked up to see her father wiping his eyes. "Dad, what's the matter?"

"Nothing's wrong. I'm just so happy. This place is a home again. I've been plumb miserable and lonely these last years without your Mama. Don't get me wrong. I'll always miss her something terrible, but I'm not so empty anymore."

Marty went over and sat next to him on the couch, laying her head on his shoulder. "I'm glad, Dad," she said. She wasn't as empty as she had been either, but neither was she full. Something was still missing and she wasn't even sure what it was.

T H I R T Y

About midnight, it started to rain, a hard steady rain from the southeast. Marty lay awake and counted the seconds between flashes of lightning and the thunder. One... two... three. The storm wasn't even directly over them yet. They were supposed to get the tail end of the tropical storms that had been drenching Florida and Georgia all week.

Thunder boomed much closer this time. Cody gave a whine and jumped into bed on top of her. "Cody, this bed isn't big enough for both of us." She tried to shove him off, but he whined and leaned into her. She could feel him trembling.

She pushed and prodded until he stretched out enough to make room for her. With his head under her chin and her arm around his shoulder, she finally fell asleep to the sound of his rhythmic breathing.

Marty woke in the morning to the sound of rain still hitting the windows. The rain kept up its steady drumming all morning. While Annie and Duke fretted over the ducks, walking the swollen creek bank until all six were accounted for, Marty paced the house like a caged tiger, looking out the windows and praying for a letup in the rain. Jeff was the only one not disgruntled. The rain had brought Stumpy back. The poor squirrel was huddled between the window and the screen, stuffing himself with the seeds Jeff had put there. He ate and left but Jeff put out more food, sure he'd be back.

Marty's mood was as dark as the clouds when Cam arrived just after lunch. He brought a new patient for Jeff, a small fur ball that he pulled from a pet carrier. The small raccoon climbed up Cam's arm to sit on his shoulder and stare at the rest of them with round scared eyes. "Somebody made a pet of him and then moved, leaving him chained to the porch. A neighbor called the police when some thugs started using him for BB gun practice. The police brought him to me."

"Great!" Marty said sarcastically. "And you brought him to us."

"I figured you had room for him, since Stumpy took off," Cam said with a grin.

"Stumpy's back," Jeff said. He told Cam the story.

"Well, what do you think about taking on this fellow? I've pried some BBs out of his hide. Other than keeping antibiotic cream on the wounds and giving him a lot of good food and water, he won't take much care." Both Cam and Jeff looked at Marty and Cam turned on the Brady smile. "Come on, Marty. Jeff will do the work and I really don't have time for this one. I've got three redtail hawks, a barn owl, a fawn, and a mother possum and her babies all recuperating at my place."

"I'll probably regret this, but all right," she said, shaking her head in mock exasperation. "Let's see. I've got four horses, a pony, a goat, and three kittens in the barn, six ducks out by the creek, three dogs that roam at will, a squirrel on the windowsill, and now a racoon in Jeff's room. I was only teasing when I said this before, but if it keeps raining, we really will have to build an ark. When you're talking to God, you might remind him that I've got an arena to build here."

It did keep raining on and off all weekend and throughout the next week, delaying the start of the indoor arena. Marty kept a wary eye on the creek. She remembered only a few times when it had flooded, rushing into the dip at the end of the road and leaving them unable to get out of their valley for a day or two. Just in case, Marty made a trip to the grocery store and stocked up on enough food and supplies to keep them for a week. Kyle did the same without checking with her, so they were well supplied for any emergency. But the idea of the arena construction being delayed rankled her. "Okay, God, please, enough is enough," she grumbled.

By Saturday morning it seemed as if the rain was over. The creek rushed by, filled to the top of its banks, but the clouds had disappeared, leaving the August sun shining out of a bright blue sky. It didn't rain again all weekend and by Monday morning, the muddy creek no longer threatened to spill over its banks.

Marty took Jeff to his first day of band practice at the high school and when she returned Kyle's work crew had arrived to start on the arena. The rest of the week she spent feeding them. It seemed every time she turned around, they needed food or drink. It amazed her that they were able to work at all, given the amount of beer they consumed. But she managed to ignore their dirty boot prints in her kitchen and cleaned up after them with a smile. She just wanted to keep them working, wanted to hear the sound of their steady sawing and hammering and shouting of instructions to one another.

Every time she looked up the hill she saw their progress. The center had finally sprung off the drawing board into wood and steel reality. Each post that went up seemed to her like a dream turned real; she'd make sure that dream was realized, no matter how many sandwiches she had to make or footprints she needed to clean or workmen she had to cajole back to work.

By the end of the week another storm, this one upgraded to a hurricane, had hit the Florida coast and was heading north, due to reach them over the weekend. On Thursday, as the workers lingered over a three-beer lunch, Marty said, "If you guys could get the roof on before the rain hits, then you wouldn't have to stop work. I mean, maybe the rain won't hit again until some-time next week. If you worked through the weekend—"

"Sis, we're going as fast as we can," Kyle said. "We all have weekend plans. And, anyway, it will take longer than another week to finish the roof."

When Friday dawned bright and clear, Marty breathed a sigh of relief, but Jeff was disgruntled. The band had only twenty kids in it and most of them were on drums. He'd been moved to sax-ophone, because he'd had several years training. Marty sat with him on the porch waiting for Amy and Joel's daughter, Casey, to pick him up for band practice. "Man…" Jeff complained, "I could use a break from our march, march, march, drill, drill, drill band practice. You'd think that garbage was more important than the music. The drill team is supposed to practice with us today, so that won't be bad."

"Because Rachel's on the drill team, right?" Marty asked. She grabbed Jeff and ruffled his hair just as Casey's car came around the bend in the lane.

"Aw, Mom," Jeff said, smoothing his hair as he ran to meet Casey.

Later as she stacked a mountain of sandwiches on a tray for the crew's lunch, Marty heard Casey's car pull up, laughter and then Jeff racing up the porch steps. He rushed into the kitchen and grabbed a ham and cheese sandwich before flopping down on a chair at the table.

"Hi," Marty said, absently.

"Today," Jeff said dramatically, "practice was so awful it was funny. The drill team is even worse than we are. Rachel's really good, but she's had years of dance, and Renee's twins, my chubby cousins, are all right. But the rest of them..." He took another bite of his sandwich. "And I got to see our uniforms today—white polyester with ratty navy and gold trim." Jeff started to laugh.

Marty reached for another loaf of bread.

"Mom, aren't you listening to me?"

Marty turned from her sandwich making. "I was listening. I'm just distracted with the construction going on and worrying about the rain starting up again. But I'm proud of you, Jeff. You're being very grown-up about this," Marty said.

"No, I hate it. I'm laughing because Rachel's drill team uniform is even worse. Get this—they wear navy blue polyester jumpers well below their knees, white button-down shirts, ankle socks, and navy orthopedic shoes."

"Well, I'm proud of you, but not for laughing at the girls; you're really trying to be happy here, aren't you?"

Jeff shrugged. "I'm doing all right. There are a lot of nice kids here. There are also more than a few rednecks, but I don't need to hang out with them. And wait until you hear this... Casey, Hap Hopwood, and me and two other kids are going to start a jazz band. Isn't that cool? Hap really plays a mean trumpet and I'm getting pretty good on the sax. I said we could practice here. That's okay, isn't it?"

Marty just nodded. Maybe they wouldn't start until life

around the place calmed down a little. She sure didn't see that happening any time soon. Not with her running to McFarland two nights a week to give lessons with Joanne, having to feed and supervise this work crew, the extra cleaning because of the wet ground, the care of the growing menagerie as well as the stress caused by the constant din of hammering, not to mention her efforts to keep that going.

"Great," Jeff said, and ran to the phone. He dialed and Marty heard him say, "Casey, we're on for this afternoon."

Marty groaned, but Jeff didn't seem to hear her. He grabbed another sandwich off the plate and poured himself a glass of milk.

"I'm going to get out of here before the 'good ol' boys' hit. I need to spend some time with Herman anyway. I know he's just a racoon and this sounds weird, but he's been acting depressed." Jeff charged out of the kitchen and Marty could hear him taking the steps two at a time. "Hey, Mom," he called from upstairs, "make sure we've got plenty of pop and chips and stuff."

Marty frowned and grabbed her purse. As much as she didn't want to have to run to the store, it beat standing around while the work crew ate and guzzled beer. She passed them coming up the porch steps on her way out. "Food's on the table," she said. "I've got to run to the store."

She walked around the side of the house and called, "Annie!" No answer. She walked around to the back of the house and saw Annie and Duke walking the creek bank up near the woods. "Hey, you two," she hollered.

"Either something is getting the eggs or these lazy bums aren't laying," Duke grumbled, as they came toward Marty.

"Dad, you've become obsessed with this," Marty said.

"Well, doggone it, I paid good money for layers."

Marty shook her head. "Annie, I have to run to the store. Jeff is having some friends over this afternoon and I have to stock up on some pop and snacks. Want to come along?"

"If Jeff's having friends over, can I invite Jen and Kika?"

"It's wonderful how the kids have just jumped right into things here, isn't it, Marty?" Duke said.

Marty had been about to say, "Not today," but her dad was right; she had to encourage them to bring friends home. "All right," she said. "Run and call them."

An hour and a half later Marty drove back up the lane, three little girls in the backseat and grocery bags in the trunk. She entered the kitchen, her arms loaded with bags, to find the crew still at lunch. "It's Friday, Marty," Kyle said. "We always take an extra half-hour or so for lunch on Friday."

Marty put her hands on her hips and glared at him. Maybe he thought he was funny, but she didn't. She was the one who would suffer if the arena wasn't done on time, not just in loss of income, but in stress and embarrassment. "You'll be happy to know it's getting cloudy. If you're really lucky, it will start to pour and you won't have to work until Monday," she said.

"Gee, Dad," Kyle said, "you're right; she's getting more like Aunt Bertie every day." Kyle turned to his friends. "You know my aunt, Bertie Crawford. She's so bossy she tells God how to run the world."

Marty left the room and went upstairs to her room, only to be ousted within a few minutes by Annie and the girls. "We were out looking for duck eggs, Mom," Annie said, "but it started to rain."

Marty looked out the window and could see the splashes as large drops fell on the creek. "Great!" she mumbled. She saw the ducks waddle up the bank for the shelter of the bushes by the unused porch steps. No wonder Annie and Duke hadn't found their nests.

She heard the distant rumble of thunder as the rain fell harder. "Okay, girls," Marty said, "I'll clear out of here."

She stopped to see Jeff. "What time are your friends due?"

"Any time now, Mom. Kyle and the 'good ol' boys' will be gone, won't they?" Jeff sat on his bed with Herman curled in his lap. Stumpy scurried up to the window and peeked in. Raucous laughter sailed up the steps from the kitchen.

"I hope so, honey," Marty said. "I'll be in the living room."

Marty went downstairs and slipped into the living room without anyone noticing her. She picked up the novel she'd been reading the night before and curled up in her favorite armchair. The rain beat against the windows, whipping itself into another summer storm.

Marty heard the dogs whining at the kitchen door and someone get up to let them in. The basement door creaked and she heard the dogs run down the wooden steps. When she looked up, Cody was peering pitifully at her over the guard gate at the living room door. "Scoot, Cody," Marty said. "You aren't allowed in here."

"Cody!" Kyle called. "Get downstairs!" He came up behind the dog and grabbed him by the collar. "Hey, Sis," Kyle said, "you could come and have a beer with us, you know."

"No, thank you," she snapped.

"Look, if we could be out there working we would be, but we can't, so what's the harm of us sitting around and having a few beers? Huh?"

Marty surveyed her brother's heavy eyelids, ruddy cheeks, and the lock of hair that looped close to one eye. He'd had more than a few. A knock sounded on the kitchen door. Marty jumped to her feet. Cody gave a bark, echoed by the two dogs in the basement. "Jeff is having friends over. Please try to behave. No teasing him, got it?" She pushed past Kyle and Cody and opened the door for Casey and a young black man who looked vaguely familiar.

"Mrs. Harris," Casey said, "this is Michael Hopwood, Jr., known as Hap to his friends. He's a trumpet-player extraordinaire!"

"Yes, I see the resemblance to your father who was a friend of mine in high school," Marty said. "Welcome to our home."

Another car pulled up the lane and stopped. Two more boys carrying instrument cases and a girl ran for the cover of the porch. Jeff let them in and then led everyone up to his room.

Later, when Marty went into the kitchen to get herself a cup of tea, the phone rang. Marty warned the men to lower their voices and grabbed the receiver. Darla sounded worried on the other end. "How high's the creek out your way?" she asked. "Someone was just in from over by Long Creek and said it's running full to its banks."

"Let me look," Marty said and looked out the dining room window. She came back to the phone. "Ours is running fast and muddy, but well below the banks."

"Tell you what, Marty," Darla said, as the line started to crackle. "I'm going to come out there and get Jen and Kika, so you don't end up stuck with them for the weekend."

Darla arrived in a short time and announced that a flash-flood warning had been issued for most of the streams and creeks in the area. That pretty much cleared the place out except for two of the work crew, Pete and the young kid, who had started to play poker and apparently felt no urgency about getting home. Jeff's friends thanked Marty for letting them practice there. She heard Jeff asking them back for the next day.

"God willing and the creek don't rise," Casey yelled over her shoulder, as she dashed out into the storm.

T H I R T Y - O N E

In the middle of the night, Annie started to cry in her sleep. "Annie, wake up," Marty said. She sat on the bed beside Annie who held her stomach and rocked back and forth, kicking free her sheet. "Wake up, Annie. You're having a bad dream."

"I'm not dreaming, Mom. My stomach hurts."

Marty switched on the bedside lamp. Annie's face was flushed, but she didn't feel feverish. "Maybe you just have to go to the bathroom," Marty offered.

Annie curled into a fetal position, holding her stomach. "It hurts, Mom... bad."

Marty rolled Annie over onto her back. "Show me where it hurts, Annie."

Annie pointed to the middle of her stomach and her lower belly.

"Not more on one side than another?"

Annie shook her head. Marty mentally ruled out appendicitis and figured Annie was probably coming down with an intestinal virus. The fever was no doubt on the way, by the flush of her cheeks.

She found a fever reducer in the bathroom and gave it to Annie with a cup of water. "Now just sip the water, honey."

Annie rolled away from Marty toward the wall. "Rub my back, Mom. It hurts, too." And so Marty rubbed Annie's back, just like Mama used to do to her when she was a sick little girl in this very room. Annie whimpered a few more times before falling into a restless sleep. Marty turned the light off and crawled back into her own bed.

But sleep didn't come as easily to Marty. She tossed and turned and listened to the rain hitting the roof and the side of the house. She turned the light back on and picked up Mama's Bible. She opened it to Psalms and started to read until she finally fell asleep.

"Mom!" Annie screamed, jarring Marty awake just in time to

see Annie leap from the bed and vomit all over the floor.

Glad she'd left the light on, Marty helped Annie into the bathroom. She cried softly and shivered as Marty cleaned her up. "It's all right, sweetie. You've got a virus. Just try to relax and ride it out. Mom's here." She carried Annie back into the bedroom wrapped in a towel. Although the night was warm, Annie kept shivering. Marty dressed her in a pair of light flannel pajamas before tucking her back into bed.

"Thanks, Mom," Annie said. "I think I feel a little better."

"Maybe something you ate didn't agree with you and now you're rid of it," Marty said, heading out of the room for a bucket and rags to clean up the mess.

But before dawn, Annie vomited again and by eight o'clock the next morning she'd started with diarrhea. Marty called Doc Harbison, who had been their family doctor since she'd been a kid and had seen the Staffords through all kinds of illnesses.

"Marty, good to hear from you," he said. "Kyle told me you were back. What can I do for you?"

Marty explained about Annie.

"I've had a couple of calls over the last couple of days about kids with the same symptoms. Just a stomach virus. Clear liquids… a lot of sleep… You know the routine, I'm sure."

"Thanks, Doc," Marty said.

"Sure thing. Glad to have you back."

Even though Annie vomited a couple of more times before lunch and continued to have diarrhea, Marty wasn't worried. Doc Harbison was rarely wrong.

Kyle left midmorning for a roping in Ohio. "I'll be back late tonight or tomorrow," he said. "Now, Sis, you're sure you don't care if I go?"

"There's nothing you can do here; and if the creek does flood, we have plenty of food to get us through a week or more. Come on, we've never been stranded more than a few days."

Kyle gave her a hug before he loaded Red onto the trailer and drove off.

Gayle called in the afternoon to see how they were doing and to give the local flood report. Quite a few of the streams were over their banks with no sign of the rain letting up. Marty assured Gayle that their creek was still contained, but she hadn't been out to the end of the road to check the low spot.

"I saw your neighbors across the way this morning at the store and they were stocking up. Said their creek is running real high and so is yours down where the two come together by the iron bridge."

"I have plenty of food to last out the weekend, even beyond if I have to," Marty said. "I had forgotten this side of country living—being totally at the mercy of nature."

"Come on, Marty, lighten up. In the city you'd be worrying about crime and pollution."

"Right now, a little filth and crime seems preferable to this chaos," Marty murmured. "Don't pay any attention to me. I'm just in a foul mood. I don't think I'd be worried at all, except that Annie has some kind of a virus and is throwing up."

"I saw Darla this morning at the store and she said Jen is sick, too. Sounds like a kid thing," Gayle said.

"That makes me feel better," Marty said. "They were together yesterday, so that confirms Doc's diagnosis of a virus." She heard Annie's footsteps charging toward the bathroom overhead. "Oh, no, Gayle, there she goes again. I'll call you later."

By late afternoon Annie was no better. Marty still wouldn't have been terribly concerned except that Annie couldn't keep even liquids down.

Even Jeff stopped teasing Annie, and in what Marty read as an act of concern, he agreed to feed the barn animals. He took off into the deluge wrapped in a slicker and rubber boots.

Duke, who never did deal well with illness, spent the day watching television in his room to avoid hearing Annie in the bathroom.

Jeff came in from the barn with bad news. "The creek's flooded down by the bridge, Mom. I could see it from the barn, but I walked down to take a closer look and the road's closed, too. It looks like water's up to the bottom of the bridge and the dip by our lane is completely under water. I think the feeder creek flooded it, because ours is still holding behind the house."

After dinner Marty walked down and took a look. The flooding was more extensive than Jeff had described. On the other side of the iron bridge, she saw a couple of police officers barricading the road. Marty must have been easy to see standing on the hillside in her bright yellow slicker, because one of the officers picked up a megaphone. "Hello, you—in the Stafford place! You can't get out this way. The upper road is under water on both ends. You guys are cut off. Are you all right?" he called.

"So far!" Marty yelled, cupping her hands to be heard above the din of the rain. She gave an exaggerated nod in case they hadn't heard her.

"Phone if you need us," he called back.

A few hours later, as Marty sat on the edge of her bed and read to Annie, she was startled by a resounding crack followed by a crash which shook the house. Cody jumped from the rug between the bed into Marty's lap. She pushed him to the floor and hurried to the window. A huge locust tree, long dead, had fallen from the sodden hillside above the creek behind the house. The top of the tree had crashed into the yard in a great splintering of branches.

Annie started to cry. "I'm scared," she said.

"It's just an old dead tree, honey. The ground got too wet to hold its roots and over it went."

"I don't care about the tree. I'm afraid the creek's going to flood."

"Even if it does, the water probably won't reach the house; but if it did, we'd move to the barn. It would never get there," Marty assured her.

In the middle of the night, Bella's barking awakened Marty. She hurried downstairs with Cody right on her heels and threw open the cellar door. Bella and Jake rushed into the kitchen. When she flipped on the light, she saw that water had seeped into the basement.

In her nightgown and rubber boots, Marty sloshed through the inch or two of water, pulling everything she could reach out of danger. Fortunately they'd learned long ago not to leave things on the basement floor. Ground water sometimes came up through the drain pipes, but never more than a few inches. Since the water level didn't seem to be rising dramatically, Marty saw no need to do anything more than place things high out of harm's way.

Then she flipped on all the outside lights and slipped a slicker on over her nightgown. Cody whined and tried to push past her at the door, but she ordered him back and went out to check the creek. The wind blew steadily out of the southeast, driving the rain before it. The creek had breached its banks. The torrent roared past, carrying branches and debris, swirling around the rocks as it surged away from her. Marty's heart pounded. She'd never seen the creek this high or wild. She forced a few deep breaths, loosening her chest muscles. The house still wasn't in danger—not yet anyway.

The wind whipped her slicker around her as she hurried back to the house. When she entered the kitchen, she could hear Annie crying. She ran upstairs and into the bathroom. Annie had had another painful bout of diarrhea, but this time, it was streaked with blood.

THIRTY-TWO

M arty told herself that the blood was nothing more than irritation or maybe a broken blood vessel. She tried to get Annie to drink ginger ale in tiny sips, but she vomited it up immediately. Dry heaves replaced the vomiting. Fearful of dehydration, Marty tried to get Annie to chew on some ice chips, but they brought on more dry heaves. All night long Annie tossed, hardly sleeping, crying out in pain when painful bowel spasms hit.

Marty prayed with Annie, hoping her prayer of, "Lord, we know you will not let any harm come to Annie," would reassure her small daughter. Silently she begged, "Lord, heal my Annie. She's little and scared and doesn't deserve this pain." By morning Annie tossed listlessly on the bed, barely able to respond to Marty's questions. Her eyes were glazed and sunken, her lips chalky white and chapped. Her face was bright red and she felt warm. Marty took her temperature—102°.

Marty went to the phone to call Doc Harbison. She picked up the receiver but didn't get a dial tone. She jiggled the carriage. Nothing. She ran upstairs and pounded on her father's door. Without waiting for his answer, she ran in. "Dad, let me try your phone. The one in the kitchen's not working and Annie's worse. I need to call the doctor." She tried Duke's phone. Nothing. She slammed it down. "The phones are out."

Her heart raced and so did her mind. What could she do? They were marooned and she needed advice. She looked into her father's face which had suddenly gone pasty pale. "Go back to sleep, Dad," she said, forcing her voice to sound calm. "The other day Doc said this was just a virus and I'm sure that's all it is. We'll just weather it through." She patted his arm and hurried from his room, confident that he had never awakened fully and would soon be asleep. She didn't need to add his panic to her own.

In the room she shared with Annie, she sat on the edge of her bed watching her tiny daughter's flushed face. She wrapped her arms around herself and rocked. She could almost hear Dan scolding her for bringing his children here. If she'd have stayed in Washington, Annie would have already seen one of the best pediatricians in the city.

Marty pressed her palms hard against her eyes and tried to think. There had to be something she could do. There was no sense in trying any fever reduction medicine; Annie would just vomit it up. A bath! Marty ran a tub full of cool water and carried Annie in to soak in it. That lowered her temperature some, but within an hour it started to climb again.

Outside the rain kept on, not as heavy as the day before, but enough to make the creek a wild series of rapids carrying off everything in their path. Jeff went to feed the animals so that Marty wouldn't have to leave Annie. When he came back he reported that the bridge deck was completely under water and a huge sycamore had come off the hillside right across the far side of it.

"Jeff, was there anyone down near the bridge?"

"I didn't see anybody, Mom," Jeff said.

"Here's a flashlight, Jeff. Please go back down there. If you see anyone, even someone surveying the damage in a plane or helicopter, try to signal them. We need help here."

Jeff charged back out into the rain and Marty began to bombard heaven with her prayers. "Please, Lord, You've taken Dan. Don't take Annie from me, too."

In her room, Annie slept fitfully, crying out and curling into a fetal position whenever a spasm hit. Marty heard something behind her and saw Duke, his face chalk white. "I've seen the creek. Our princess is real sick, isn't she?"

Marty nodded. "I don't think this is just a virus, or if it is, it's a bad one. She's dehydrating. I need to get her to a doctor."

Duke came out into the hall and stood by Marty. He looked in at Annie and Marty saw his hands shaking.

"All right," he said, taking a deep breath. "I'll carry her out."

"Dad, don't be ridiculous. That's not our gentle creek anymore. It'd carry both you and Annie to your deaths, if not by drowning then by battering you against the rocks."

"There's got to be something we can use to bridge the creek and get over onto the hillside. From there it wouldn't be such a hard climb out to Morgans. The back road should be clear to the hospital."

Marty hugged her father. "Dad, you can't do it. I'm going to try to ride out. Sass isn't reliable and Glory's too feeble. I'll take Grandma. But I'm going to leave Annie here with you and Jeff. I'll try to get to the old Wilson place on the upper road. Maybe their phone is working and I can call for an air ambulance. Please tell me Washington Hospital uses one."

"Sure, they've got one, but the Wilson place has been boarded up for the last three years. There's not another house on that road between here and the creeks—ours on one end and Long Creek on the other. We've got to go over the hillside to Gayle's."

Marty glared at her father. What did he expect her to do? Fly out over the cliffside to Gayle and Mac's? An idea hit her with the force of a punch to the solar plexus. She couldn't fly, but maybe there was another way. Marty ran to the window and looked at the fallen tree. "I'll be right back," she said. She grabbed her slicker and ran out into the storm for a closer look at that tree. The creek still roared through the valley and the rain beat on out of a sky as dark as twilight.

Jeff followed her into the backyard. "Mom, don't be crazy."

"What's crazy, Jeff? The trunk of that tree is out of the water. I'll climb out that way."

"Mom, what are you going to do if the Morgans' phone is out, too?"

That hadn't even occurred to her. "I'll take Annie with me. There are no major streams between their place and the hospital. Gayle can drive us there."

Marty got as close as she dared to the wildly rushing water. The tree had grown halfway up the hillside and had fallen so that the trunk lay at a gradual angle to the yard below. With Annie tied to her back, she could probably climb it without too much trouble. But most of the bark had long ago peeled away, leaving a trunk of smooth wood, sure to be slippery.

"Can't do it, Mom," Jeff said.

"I know," she mumbled. "But I have to try something."

"Kyle's ladder," Jeff yelled.

"What?"

"Come on, Mom," Jeff called over his shoulder, as he ran toward the barn.

Kyle had left his forty-foot aluminum ladder where he'd been using it on the construction of the arena. Together Marty and Jeff carried it down to the house. They found a place where the bank was high. The creek normally only twelve feet across had swollen to twenty. But still, this place was narrower than anywhere else. By wedging the bottom of the ladder against the trunk of a tree just out of reach of the water, the top hit low on the hillside, but well above the torrent. Marty hugged Jeff. "I can do that, Jeff. I know I can."

"Mom, let me go. I'm stronger than you are."

"No, honey, no. I have to do it. I'll put Annie on my back and climb right out of here."

She ran into the house and explained the plan to Duke. "Marty, let me take her. I'm the man of the house. I think I could make it without much trouble."

Marty took his trembling hands in hers. She looked into his face which was still pasty, but now with a grayish tint. His chest rose and fell as he struggled to get enough air. "Dad, you're not strong enough. You'd never make it. Jeff thinks he should go, but you and I both know he's too young. I have to do it."

Duke buried his face in his hands and cried. "I'm sorry, Marty. If I were younger, I'd be able to make it."

"I know, Dad, it's okay. I really need you to stay here and take care of Jeff and the house and the animals," Marty said, ushering him out of the room.

She pulled a warm sweatsuit on Annie, heavy socks and tennis shoes. Annie didn't seem to understand what was happening and whimpered as Marty dressed her. She felt terribly hot and was obviously too weak to help Marty by holding on. She put Annie in her purple hooded slicker and almost cried at the contrast her white face made against it. "Jeff," she called, lifting Annie from the bed.

"Here, Mom," Jeff said, running into the room. "Listen, I wedged the other end of the ladder under some rocks on the far side. I tried the first couple of rungs. It's real stable. Let me go, please."

"Jeff, no! I can make it. I know I can."

"All right, let me carry her and you come with us. That hillside is steep, Mom, and wet."

Marty put her arms around him and hugged him tight. "Jeff, if you go your grandfather might try it and he'd have a heart attack. He's already looking pale and gray. I need you here to keep an eye on him and to feed the animals." She took his face in her hands, kissed his cheek and said, "I'm counting on you."

Tears rimmed Jeff's eyes, but he blinked them back. "You'll be fine, Mom. You're strong and so is Annie. And Grandpap and I will be all right."

"That's the spirit, Jeff. Now get me a couple of sheets... the ones we use on Grandpap's double bed. Hurry." She carried Annie downstairs followed by Duke and Cody. "Dad, hold her a minute," she said, handing Annie to her father. She grabbed Kyle's lined jean jacket from the closet. It would be easier to climb in than her slicker and less slippery against Annie. Jeff ran down the steps with the sheets.

"Here, Dad, stand Annie here and hold onto her."

Annie whimpered slightly and Cody whined and pawed at Duke's leg. "Cody, quiet! Sit!" Marty commanded. Cody did but Bella took up the whining in the kitchen as the rain started to hit harder against the side the house.

Marty kissed Annie's forehead. "Be brave, sweetheart," she said, but her own heart pounded hard all the way to the back of her throat. She wrapped the sheets around Annie, between her legs, around her arms, making a sling for her seat. She tied tight knots as she went until she had what looked like a large version of the backcarrier she'd used to tote Annie around as an infant. "Dad, lift her high onto my back," Marty said. "Jeff, bring the sheets over my shoulders, cross them over my chest and tie them behind, under Annie if you can."

The sheets just reached, but Jeff tied the knots tight. "They'll hold, Mom," he said, giving them another pull.

"Good, Jeff. Now take the bottom corners and tie them around my waist." Jeff did as he was told. "Annie," Marty said. "Hold on around my neck, if you can." Annie's thin arms circled Marty's neck limply.

She walked out into the rain and shivered, but not from cold. She could hear the roar of the creek and the wind moan through the treetops. She set her jaw and strode to the ladder. Annie was a light weight, too light.

Jeff hugged her and kissed Annie's cheek. Duke hugged and kissed both Marty and Annie while Jeff checked to make sure the ladder was still secure. Before she could reconsider, Marty started to climb. The wet rubber of her tennis shoe soles slipped against the metal rungs of the ladder, slowing her. Marty looked down. The turbulent water ran brown and frothy underneath her. Her arms and legs shook as she climbed faster. "I can do this!" she repeated over and over, making her arms and legs respond.

Behind her she heard Jeff yell. She looked over her shoulder to see Cody leap from the bank into the stream. Instantly, he was dragged under and then popped up again, his legs pumping furiously before he disappeared behind a boulder.

She put her face down on her arm and cried. Crazy dog. She saw him resurface again farther down stream. His body slammed into an exposed rock and then again he was gone from view. Her stomach seemed to plunge into the water below, but she kept climbing. Halfway across the span, Marty's foot slipped off a rung just as she was reaching for a higher one. She fell onto her stomach against the ladder and froze. This time a quaking started in her knees, spread down and then up her legs, over back, up her arms. Below her the water rolled, tearing bushes and branches from the banks, swirling around the boulders, making whirlpools that could drown them in an instant after smashing them against the rocks. Marty squeezed her eyes shut. One large tree branch tearing down the valley could hit the ladder and throw them into the water. Behind her she could hear Jeff and Duke yelling to her, but she couldn't make out their words.

She knew they were telling her to keep going, but she couldn't. She couldn't move. The rain beat down on her and Annie. Through the coat and the sheets and all their clothing, she could feel the heat of Annie's fever. Still she couldn't move. Why had she ever thought she could do this? She and Annie were going to die and it was her fault. Her fault for ever coming back to this God-forsaken place.

A tiny voice in her ear whispered, "The Lord is a shepherd, Mommy…" and then it faded away.

"Yea, though I walk through the valley of the shadow of death, I will fear no evil," she muttered the words over and over to herself, until they began to make sense. "Surely only goodness and mercy shall follow me all the days of my life," she finished. Marty stopped shaking. She took a deep breath. "Lord, forgive me my pride," she said aloud. "We are yours and are in your hands. Lead me, please, for my daughter's sake, if not my own. I can't do this myself."

Marty reached above her head without looking and found a higher rung. Her foot found the next level. She climbed with her eyes shut, whispering only, "Jesus, my Lord and my God." She was startled by a bark close to her ear. She opened her eyes. Cody stood wet and bedraggled on the bank just above her. Only a few more steps and she'd be off the ladder.

She reached for the pup's collar and he braced himself as if he understood what she needed, as she pulled herself and her daughter from the ladder to the hillside. Just above her a worn deer path criss-crossed the hillside and would provide a way to the top. Cody's warm wet tongue slapped across her face. She wrapped her arms around his neck, kissing his forehead.

Quickly she shut her eyes and bowed her head. "My Lord Jesus, I thank you, with all that I am, for delivering us." Still she couldn't shake the feeling that something even more important than crossing a flood had occurred on the ladder. She could think about that later. Right now she had to get help for Annie. Although her legs and back ached, she began to scale the hillside.

THIRTY-THREE

Marty stood on the hillside above the Morgan place. Lights glimmered from the house and barn, and Cam's truck was parked outside the barn. Help was just ahead. With the rain pelting her face, she ran until the footing became treacherous on the steep slope. Cody ran ahead of them toward the house, baying the whole way.

Before she even reached the house, Gayle ran out to meet her. "Marty! What's happened?"

No words would come. Marty clung to Gayle sobbing.

"For Pete's sake, what's going on here?" Mac called, running toward them from the barn followed by Luke and Cam.

"Let's get them out of the rain," Gayle said. Cody, wet and covered in mud, tried to push past Gayle into the house. "Luke," Gayle said, "take him up to the barn and dry him off and then bring him down."

Luke grabbed Cody's collar. Cody planted his feet and growled.

"Cody," Marty ordered, "go with Luke." The dog quit growling, but Luke had to drag him away from Marty and Annie.

Inside Gayle's cheery kitchen, they unwrapped Annie whose body had stayed remarkably dry inside her sheet cocoon. Her cracked lips curled into a faint smile. She raised one small hand and whispered, "Hi."

As Gayle pulled off Annie's sweatpants, Mac grabbed a throw from the back of Gayle's reading chair. He wrapped it around Annie and pulled her onto his lap, holding her close. "How about a glass of ginger ale or something, sweetie pie?" he asked. Annie shook her head and leaned back against him, her eyes closed.

Gayle handed Marty a mug of coffee just the way she liked it—hot with plenty of fresh cream. She slipped off her jacket with its wet sleeves and front and took a long sip of coffee letting it warm her. Then she quickly told them what had happened, and asked to use the phone. Annie needed help.

"Our phone's out but come on. Let's get her to the hospital," Gayle said.

Luke came into the kitchen. "Marty, I locked your dog in a stall with his brother. He was so worked up I was afraid he'd try to head back to your place."

"Cam…"

He took her hand. "I'll check him out and take him home with me."

Marty nodded.

"Hey, Luke, hand me one of your mom's clean dishtowels," Cam said. When Luke tossed him a blue checked towel, he wiped it first over Marty's face and then used it to dry her dripping hair.

Too worn out to protest, Marty leaned back in the chair and let him. Gayle rushed in, her raincoat on, her purse over her arm. Mac stood with Annie.

Cam peeled off his slicker and then unbuttoned the denim jacket he had on underneath. He helped Marty into it, the red and black flannel lining still warm from his body. "This will keep the wet out," he said with a smile.

Marty smiled at him. "Thanks, Cam." She followed Mac and Gayle out to the car. Getting in the back, she took Annie on her lap as Gayle got in the driver's seat.

"Marty, is everything all right down at your place? Do we need to get help in there?" Mac asked.

"As long as the creek doesn't reach the house, they'll be fine, but someone please keep an eye on it. If it rises any higher, get Jeff and Duke out of there. And the animals."

"I don't think we can get the horses up the ladder, Marty, or out in a helicopter, but we'll think of something," Cam said. "I'll call Doc Harbison from my truck phone and tell him to meet you at the hospital. As soon as I'm done treating Mac's calf, I'll take Cody to my place and meet you at the hospital."

"And I'll climb the hill and check out the creek," Luke said.

"And I guess that leaves me to hold down the fort here," Mac said.

Gayle nodded and off they drove through a rain that seemed to be letting up a bit. Annie wiggled off Marty's lap and stretched out on the seat. Marty tucked the throw in around her and then sank back against the upholstered seat, too exhausted for words.

When they arrived at the hospital, an emergency room crew was waiting for them. They whisked Annie into an examining room and tried to usher Marty in the opposite direction. She started to protest, but when she saw Gayle disappear down the corridor after Annie, she moved zombielike into the office to fill out papers and answer questions.

By the time they released Marty to find her daughter, Doc had arrived. "Marty, I've been trying to get you on the phone. This isn't a virus. It's a parasite that slipped into the water system in town with the heavy rains. At least, that's what the little Patterson girl had, and she tells me that last week she and Annie were drinking from their pump."

The IV team was hooking Annie to bags of fluid. Marty stood close to Gayle who held Annie's hand. Doc moved to the other side of the table to examine Annie. All Marty could do was watch the nurse getting the needle ready to push into Annie's arm. Marty remembered all the times she'd seen this scene played out with Dan. She started to shake.

"We need to hydrate her," Doc said. "I'm having some tests run, but I'd bet my practice it's the same parasite the Patterson girl had, the one that's been making people sick all over town. Nobody's quite this ill, but then they were able to get help."

"But, Doc, what—"

"Shhh," he ordered. "I'd also bet my practice that Annie will be just fine in a few days. Her fever's not that high. Before this, was she healthy and strong?"

Marty nodded and noticed that Gayle did, too. Annie tried to smile at her mother, but pain and fear showed on her small pale face. Gayle placed Annie's hand in Marty's and took a step back. Annie turned toward the arm being punctured for the IV. "It's all right, Annie," Marty said. "Don't look at it. One prick and then you'll hardly know it's there." Marty bent and kissed her forehead.

"There, now," said the nurse, "all done. That's not so bad, is it?"

Annie stared at her arm and the tubing running into it. "I don't like it," she said.

The whole idea of Annie punctured and fluids running into her made Marty's stomach clench. She focused on her daughter's face. Dan's eyes had carried that same glazed look before he died. A look of utter terror washed over Annie and Marty realized that Annie was picking up on her fear. Marty forced a rusty sounding laugh from her throat. "Me either, sweetie, but you've got to have it. It's going to make you feel a lot better."

Marty and Gayle followed the nurses as they pushed Annie's gurney to her hospital room. Gayle ran to call Cam's truck phone, so he could tell Mac the news. Marty settled into a vinyl armchair next to Annie's bed. A nurse came in and offered Annie some ice chips for her dry mouth. She sucked them greedily, but when she tried to swallow, the water came right back up. Annie began to cry softly, almost like a kitten mewing, but finally drifted off to sleep.

Marty pushed back on the chair so that it reclined a bit and dropped off to sleep. She was vaguely aware that Gayle came into the room and covered her with a blanket and eased a pillow under her head.

Laughter and voices woke her. She opened one eye a slit and saw Mac standing over her.

"I'll be darned, Stafford! You snore!" She opened her eyes to see who was laughing at his comment. Gayle and Cam stood at the foot of Annie's bed. Annie lay in bed propped up on pillows, looking at her mother with bright eyes. A healthier color had returned to her cheeks.

"The name's Harris, Mac, and I do not." Marty stood and stretched the kinks out of her limbs.

Mac hugged her, thumping her back. "To me, you'll always be little Martha Stafford, my next-door neighbor."

Marty shook her head and frowned at him. "You're impossible. How long was I sleeping?"

"A couple of hours," Gayle said. "Annie and I got tired just watching you. Right, Annie?"

Annie nodded. "Mom, Dr. Brady says it's stopped raining."

"I was still at Mac's when Gayle called," Cam said. "Luke and I climbed to the ridge and followed the path down to your ladder." Cam shook his head. "You're something else, Marty."

"Anyway," Mac continued, "Luke hollered until Jeff came out."

"I couldn't believe he heard us over the noise of the creek," Cam said, "but he did. He came to where he could hear us better and we told him you and Annie had made it and Annie was going to be fine. He said to tell you, 'Good going, Mom,' and that he and Duke are fine. He said something about Duke and him cooking dinner."

Marty laughed. "Burgers and beans, no doubt."

Gayle handed her towels, a washcloth, and soap. "The nurses are going to sneak you into a shower down the hall."

Marty ran a hand over her head. Bits of mud and debris came away in her hand. "That bad, huh?"

"You're a mess, Mom," Annie said.

Mac handed her a bag. "I gathered up some clothes at home that I thought might do you."

"Thanks, everybody," Marty said, as she followed Gayle to the nurse's station.

She let the steamy shower flow over her head and shoulders and down her back, relishing its soothing warmth. It eased her aching muscles and restored her energies, but she still felt as if her brain had numbed and that there was something important she'd forgotten. Her stomach growled. She had forgotten about food, but there was something else she needed to remember.

She dressed in what had to be a pair of Luke's old jeans. They were a bit big at the waist and she had to roll the legs up several turns, but they'd do. At least, Mac had realized that she'd never fit into Gayle's small clothes. She pulled on the sweatshirt Mac had picked for her, bright green with John Deere printed over a huge tractor on the front. It was far too big for her and had to be Mac's. She turned it inside out to hide the tractor.

Gayle and Mac insisted on staying with Annie while Marty and Cam went to get something to eat in the hospital snack bar. They chose the special—chicken stew and biscuits. Like Cam's comfortable company, it warmed and soothed.

When they went back up to Annie's room, Mac and Gayle were in the hall. The white curtain was around Annie's bed. "She's having some cramps," Gayle said. "The nurse is checking her."

Another nurse came bustling down the hall. "I heard you all were here," Patsy Malone said. "What are you holding? A class reunion committee meeting?"

So Patsy hadn't given up her dream of being a nurse. No wonder Marty hadn't seen her the few times she'd stopped at the restaurant.

"Hey, Patsy, who's slinging pie tonight?" Mac asked.

"Mom. Who else? She bakes them, so she's the best one to serve them. Hah!" Just like in high school, Patsy punctuated her sentences with a short laugh, making her sound a lot tougher than she was. Almost as wide as she was tall, she stood with her hands on her broad hips looking up at Mac.

The nurse came out of Annie's room with a bedpan. "We'll get a good sample out of this, but if I'm any judge, it's the parasite for sure."

"That's it," Mac said, making a face. "I'm out of here. Let me say goodnight to my little friend." He went into the room followed by Gayle. They hugged Annie.

Cam followed them in to say his goodnight as well. On the way out he gave Marty a hug and promised to check back with her.

"I'll be back tomorrow, Annie," Gayle said as she hugged Marty. "I'm guessing you want to stay, but you know you're welcome at our place."

"We'll take good care of Annie, if you want to get a night's rest," Patsy said.

"I know you would, but I need to be here. I'm sure I couldn't sleep anyway." But after their friends left and Annie fell asleep, exhaustion washed over Marty and she, too, was soon sleeping.

THIRTY-FOUR

Marty woke up in the middle of the night to the sound of someone in the room. She saw Patsy grinning at her while taking Annie's blood pressure.

"Oh, if only Derry Brady could see you now. Hah!" Patsy said.

"That's over, thank you, and I managed to escape with my pride and virtue intact," Marty said with a yawn.

"Amen to that, sister," Patsy said. "Besides, Ceci Collins would have probably had you bumped off." She read the dial on the blood pressure cuff and wrote on the chart. "This little pumpkin is doing fine." Patsy patted Annie's cheek and pulled the covers up under her chin. "I'm due for a break. I'll buy you an herbal tea or something equally dull. Hah!"

In the lounge, Patsy kicked off her shoes and rested her chubby stockinged feet on the coffee table. Over tea she told Marty about how she'd finally made enough money from the restaurant to be able to afford nursing school and had graduated five years ago. "When it became clear that I couldn't afford school right after graduation, I had no choice but to just turn my future over to God. If that meant I ran the restaurant forever... oh, well... but he apparently wanted me to be a nurse, so here I am."

Marty just looked at Patsy for a moment, wishing she'd been a better friend to her in high school. "I'm happy for you, Patsy. You seem comfortable with your life."

"Well, look at you! I heard about that Center you all are building on your place. There's such a need for it around here, Hah! See, no doubt about it—God sets us down where we're supposed to be—in his time, not ours."

"Aunt Bertie's always saying, 'When God closes a door, he opens a window.' Maybe she's right. Maybe you're right."

"Hah! Have you ever known me to be wrong?"

"Patsy, I think I need to visit the chapel," Marty said, again having that uneasy feeling that she'd forgotten something. Maybe she'd find it there.

She followed Patsy's directions to the hospital chapel. Inside the tiny room, Marty looked at the altar with its fresh flowers, the symbols on the walls of the various faiths—Christian, Jewish, and Islamic. A banner over the altar proclaimed, "All who love the Lord are welcome here." In the front pew an old woman was reading from a prayer book.

Marty sat in the back and bowed her head to pray, but no words would come. Random thoughts floated through her mind in a jumble. Did she love the Lord? Maybe. She hoped so. But Karl Marx had been right. Well, sort of. Religion or God often *is* the opiate of the people. That's how Marty had used him. He was like a drug to keep her going, a magic talisman in her pocket. It was as if she had believed that if she tagged, "Dear Lord, please," before a request, her dearest wish would come true.

She thought of Annie and her simple but absolute faith. She'd been like that when she was little. The weak need faith to make them feel strong, protected, safe. But true faith must grow into the reality beyond the need. Her faith never had. She'd replaced God with Dan, and he'd made her feel safe and protected. Then Dan had died and she needed God, needed him again as her opiate to make everything right.

She found a prayer card in the holder in front of her. On it was printed a verse from Micah, "This is what God asks of you: only this, to act justly, to love tenderly, and to walk humbly with your God."

Oh, how hard walking humbly was for her. As immature as her faith had been, she had never intended to offend God. Now she realized that in her ignorance she had been making herself her God. *She* was going to take care of her children, her father, and Kyle. *She* was going to save Derry and bring him to the Lord. *She* was going to make all the wrongs in their lives right.

Visions arose of muddy brown water raging underneath her, Annie tied to her back, fear overtaking her heart... until? Until she handed herself and Annie over to Jesus, put their lives in his hands. That's what God had shown her on that ladder over the flooded valley. That's what she had shoved out of her mind, because it carried with it a pain almost too enormous to be borne—the limits of her own humanity.

Ashamed, Marty once again bowed her head. "Forgive me, Lord," she whispered. She strained, lifting her heart toward a wordless image of holiness. What loomed was the gentle bearded vision, the artists' rendition of the physical appearance of Jesus. But even as she pictured him, she knew that image wasn't really Jesus, but only her imperfect image of who she thought he might be. The unknowing—the separation between her and her God—was more painful than anything she'd ever felt before, and she wept.

When her tears had run their course, Marty threw back her head and opened her arms. Humbled, she shut her eyes and whispered, "Lord Jesus, help me to love you. My Lord, my God, teach me your ways." Her heart was flooded with peace, filling that empty place in her heart in the only way it could ever be filled.

It lasted only a second. The old woman rose from the front pew, still crying. Her long dry sobs of despair pulled Marty back to a place of sorrow and worry. But now Marty had been given a glimpse of the promise, of the peace and fullness that only the Lord can give. Her Lord was with her.

THIRTY-FIVE

The rain stopped and within a few days the creeks receded. Kyle arrived at the hospital Monday morning, right after he found out from Gayle what had happened. He promised to get back to the farm as soon as the creek allowed. Annie was decidedly on the mend and the doctor expected to release her Tuesday.

Mud still covered the road on Tuesday morning when Gayle drove Marty and Annie toward the iron bridge. Miraculously, it had held, although its surface had been under a foot or two of water. Gayle drove across the bridge and turned into the lane. They drove to the house through the drying mud and debris. As they got closer to the house, Marty heard the blare of Kyle's chain saw. When Gayle stopped the car by the house and Marty stepped out, Bella and Jake caught sight of her and started to run. They arrived, wiggling and whining around her legs, sniffing to see where she'd been. "Don't worry," she said, patting them each in turn. "Cody's fine. He'll be home soon."

She was surprised to see Jeff backing Kyle's truck close to the fallen locust. "Hey, kid, you don't know how to drive," Marty yelled.

"I do now," he called back. He leaped out of the truck and ran to meet her. Behind him she saw Kyle lay down his saw and Duke drop a bundle of sticks in the truck bed. They hurried to meet Marty and Annie, too.

She hugged them all tightly and then held onto them, so thankful that they all had weathered the storm, that the Lord had pulled them all through.

"I leave you in the loving hands of your family," Gayle said. "And I have to get home to mine."

Marty hugged her heartily before she let her go. "You are the best friend in the world."

As soon as Gayle had driven off, Marty said, "Let's get Annie into bed." She started toward the house. "Then I'll fix lunch."

"Good thing," Duke said. "Jeff's getting sick of my cooking."

"True, but in self-defense I've learned to make a few things myself—like spaghetti and meatballs and scrambled eggs," Jeff said.

"Yeah, well," Kyle said, "I had his spaghetti last night and, let me tell you, it won't win any prizes."

"If you didn't like it, you shouldn't have eaten three helpings, you hog," Jeff snapped, taking a fake punch at his uncle. Kyle leaped and grabbed Jeff around the neck. They tussled, laughing and trying to trip each other all the way to the porch.

"Boys will be boys," Duke said, his voice full of authority "Come on now, you two! Behave! We've got too much work to do to be clowning around."

Marty looked at her father in surprise.

"Well, someone had to take charge while you were gone," he said.

Marty laughed. "Now you're sounding like Aunt Bertie."

"Your Aunt Bertie's not so bad. She stopped yesterday after she'd been to see you at the hospital. Brought us a pie, even. Besides, if everybody'd do what they were supposed to, no one would have to be the boss. That's what your Mama used to say." Duke pulled himself up to his full height and, for the first since she'd moved home, Marty remembered Duke was a tall man.

"You're right, Dad," she said. "Hey! Where's my porch furniture?" Only the swing hanging from the ceiling remained.

"We moved it into the dining room," Jeff said. "The wind was blowing a lot of water around so . . ." He shrugged.

After she put a tired Annie to bed, she joined the rest of them in the kitchen. Kyle poured her a tall glass of bottled water from the fridge. "I took a water sample in early this morning. Chances are our well is fine, because none of the rest of us got sick. To be safe, though, we'll drink bottled water until the results are back."

Marty opened the door to the basement. Damp mud covered the floor, but someone had already started to shovel it into a wheelbarrow.

"No serious damage down there," Kyle said. "We were lucky."

"We were blessed," Marty answered, "in so many ways."

They ate a hearty lunch together of leftover spaghetti and meatballs. Jeff had made enough to feed an army, and it wasn't bad. Over lunch Kyle explained about the work on the arena. "All the fellows have cleanup to do at their own places or regular customers who need their help. The entire county was hit pretty hard. I told them we'd resume work next Monday. That will give the ground up on the hill time to dry out and us time to get this place in order."

Impatience pushed at Marty, but she banished it. Kyle had made a wise and just decision that took everyone into account. The arena had to wait. Besides, Marty was trying to learn to give it all up to God's will, not hers.

Jeff began the animal report. Stumpy was still around. During the worst of the storm he huddled between the screen and the window until Jeff made him a little shelter out of scraps of plywood. He seemed to like it and had made it his home. The storm seemed to have convinced Herman that he never wanted to go outside again. He even ran upstairs if anyone opened the door. "Let's face it, Mom," Jeff said. "He's too far gone; he's here to stay."

Marty shook her head and put her face in her hands, but only so Jeff wouldn't see her smile.

"We lost a pair of ducks, the little ones," Duke said. "Think the fox got them. But the older female has made a nest under the old porch and it looks like she's getting ready to lay."

"The horses are fine," Kyle said. "I turned them out for a couple of hours yesterday, just so they could move around a bit. The hillside was too muddy and slippery to leave them out all day."

"And the goat's walking pretty well," Jeff said. "I think Grandpap was right. She's going to be fine."

"And tell Annie that her kittens are growing and they miss her," Duke added. "I'll bring them down to see her later."

The next day, Cam's truck with a horse trailer behind it was parked by the house when Marty came down from feeding Annie breakfast. As she stepped out onto the porch, Cody charged from behind the house, jumping and wiggling and dancing around her legs.

"Get out of there, you crazy dog," Duke called.

"No, Dad, let me see him," Marty said. She sat down on the bottom porch step and threw her arms around him. He jumped up across her lap and then slid off to roll onto his back for a belly rub. "You are a wonderful dog, you good boy, you," Marty said. He went to the screen door where he whined and scratched. Marty opened the door and he raced up the steps. She and Duke went into the kitchen. The sound of Annie laughing floated down the stairs.

"Jeff, Kyle, and Cam are in the barn putting the new horses away," Duke said.

"New horses?"

"Apparently someone's barn got washed out. They had a couple of riding horses and decided they weren't using them enough to justify rebuilding so . . ."

"So Cam said we'd take them?" Marty said, finishing his sentence.

"You got it. They look like pretty nice horses. They're supposed to be real quiet and not too old."

"Well, that's a plus," Marty said. "How about you keeping Annie company and I'll see what's going on?"

Jeff and Kyle, with Cam and Kika, were already coming from the barn as Marty stepped out onto the porch. Everyone but Cam ran up to see Annie. Marty put on a pot of coffee and turned to her friend. "So how many more horses are you going to send me?" she asked.

"How many do you need?"

"I'm not sure yet, so we better put a hold on them until we open. I sure don't want to be feeding horses I don't need," Marty said.

"Actually, you need another pony," Cam said.

Marty put her hands on her hips and raised an eyebrow. "Oh?"

"Some friends of mine have this terrific pony, big enough even for larger kids. Their kids have outgrown her and they don't want to just sell her to someone they don't know. They'd rather give her to the right home. She pulls a cart as well as rides like an angel."

"When's she coming?"

"Tomorrow," Cam said, his dimples deepening at the edge of his beard.

"All right, but no more for a while. Agreed?"

"Agreed, but actually…"

"No way, Cam. With the addition of that pony, I'll be cleaning eight stalls a day. That's plenty."

"You've got a few boarders coming—some kids who show 4-H horses were real excited when they heard you're building an indoor arena so they could ride all winter. They've been paying a pretty steep price for a place with no turnout and only an outdoor arena, so you can make some money there."

Marty stared at him. How could she complain about paying customers? But how could she do all this work and get the Center started?

"Now, I talked to Sam before I okayed the boarders and we agreed that you needed some help, so…"

"Don't tell me you've hired someone, too."

"No, Sam wanted you to do the interview, but she's coming by this afternoon. He said to tell you that the Foundation will pay her salary. Offer what you think is fair. Actually, Marty, this kid needs a job bad… and a place to stay."

"Cam, we don't have any extra room to put somebody up."

"All she needs is a hookup. She lives in a camper on the back of her truck."

Cam and Kika were long gone when the girl arrived in a smoke-spewing pickup that coughed the whole way up the drive. Marty cleared Dad, Kyle, and Jeff out of the kitchen, so she could deal with her without distraction. The girl knocked so lightly on the door Marty wouldn't have heard it if she hadn't been standing nearby. Marty opened the door and let in a pale, malnourished waif who looked to be about sixteen and said her name was Catherine O'Reilly.

"But everybody calls me Cat," she said.

Marty studied her. Cat's large black eyes studied Marty in return, in a direct unwavering stare. "You look very young, Cat," Marty said, sorry to sound so skeptical.

"No, Ma'am, I'm nineteen," she replied. "And I've been on my own a long time. I'm a whole lot stronger than I look, and I expect to work hard for my money. I know about horses, been working at the racetrack the last little while, but I know a lot about all kinds of animals. Worked once in a pet store and another time on a working farm that had just about every farm animal you could think of."

Marty's inclination was to turn her down. There was a whole lot of misery behind those black eyes and the Lord alone knew what kind of trouble followed this kid.

She called Kyle and asked him to show the girl the barn while she gave some thought to hiring her. Marty watched out the window. Although a good head shorter than Kyle, Cat strode step for step with him up the hill. Marty looked at the rusted and dinged camper on the back of her dilapidated pickup. "Could you really send her away?" questioned her conscience. And then she heard an answer, "Whatsoever you do for the least of my brothers, you do also for me." She'd taken in all kinds of sorrowful animals. Weren't people more important?

Marty headed up the hill to tell Cat she was hired. But she'd have to ask Kyle how much extra it would cost to add a two-room apartment to the complex. And then she'd have to okay it with Sam. That was how it would have to be, so Marty was sure they'd find the money somehow. There was no way she could let a kid live in that awful camper all winter.

E P I L O G U E
Thanksgiving Day

On Thanksgiving morning, Marty stood in the municipal building parking lot waiting for the parade to begin. Although the sun shone brightly, an occasional snowflake drifted by on the icy air. She watched Mac and Luke hitch the team of Belgians to the big hay wagon that carried the Center's entry in the parade. Duke bent over, using the car window as a mirror to make sure his authentic Indian war bonnet, given by a chief of a Western tribe to some long-ago Stafford, sat just right on his head. On top of the wagon Kristen and Gayle bustled from child to child, making sure the Pilgrim hats and the Indian feathers were all in place. Also on the wagon, Kyle knelt under the picnic table, hammering in extra nails to keep it from wobbling and dumping its faux feast on the young Pilgrims and Indians.

Sam came up behind Marty and handed her a hot chocolate. "So, what do you think?" he asked.

Marty just smiled. She could only feel, not express, what she thought about this miracle. The Lisa Center at Stafford Farm had finally opened the end of October with a great deal of fanfare, a good volunteer staff, and a waiting list of riders. Kristen's fund-raisers had been such a success that it seemed possible that very little of Sam's money would go to the initial support. And Sam and Kristen were busy building an endowment to secure the future. In her heart Marty said a prayer of thanks to suit the day. The one thing she'd learned on that terrifying bridge over the flooded creek was that the Lord had more in mind for her than she ever could have dreamed of for herself. Her life was much better off in his hands.

Lisa, dressed as an Indian, tossed her head and jiggled in place as she waved wildly at her Grampy. Sam waved back. Annie, dressed as a Pilgrim, held Lisa's hand. Next to her Jen and Kika stood like smiling statues in their costumes.

"Kyle," Sam called, "make sure Julie's wheelchair is locked into place."

Sam climbed up to help. He and Kyle bent and locked the wheels and checked the wood blocks that prevented the wheelchair from moving. Twelve-year-old Julie, her body rigid with cerebral palsy, grinned. Glory was Julie's favorite horse and they'd become quite a team.

Jim, who was thirteen and autistic, stood woodenly near the back of the table. Marty caught his attention and smiled at him. "Say, Marty," Jim called, "is this where I'm supposed to stand? And how did you want to me to wave? Like this?" He pasted a smile on his face and waved stiffly from his elbow, left then right then left.

"Very good, Jim," Marty said with an encouraging smile.

On the opposite sidewalk, draped in a voluminous mink coat, Ceci wobbled on three-inch heels. Derry, wrapped in a trendy fur-lined leather trench coat, held her elbow to steady her as he trotted along beside. The new Mr. and Mrs. Brady were to ride in a vintage car to lead the parade. They had been invited to repay Ceci for the money she had shelled out to buy new band uniforms, a gesture that had been intended to end the tongue-wagging over the way she and Derry had carried on.

An arm linked through Marty's. Cam. "Do they bother you?"

Marty shook her head. "Not at all. I wish them every happiness."

"I'm glad you do. I think Derry and Ceci together may have a chance. They seem to understand each other."

"They fit, Cam. Derry and I didn't."

"Hey, Cam," called Mac, "what's holding up the parade?"

"Actually..." Cam grinned, the corners of his eyes crinkling in mischief, "Renee. She's got the drill team holed up in the basement of the municipal building, making some last-minute adjustments in the girls' outfits."

"She's your cousin, Marty. Can't you do something with her?" Luke said.

"No way," Marty said. "This is her big moment. She's been working on altering those outfits for over a month, ever since the band's new uniforms came in. I'm staying out of her way."

At the other end of the parking lot, the band began to tune their instruments. Parade officials bustled between entries, ordering all to line up on the side street in proper order. The vintage car with Ceci and Derry rolled into place and stopped at the corner. Derry grinned and waved at all of them. Luke, Mac, and Kyle hooted and teased. Marty and Cam and the rest smiled and waved back.

Marty gave the Center's wagon a quick glance. It felt odd not to be up there working with them, but this was Kristen's idea and she had things well under control. Marty smiled, guessing that maybe she was learning something about humility. Now that she'd agreed to let God run the universe, she was also content to step back and let others act in his name.

Marty turned back to watch the lineup for the parade. Just behind the car with Derry and Ceci came the firetruck carrying the football team—their trip to the state finals in two days a special reason for the parade. The cheerleaders followed in two white convertibles from a local car dealer.

Renee stepped up beside Marty and threw her the victory sign. "Wait until you see our girls. They'll set this town on its ear!"

Catcalls and whistles preceded the fifteen-girl drill team as they came around the corner, strutting higher than Marty had ever seen them at a football game. "Renee, they look great!" Marty said.

"You're darn right they do!" said Aunt Bertie, joining them.

The girls marched by proudly waving their flags, dancing in formation, wearing the same old jumpers but shortened to a reasonable length halfway up their legs. The old shirts had been replaced by satin blouses with shiny gold satin stars on the big sleeves. Navy tights and the same gold stars on white tennis shoes finished the outfits. The girls stopped at their place in line, staying in formation but laughing and talking.

The band marched into position, looking wonderful in their navy satin uniforms trimmed with white and gold braid. They practiced as they went and Marty had to admit they didn't sound half-bad, just a bit heavy on the percussion. Jeff, Hap, and Casey did a fancy spin-around and high-step when they passed the Center's wagon.

All the kids on the float laughed and clapped, except Jim who waved and almost smiled, a small miracle in itself. Marty smiled and nodded to reassure him.

Duke started to climb up on the wagon. "Just a minute," Aunt Bertie demanded. She bustled over and started to straighten Duke's headdress. She fluffed the feathers that hung down his back.

"We've got to get in line now, Bertie," Duke complained.

"I spent two weeks sewing you this Indian outfit to go with the headdress," she said. "And you're not going anywhere until I'm sure you've got it right." She pushed him around to check the back of his fake leather tunic, complete with beading and fringe. She gave the bead design a pat and then the hem a quick tug to help smooth it over Duke's back. "There," she said, smiling and patting his shoulder. "You look splendid."

Kyle jumped off the wagon to join Marty and Cam. "Dad and Bertie getting along may be the biggest miracle," she said.

"Well, time heals all wounds. Besides, they were sweethearts once," Kyle said.

"What?" Marty spun to look at her brother and heard Cam laughing beside her.

"Yeah, Mama told me about it. Duke dated Aunt Bertie long before he ever dated Mama."

Marty stared at her father. He sat grinning on the wagon seat next to Mac who mugged while adjusting his Pilgrim hat. Marty wasn't sure, but she thought she saw Aunt Bertie wink at her father. Mac turned the team of horses and clucked to them. They pulled the wagon out of the parking lot into place. Luke stayed by the horses' heads. Sam and Kyle fell into place to walk along one side of the float, with Kristen and Gayle on the other.

"Marty!" Kristen called. "I forgot the candy. It's in my car."

Marty sprinted to the car and returned with the bags of candy for the kids to toss from the wagon. She handed them to Kristen and hurried back to Cam and Renee and Bertie.

"They're about to start," Marty said.

"Come on, let's find a place on Main Street so we can watch the whole thing," Cam said, taking her arm.

Renee and Bertie hurried along beside them as the band began to play. "Oh, let's hurry," said Renee.

Aunt Bertie bustled ahead of them with Renee scurrying after her. Cam laughed and pushed Marty ahead of him as he jogged up the street. They joined the Pattersons on the porch of the hardware store.

"Come on," said Darla, "we've got plenty of room. Kids, squeeze over there. Pudgy, step back and let Renee and Mrs. Crawford in."

Marty looked up and down the crowded sidewalks. It seemed that the whole town and half of the county had turned out for the parade. Joel and Amy Cramer ran toward them, laughing and holding hands, and came up on the porch.

Across the street, Cat O'Reilly stood high on a garden wall waiting for the parade to start. What an odd child she was, quiet and a loner, but hardworking and good-hearted, wonderful with the animals and the children. Marty increasingly depended on her, not just her help but also her judgment.

As the parade came toward them, Marty found her heart responding. "You know what, Cam?" she said.

"What?" he asked, smiling back at her.

"I love it here."

Cam's hearty laugh warmed her. "Me, too, but I never thought I'd hear you say that."

"No, it's just that... I think it's right where I'm supposed to be."

Cam nodded. "I understand."

"Look, here they come," she said, and linked her arm through his.

He reached over and patted the hand hooked on his elbow. They waved and laughed as Derry and Ceci passed, and then the football team, and the cheerleaders, the wonderful drill team, and the band. They kept waving as the local dance school group sashayed by and all the cars advertising various local businesses.

When a gusty wind blew down the street, Marty huddled against Cam's shoulder. She realized for the first time how good it felt to stand next to him. He was a bit taller than she and a lot stronger physically, but she didn't want him to take care of her. "Hey, Cam, look at me," she said.

He turned and smiled at her, his blue eyes warm, his smile genuine with those cute dimples flashing by the edge of his beard. And she didn't want or need to take care of him.

He laughed and threw an arm around her shoulder. "Are you flirting with me, Marty?" he teased.

"I'm not sure yet."

"Is it all right if I stick around to find out?"

"I'd be hurt if you didn't." She liked how her arm just reached around his waist.

The two big Belgians plodded toward them, the warm mist from their nostrils curling away like smoke. Duke's headdress had blown slightly askew in the wind, but he waved and smiled, not seeming to notice. The smiling faces of the children on the wagon held a ruddy glow of health as they tossed candy to the scrambling children on the sidewalks. How she loved all of them, not just the children but the adults, both family and friends, the whole town.

"Isn't this grand?" said Cam. "This is the kind of day that reminds me that 'God's in his heaven and all's right with the world.'"

"Amen," Marty whispered, letting the love of the Lord fill her heart.